"A SINGLE DANCER, SWAYING LIKE A LILY."

(*See page 92.*)

Omar the Tentmaker

OMAR THE TENTMAKER

A Romance of Old Persia

By

NATHAN HASKELL DOLE

Illustrated by

FRANK T. MERRILL

GYAN

Published by

GYAN

Gyan Publishing House
5, Ansari Road
Daryaganj, New Delhi-110002
Phone: 011-47034999, 9811692060
E-mail: books@gyanbooks.com

Distribution Network
gyanbooks.com
India, USA, Canada, UK, Australia, France

ISBN : 978-81-212-6248-4 (PB)
First Published, 1899

2nd Impression 2022

Printed at: Gyan Press, Delhi.

OMAR THE TENTMAKER
Author: NATHAN HASKELL DOLE

OMAR THE TENTMAKER

A Romance of Old Persia

BY

NATHAN HASKELL DOLE

Illustrated by

FRANK T. MERRILL

1899

TO

The Omar Khayyám Club of London

AND TO ALL ADMIRERS OF THE POET-ASTRONOMER

THIS STORY IS RESPECTFULLY

DEDICATED BY

THE AUTHOR

CONTENTS.

ILLUSTRATIONS.

OMAR THE TENTMAKER.

CHAPTER I.

SULEYMÂN'S MAGIC CARPET.

The Unchanging East!

Those who look at the constellations say that the stars are always the same: the belt of mighty Orion glitters as it did in the days of Pharaoh; Cassiopæa still sits in her jewelled chair. Only the planets wander in their fateful and fated courses. Yet astronomers tell us that even the fixed stars are wheeling in mazy dances and are altering their relative positions each second of hurrying time.

So with the unchanging East. We may not detect any variation in a lifetime; a century may bring about no marked alteration in the manners and customs of the people, but to the eye of wisdom improvement or retrogression is visible on the mighty chart of history. What mysteries lurk under those heaps of ghastly ruins that make desolate the lovely valleys of Irân? What melancholy tales are whispered by the rushes that nod in the soft breeze rippling the waters of her crystal rivers? These ruins are the hieroglyphics of a civilization now forgotten; these rushes mourn for a prosperity long since swallowed up in the black gulf of anarchy; could you understand their tongue you might learn of terrible tragedies succeeding happy days of comfort and refinement.

The great Clock of the Ages had scarcely more than marked with its hour-hand the beginning of its second revolution since the birth of our era. In England, Edward the Confessor was just closing his long and virtuous reign, and William the Conqueror was setting sail from France with his suite of Norman knights; Sancho III. was king in Spain; Henry IV. was king in Germany, and Philip I. in France. The mighty impulse that led to the Crusades, and sent millions of men to fight and die in the ideal cause of freeing the holy places from the contaminating control of the Saracens, was already beginning to be felt throughout Europe.

The sceptre of power had dropped from the weakened hand of the Arab in Syria and Irâk. The dynasty of Seljûk, the Turk, was established in Asia. Togrul Beg had obliged the Khalif of Bagdâd, Al Kaïm-bi-amr Allâh, to grant spiritual confirmation of his wide conquests, to acknowledge him as Sultân of the East, and to give him his daughter in marriage; but before his ambition was gratified he had died, in 1063, and had been succeeded by his nephew, Alp Arslân, son of Chakir Beg. Alp Arslân, with his Amîr Atsiz, had still further spread the glory of the Seljûk banner, had captured Aleppo, had conquered Syria and Palestine, and in battle with the Greeks had taken prisoner the Emperor Romanus Diogenes. But in the very hour of triumph he had been killed by a captured Turkoman chief, Jusûf Barzâmi, who had concealed a dagger in his greaves. His son, Malíkshāh, after a brief struggle with Alp Arslân's brother, Kâwurd, defeated him at Kamadân, and put him to death by the bow-string. Then he took peaceful possession of the throne, and, aided by Alp Arslân's minister Hasan, known as Nizâmu'l-Mulk, the regulator or supporter of the realm, the ablest and most liberal Wazîr that ever held up the arms of an Oriental potentate, brought the Sultanate to the highest pitch of celebrity.

As it often happens that, while a large part of a continent is covered with a dense pall of clouds, some happy valley still enjoys unclouded skies, so it happened that in this eleventh century, while Europe was intellectually half barbarous, while learning was practically confined to the scattered monasteries, while no great poet was writing immortal verse, no great artist was handing down the lighted torch of genius, the distant province of Khurāsân in Persia, though it was tributary to a ruler of another and alien race, was at the height of splendor and prosperity.

The Romancer possesses by right of his imagination Suleymân's famous carpet. He may invite his reader to sit upon it and allow himself to be transported back and away to that distant province of Khurāsân, to that long past epoch in the history of man.

CHAPTER II.

THE MOUNTAIN-PASS.

It was a perfect day in early spring. Not a cloud flecked the tender blue dome of the sky. The sun, as if conscious that he was looking down on his own particular land,[1] where not so many generations before the fire towers had blazed in his honor, poured down the fullest benediction of his radiance.

An imposing caravan came laboriously to the crest of the pass that conducted the road from Marp to the valley of Nishāpûr. It could be seen at a glance that it was no trading caravan. The magnificence of the horses, of the purest Arabian breed, the richness of the trappings, the abundance of farrâsh-hâ or servants, the throng of evil-faced camels loaded with the appurtenances of a multitudinous camp, the brilliantly decorated palankins, called takht-i-ravân-hâ, slung between sturdy and well-conditioned mules, proved beyond a doubt that some princely or even royal party was making its way over the mountains.

[1] Khur-āssân — the land of the sun.

It was indeed a royal party. The Seljûk Sultân Malíkshāh, with all his court, was bound for the city of Nishāpûr, and as the foremost of the procession reached the edge of the ridge, the view of the happy valley was suddenly unrolled before their eyes, as if by enchantment. A halt was ordered so that all might enjoy the spectacle. To right and left rose noble mountain peaks still white with the unmelted winter's-snow. At their feet, far down lay the plain, as if in the palm of the hand, — scores of flourishing villages embowered in groves and fruit orchards with the gleam of azure waters. To the right was Nishāpûr, "the Vestibule of the East," surrounded with its embattled wall, its masājíd or mosques, with their bulbous-tiled domes shining in the sun. As far as the eye could see there was evidence of a thrifty population, of a fertile region rejoicing in its prosperity.

Ibrāhîm Niyâl, nephew of Malíkshāh, and Governor of Khurāsân, informed of the Sultân's projected visit, having made all provision for the reception of his uncle and all the retinue, had set forth from Nishāpûr the day before, and had so timed his journey that, just as the royal party halted, the bravery of his banners and regalia gleamed in the morning sun as he came riding up the road from the valley. He had come to perform the ceremony of the istikbâl. Nothing could have been more imposing than the meeting of the two trains, on the little plateau of observation. Ibrâhîm Niyâl, attended by a brilliant cavalcade, dressed in most picturesque costumes, came riding up, mounted on superb steeds the very names of which attested the purity of their descent. Ibrâhîm Niyâl, dismounting from his horse, which he left with a zindâr, approached the Sultân, and, bending low before him, kissed the ground and addressed the formal words:

"*Salâm haldi-kum* — Peace be with you."

The Sultân, giving the return salâm, raised his nephew to his feet and kissed him. They then entered into an animated conversation in Turkish. It was evident that nothing disturbed the cordiality between the two august relatives. Malíkshâh's brow was serene and Ibrâhîm Niyâl's face beamed with satisfaction. The Sultân was in the very prime of life. Though somewhat stout, he was well portioned and alert in his motions. He had a keen, black eye, and long, thin mustachios; but his face was neither cruel nor sensual. There was about his whole person an air of refinement unusual to find in an Oriental potentate whose hands held the keen sword of unrestricted power.

The nephew bore a striking resemblance to the Sultân, but had a less intellectual face; there were harder lines about the mouth, his eyes were restless and cruel. His look was haughty. The power he had to wield he would wield with greater caprice and harshness.

"Nature herself seems to be aware of your illustrious arrival," he was saying, "and has granted such a day as even this happy valley, famous for perfect days, not often gives us."

The Sultân replied in appreciative mood, and then Ibrāhîm Niyâl explained the arrangements that had been made for his reception and entertainment in the city.

Meantime, at a little distance away, a more significant meeting had occurred. The Sultân was accompanied by his whole court, and by an immense retinue of servants of every kind. The officer who had charge of the arrangements, and who was responsible for everything being carried out with perfect smoothness, was the Wazîr Nizâmu'l-Mulk, who by his genius for system and his skill in carrying on the complicated affairs of State, had made himself indispensable to the former Sultân, Togrul Beg, but even more so to Malíkshāh, who had come so unexpectedly to the throne. Though a comparatively young man, he was capable of bearing every responsibility that might be thrust upon him, and of fulfilling all his duties with little apparent friction. So able a man arises not more than once in a century. His ability was evident at a glance; by the keenness of his calm and brilliant eye, by the breadth of his noble brow, by the long and handsome nose with sensitive nostrils, by the firm and beautiful mouth which showed a barrier of the whitest teeth when he laughed, as happened not infrequently, since being a Persian of purest blood, he was fond of a jest, and by his commanding stature and admirably proportioned figure. His complexion was dark, but his features all told that he was of the noble Aryan race.

In the suite of Ibrāhîm Niyâl came one of the most remarkable men of Nishāpûr. He bore an imposing array of names that bespoke the excellent ancestry which he might have boasted of, if he had ever cared to boast. He was known as 'Umar al Khayyâmi, or Omar the Tentmaker; but this was a takhallus or poetic name which he had chosen because his father bore the name before him, not because he himself, or his father, had ever engaged in the work of making tents. He plays on the meaning of it in one of his earliest poems:

> *Khayyâm ky khaymhâ hykmât mi-duht:*
> Khayyâm, who at the Tents of Wisdom was sewing,
> Has fallen into Adversity's Furnace glowing.

The "Tents of Wisdom" represented his interests in scientific subjects and especially in astronomy. At the same time he was no recluse or dry-as-dust scholar. One could read his qualities in his face. He had contemplative, yet laughing, dark-brown eyes;

a smooth, unruffled brow; a mouth which easily curled with scorn and yet was never ill-tempered, because of his naturally genial humor. His features were regular and refined; he was tall and athletic, yet it could be seen by his motions that he was not averse to the comforts of indolence. Above all, fanaticism was absent from his mental or moral make-up. He had come in Ībrāhīm Niyâl's suite with less than what would have been his ordinary reluctance to put himself forward in any way, from the fact that a special messenger had several days before brought him from Nizâmu'l-Mulk notification of the imperial journey and of the pleasure that the Wazîr would take in renewing acquaintance with his old schoolmate.

The two were now just meeting. There was no condescension on the part of the powerful minister; there was no subserviency to be seen in manner or words of the modest scholar. They had been friends years before, and it is the divine nature of genuine friendship to keep unimpaired by time or separation. They drew a little aside from the rest, and by a mutual impulse, sitting on a great block of reddish granite which stood like a monument dominating the pass, engaged in eager talk.

"Indeed, I appreciate your courtesy," Nizâmu'l-Mulk was saying, "in leaving your studies and laboriously climbing to this height to answer my missive. I had expected only that you would let the light of your face shine on me after we were established in the palace; but here you come to the mountain-top to greet me."

"Surely the kindness of your letter deserved tenfold more pains than I have taken to give you my salâm," replied Omar. "The splendor of your fame has spread over the whole realm; it fills our valley even as the golden sunlight fills it this auspicious morning, and could I have failed to wish to see the Sun which spreads abroad such a beneficent light?"

The Oriental mind is prone to exaggeration, and delights in far-fetched fancies and hyperboles. But at this period there was much greater restraint than would be found even a hundred years later. Omar's speech was more flowery than was his wont, and Nizâmu'l-Mulk listening to him, and with his keen insight detecting no trace of hypocrisy, yet thought it savored a little of sarcasm, or at least of irony. But he remembered Omar of old, and being perfectly free from conceit he was amused rather than annoyed.

But Omar went on, after a second's pause:

"To an indolent person like myself, having conquered the inertia that keeps mortals naturally at the bottom of the valleys, like eels at the bottom of the stream, I should be rewarded if by nothing else than by this superb view; but to have, in addition, the sight of my old friend whom I have not seen for twenty years — and who in the midst of all his cares and responsibilities has not forgotten me—this is indeed an honor and a delight."

There was no mistaking the heartiness of tone in which this was spoken or the glow of pleasure on Omar's face.

"Well," said Nizâmu'l-Mulk, "we shall have a thousand interesting things to talk over, a thousand recollections to bring to life again, and you must give me all the time you can spare. I wish to present you to his Majesty, but while he is engaged in talking with Ibrāhîm Niyâl we may at least make a beginning. You have kindly told me that you know something of my course in life; now tell me of yourself. Is your worthy father, whom I remember so well—Ibrāhîm Khayyâm—is he still in the land of the living?"

"Nay," replied the Imâm; "he died five years ago, full of years and the respect of his friends. He bore the burden of ninety winters."

"May Allâh show him mercy and bestow on him the treasures of Paradise!" exclaimed Nizâmu'l-Mulk, piously; "and your worthy mother?"

"My mother still lives and is in possession of all her faculties. She well remembers you and often speaks of you."

"And you? Are you contented? Does your ambition never prompt you to seek to better yourself?"

The color glowed in Omar's cheek; a fire flashed for a moment in his eye; rising to his feet he pointed down to the city, and said:

"My friend, do you see that gleam of silver that like a ribbon ties together the bouquets of foliage here and there on the plain behind Nishāpûr? That is the Seghâwer River, — a stream of crystalline waters. On its banks I love to sit and dream. Is ambition compatible with sitting beside a crystalline stream and dreaming away a summer's day?"

"Forgive my freedom, friend Omar; but have you sufficient of this world's goods to enable you to dream thus at ease? For without means bad dreams mingle with summer siestas! You remember our compact of long ago, when we sat at the feet of the Imâm Muwaffak? 'Tis yours to ask; mine to grant."

"Let us not talk about that now. Wait until you have seen my needs," said Omar, with a winning smile.

"Nor should we have time now," said the Wazîr, "for the Sultân looks this way. I wish to present you to him. Let us go!"

A sultân's look is a command, and Nizâmu'l-Mulk, taking Omar with him, joined Malíkshâh, who, having satisfied himself with the distant view of the beautiful valley, and the great city that he was to visit for the first time, was growing impatient to continue on his way. Nevertheless, he paused long enough graciously to receive Omar ibn Ibrāhîm al-Khayyâmi, whom Nızâmu'l-Mulk now introduced to him as the Imâm of Khurāsân, the light of science, the worthy successor of Abu 'Ali Sîna (Avicenna), not only a great mathematician, but also a prince of poets.

"I have long wished to know you," remarked the Sultân. "Your praises, sung by this truest of friends, have been sweet in my ears, and one of the attractions that brought me to Khurāsân was the thought that I should see you, and, perhaps, win your good-will."

Such flattering recognition from a sovereign's lips was like honey, but Omar was not a man to let his head be turned. He replied with wise dignity, and thus confirmed the good impression that his appearance made. From that moment Malíkshâh was his generous patron and friend.

The signal was now given for the caravan to start on its downward way.

CHAPTER III.

THE PARK ON THE HILL.

FIRST, the guards armed with tall decorated lances rode forward on noble white Arabian steeds; then followed the musicians whom Ibrāhîm Niyâl had brought with him, and they discoursed strains which, if not harmonious, were at least inspiring and loud; then more guards, and more, in military order and controlling with perfect horsemanship their eager horses, going six and six, matched in size and color, and all adorned with trappings of the best Bukhâra work, — embroidered cloths, and richest of leather. At a suitable interval Malíkshâh and his now enlarged suite followed, the Sultân riding as splendid a charger as the Orient could furnish; black as coal, glossy, and well groomed, his trappings glittering with precious stones, but worth more than precious stones, by the intelligent keenness of his liquid eye, the perfect proportion of every part, the high-bred elegance of his slender limbs, and the sureness of his gait. Well might Omar and others who believed in transmigration declare that the soul of some great warrior dwelt for an incarnation in Sâdet Joghân! No wonder the Sultân preferred to back such a horse rather than be carried inglorious in a palankin.

Immediately behind him and his suite, separated only by another relay of guards, came the brightly painted and decorated takht-i-Rawân-hâ of the ladies, who, careless of showing their faces, looked eagerly, but with no little apprehension, at the steep path and the formidable gulfs yawning below them, at the splendid plain, and the noble city to which they were going. Behind them came the ungainly red camels, with their lurching gait never improved since antediluvian days, their wicked eyes glaring at their drivers, and ready for any chance to snap and scold. These were laden with all imaginable treasures, — rugs and carpets, provisions and luxuries, whatever might be needed for hunting or camping, for rewarding faithfulness or doing justice. Priests and all the ministers of the service, servants of every sort and camp-followers, dressed in most picturesque garbs, brought up the rear, — a travelling city was on its way down the mountain-side, and, as it was a visit of pleasure, there was nothing visible but gaiety; whatever jealousies were felt were for the time hidden; no possible danger of attack from mountain tribes threatened; the sun still shone with unabated splendor, and the farther down they came, the more beautiful became the rich and varied vegetation.

By pushing forward rapidly, those on horseback might have reached Nishāpûr early in the evening; but there was no haste, and Ibrāhîm Niyâl had arranged that the caravan should encamp in a park situated on one of the lower foothills, and offering ample accommodations for the whole train, while his Majesty, the Kyblá-y Hālám, that is to say, the "Centre of the Universe," together with his immediate followers, would be entertained in a hunting sarâi or imperial-lodge which had been especially furnished for the purpose.

This plan was agreeable to Malíkshāh, and shortly after the sun stood on the meridian the great caravan was entering the gates of the park. As by magic, camel's-hair tents were pitched on the level plateau, and a busy camp like a small city, with all its industries, was created, as if a powerful Jinnî had created it out of air and set it down glowing with life. The sound of hammers on anvils was heard, for horses had to be shod; armorers were soon engaged in polishing and sharpening weapons, for it was known that on the morrow a great hunt would take place. It was no small enterprise to feed such a multitude, and the cook's quarters were soon sending forth appetizing odors. Nothing was neglected that might add to the comfort of any.

The sarâi itself was an enormous building, but low; it was built of sun-dried bricks decorated with brilliant tiles. A large front room or hall, resting on carved pillars, received the whole suite of the Sultân, and here he might have given audience to a thousand. Everything was so well managed and anticipated that the guests were shown to their apartments by dozens of noiseless servants, so that there was no confusion or delay. Baths were provided for those who wished to perform their ablutions, and wash the dust of travel from their hands and faces. A sumptuous feast was provided. The principal dish was a whole mountain sheep stuffed with pistachio nuts and almonds, and served with raisins, apricots, preserved plums, and covered with rice mixed with pomegranate seeds. Fowls, roasted on live embers and swimming in melted butter, fish from the mountain torrent, and a multitude of delicious fruits, preserved and fresh, added zest to the meal. The visitors were surprised that such variety and so well cooked dainties could have been served seemingly at a moment's notice, so far away from the capital.

The Sultân was graciously pleased to ask Nizâm-u'l-Mulk to join him and his nephew, and to bring his friend Omar with him. Such condescension was remarked by many, and the rumor of it soon spread among the party of notables from Nishāpûr; some naturally felt envious of Omar's good fortune, and ever afterward were not slow to make capital of it in their criticism of him. Others felt proud that a son of Nishāpûr should be so distinguished.

The evening was given up to talk and music. Under the light of flaming torches casting a ruddy glare, and weird shadows enhanced by the firelight, for the night air was still cool, girls, that had come with some caravan from India, danced strange, languorous, voluptuous dances. When these were dismissed with rewards, the Sultân had his story-teller summoned, and against him was pitted the great nakkāl of Nishāpûr whom Ibrāhîm Niyâl had brought with him; for in those days, as now, the Orientals were excessively fond of stories, and, like children, were content to hear the same ones told and retold dozens of times. When this exciting duel of improvisation was over, amid the applause of all, the Sultân, suddenly addressing Omar, who had sat listening with keen enjoyment, said to him:

"Our appetites have been pleasantly stayed; we have feasted our eyes with graceful forms and motions; we have heard with our ears entertaining stories; now 'tis your turn, you who are called Malík-al Shoharâ — Prince of Poets. Repeat for us one of those famous quatrains, the fame whereof has reached across the mountains, even to Marv — it is your turn, I say, to add cheer to the evening by repeating a quatrain or two in the musical Palahvî that I love so well."

Omar Khayyâm, serene in his simplicity and lack of self-consciousness, waited not to be urged. Putting his hand to his breast and bowing low, he replied, beginning with the conventional phrase:

"*Tabārák Allâh! házza wa jáll!*—Praise God! mighty and glorious is he! 'Tis indeed an auspicious day that has brought Malíkshāh in safety to our beautiful valley. Would that his unworthy servant had the fiery tongue to sing his praise aright. But since I am ordered I will obey. I crave indulgence for the feebleness of this hasty impromptu."

Then, to the wonder of all, he repeated, with absolute dignity, in a clear, melodious voice, in that Persian tongue, so full of musical inflections and cadences, a quatrain still preserved in the oldest of all known manuscripts:

O Shâh! Thy stars appointed thee to Sovereignty,
And placed thee on the saddled steed of Empery;
And when thy charger, golden-hoofed, beneath thee moved,
The clay whereon he set his foot turned gold for thee!

It was so charmingly spoken, composed with such elegance and propriety, that Nizâmu'l-Mulk was prouder than ever of his friend's well-remembered genius, and the Sultân begged Omar to make a fair draught of the rubâ'i and present it to him as a remembrance of a happy evening. He then gave the signal for the festivities to close, and retired for the night.

CHAPTER IV.

A MEETING OF OLD FRIENDS.

THE chase has ever been regarded as the noblest sport of kings. It is not merely the instinct of destruction that animates the mind, though that is not absent, implanted by nature herself, who sets the hawk chasing the sparrow which in turn chases the moth — an almost endless chain of cruelty and extermination; but there are also the loftier elements of adventure and danger; the exhilaration of the dash across country with no care for dykes or bounds; the chiming music of the hounds, and the poetry of the swift darting falcons.

The province of Khurāsân was at this time so populous, and the mountains whereby it was surrounded on three sides were cultivated to such a height, that game was not easily found; only by striking off beyond the great Turquoise mines, far up on the snow-clad ranges were the wild sheep called bakhta, or the ibex called būz, to be found by the ordinary huntsman; but many specimens were collected in Ibrāhîm Niyâl's park, and the Sultân was promised a morning of exemplary hunting with dogs and hawks.

A perfectly windless night was followed by a morning such as delights the huntsman's heart. The muazzîn from the top of a tall tower of observation that flanked the palace suddenly broke out with the musical call to morning prayer :

"*La-ilâha il-lal-lâhu ! Muhammâd-ur-rasul-ullâh !* — There is no God but God and Muhammâd is the apostle of God ! "

Then the sun rose from behind the snow-topped mountains, his jolly face glowing with satisfaction at seeing such a beautiful world. Light mists hung in graceful lines over the watercourses in the valley, or collected here and there, giving the eye the illusion of large ponds ; but these soon dissipated and rose to heaven in the shape of swan-like clouds that slowly sailed away and vanished.

Soon all was astir in and about the palace. After a light breakfast, the hunting-train was collected, and with little delay, because Nizâmu'l-Mulk disliked any hitch in carrying out his plans, they rode down the hillside and up the opposite mountain. Either by carefully prepared accident or by the will of Heaven, the mountain-goat which they proposed first to hunt was soon detected trying to escape up the steep escarpment of the cliff. No creature is swifter ; none surer-footed. With horses alone the chase is impossible; even the agile greyhound is slow compared to this wild creature. But inventive man can train the jerfalcon and make it his minister to hinder the flight of the goat.

As soon as Malíkshāh's eye caught sight of the beautiful horned prey bounding along with untrammelled grace, he gave the signal for the two hawks to be unhooded. Their trainer, the Kushchi-bashi, smoothed their glossy feathers, spoke a few encouraging words to them, then let them loose. They circled up into the air, and, as if by some reasoning-power diviner than instinct, the twin hawks flew straight for their quarry. All that they could do was to harry the game, to flap their wings in its eyes, to delay its course; but meantime the dogs, sending forth their deep bell-tones, woke the echoes from the precipices and were following up to make good the work of the hawks; and closely at their heels rode the imperial party, full of exhilaration, owing to the winy clearness and coolness of the mountain air and the zest of the sport.

Nizâmu'l-Mulk, of course, was in the chosen party, and he took Omar under his special care. Omar was glad to go because he liked to see all phases of life. But a singular incident kept the two friends from being in at the death. Accompanied only by one or two servants, they were riding side by side, a little in the rear of the rest, when, as if suddenly created from the very air, there stood before them a man with all the appearance of a beggar, though dressed in the ihrâm or pilgrim-robe that consisted — if anything so filthy and tattered could be said to consist — of two cloths, one extending from the shoulders to the waist, the other from the loins to the feet. A tall cap of lamb's wool was thrust carelessly on the head; the long hair was matted, and he wore a marvellous flowing beard dyed yellow with henna; fierce, curling mustachios crossed a face cadaverous in its thinness, and strange in its swarthy hue, while a pair of dark eyes glowed like coals of fire in the cavernous depths of their sockets. His feet were shod in sandals, but he was careful to show the instep and the soil-stained heels. He was evidently tall, but his stooping shoulders gave the impression of age. This singular figure blocked the way of the two huntsmen's horses, and, lifting up his hands, cried in a voice of singular power and clearness:

"*Hân hân! Hodâyā! Gurysnâm! Kâdrī nân ba-mân bī-dihēd!* — Listen! Listen! O God, I am hungry! Give me a piece of bread!"

The riders, wondering how such an importunate beggar had managed to make his way into the guarded park, would have ridden on, paying no attention to him, but a keener flash came into the man's eyes when he saw their determination:

"*La'natul-l-lâh!* — Be accursed of God!" he hissed

"THIS SINGULAR FIGURE BLOCKED THE WAY."

between his clenched teeth, and he seized Nizâmu'l-Mulk's horse by the bridle.

Here the keenness of the Wazîr's intellect shone forth:

"You are an impostor," he cried, and instinctively he looked around, to see if there did not suddenly dash, from the surrounding underbrush, a body of cut-throats, who would, perhaps, first assassinate the minister, and then overpower the Sultân.

The apparent beggar then drew himself up to his full height. "*Vâ vâilā!* Woe is me, that Hasan, the great Wazîr, the famous Nizâmu'l-Mulk, should call his servant an impostor. Do you not remember me — Hasan ibn Sabah? For it is I! I, who after undergoing a thousand perils, and escaping a thousand deaths, have at last come to remind you of your forgotten promise!"

It was then manifest that the beggar was not what he seemed. He was, indeed, a pitiable object; he had evidently been through strenuous trials; but when he stood straight he was no longer old, but a man in the prime of life.

Nizâmu'l-Mulk bade his body-servant take word to Malîkshāh that he was called back to the sarâi, but would join him again later.

Another servant was ordered to bring a led-horse as speedily as possible. When it was brought, the three old schoolmates, now so extraordinarily reunited, rode slowly back to the palace on the hill.

Hasan ben Sabah had always been of a selfish, moody, and taciturn nature, even when, as lads, the three had been under the instruction of the celebrated Imâm Mowaffak, in the school at Nishāpûr. He had been the one to propose forming the compact, in accordance with which the one that first arrived at wealth and power should share his advantage with the others. It was characteristic of him to assert his claim; but Nizâmu'l-Mulk had not forgotten it, as we have seen. And now, as Hasan rode between his old friends, so shabby and disreputable in garb compared with their courtly elegance, though in hunting costume, the contrast seemed to make deeper the scowl on his brow and to intensify the fever that glowed in his black eyes. Had life been going hard with Hasan ben Sabah?

That was what both Omar and the Wazîr were asking themselves, and what with instinctive delicacy they disliked asking him outright. So they rode not only slowly, but in silence. The pilgrim garb served as an excuse for a question:

"Has our worthy friend, Hasan ibn 'Ali ibn Sabah er-Razî, been on a pilgrimage?"

Nizâmu'l-Mulk repeated his whole name to show how well his memory served him, and, perhaps, also to flatter.

"Life is a pilgrimage: I have been going through life," replied Hasan, sententiously. He seemed not inclined to speak, and they got nothing further from him till after they had dismounted at the entrance to the sarâi. Even in his unkempt and wretchedly ragged attire Hasan was not a man to cause ridicule. It could be seen that he was no ordinary mortal. Nizâmu'l-Mulk had him first conducted to the *hammâm*, where he was given a bath. Fresh clothes were furnished him, and when he was suitably clad he was fed. He ate like a starving man, and when he had satisfied his hunger he was more ready to talk.

Nizâmu'l-Mulk, at Omar's suggestion, decided not to rejoin the hunt: a messenger was despatched to inform Malíkshāh that, owing to the presence of an honored guest, he would remain at the sarâi until the Sultân returned. It was a mere matter of form; he knew well enough that Malíkshāh, carried away by the zeal for the chase, and well attended as he was, would not notice his absence. If he confessed inwardly to a sense of disappointment at missing the boar hunt that was to follow that of the wild goats, he did not show it in his face or manner. Omar knew nothing of that proposed delectation, but being a studious man, fonder of mental studies and speculations, of quietude, than of active exercise, he was perfectly satisfied with what he had already seen.

The picture of the well-trained and beautiful hawks flying after their flying quarry remained vividly in his mind, and he saw in it an opportunity for an illustration to use in one of his quatrains. The musical cadence of the quintuple rhyme was already beginning to dawn in his mind.

But he had not got further than the first two lines when his mind was wholly concentrated on the story that Hasan ibn Sabah was beginning to relate. Allâh alone knows how much of it was true!

CHAPTER V.

HASAN BEN SABAH'S STORY.

"WE all remember," said Hasan ben Sabah, "the days which we spent at the feet of the greatest of the Ulamâh, with the venerable Imâm Muwaffak-ed-dîn. Can you not recall his weak and trembling voice, when, at the age of five and eighty, he still poured forth the treasures of his eloquence and expounded for us the subtle meanings of the Law? And what dreams of ambition did we not cherish! For we well knew that the pupils of the Imâm not infrequently went high on the mountain-side of Fame. You remember our compact. 'One of us three, if not all of us, will assuredly attain to fortune. Let us make a compact,' I said, 'that whatever good may be granted to any one of us shall be equally shared by him with the others, and the possessor of the good shall give himself no preference!'"

"We were then young and enthusiastic boys," remarked Nizâmu'l-Mulk. "We were not wise. Rash promises made in childhood may not hold in maturer years."

He said this with a view to test the patience of the

claimant. Omar, to whom the idea of reminding the generous Wazîr of a promise made so long ago was repugnant, looked at Hasan and wondered how he would take the rebuff. Hasan said naught. There was silence again. But Nizâmu'l-Mulk was not going to be deprived of the pleasure of listening to Hasan's story.

"Can it be," he asked, "can it be that a man of such supereminent talents as you possess, has not profited by the teachings of our hāl'ym? We predicted that you would go far, rise high, reach fortune. Has then the world gone wrong with you? Have the planets poured counteracting influences? Did not Omar, the son of Ibrāhîm, read in the stars that you were born under happy auspices? Has not your dream been attained? Tell us of your career during all these years."

"Verily I will," said Hasan. "After I had for four years drunken at the fountain of learning that poured forth so abundantly from the Imâm Muwaffak's lips, I returned to my father's home at Rey in the province of Irâk. My father was then possessed of abundant means."

Omar recalled that Hasan's father 'Ali bore but a doubtful reputation — a reputation that came with poor Hasan even from the distant home in Irâk.

"My father said to me," continued Hasan, "'My son, travel gives the final polish to the mind. I am satisfied with the progress that you have made in your studies; you are fitted for the career of a kātib; you might teach in the mosques all the beauties of the Arabic language and literature; your penmanship is perfect; you are a skilled accountant; you might take your place as the right hand to the governor of the province; you are equally well-fitted to be muftî or even wazîr. You are sure to rise. But that you may put the final polish on polish already so eminent, take this purse of gold and see the world for yourself.' I was nothing loth. I was young and full of life. I engaged a servant, and taking my father's best horse I set forth. Where should I go first? Irâk, of all the provinces of Irân, is most extensive and most fertile. I had done better to make myself acquainted with its possibilities; but my eyes were dazzled by the fame of Bagdâd which lies in another Irâk — Bagdâd, which I had heard called Daressalâm, the House of Peace. But why should I tell the great Nizâmu'l-Mulk of its tiled wall of fifteen thousand ells, its two hundred towers? He, of course, has seen its splendid palace, the Daresh Shedshret, the House of the Tree, with its pillars of gold and silver ingeniously contrived to take the form of trees loaded with jewelled fruits, where jewelled birds sing songs of fantasy under emerald leaves, guarded by effigies of knights clad in richest robes adorned with pearls and gems. Had not the report of these glories reached Isfahân? And I was sent by my father to see the world. I travelled to Bagdâd. I was fortified with letters and hoped great things from the Kaliph. I was kindly received and my knowledge of the law and of polite Arabic stood me in good stead. But my success aroused jealousies. I had no chance to show proof of my abilities, because the Kaliph's ears were poisoned against me. I was ever modest, and I had no desire to contend against a fate that I saw was threatening me. I fled from the city not poorer — for I had enjoyed some chances — and precious stones are easily stowed away. I went to Egypt and there increased my knowledge of mysterious doctrines. Egypt still retained some relics of the wonderful teachings that made our prophet Mūsâ preëminent. I found there priests that were adepts in the mystic teachings. I saw the pyramids, those solemn memorials of a forgotten past. I was taught the riddle of the Sphynx. At Cairo I was admitted into the grand lodge of a secret order. I absorbed all the lore to be had in Egypt: verily I believe I could perform miracles!"

As he said these words, the fire again glowed in his cavernous eyes. Mayhap it was the fire of insanity! Or was it genius? At any rate it made his hearers uncomfortable. Neither of them felt at ease with their old friend.

He went on:

"I heard of the fame of the caliphate of the Saracens in Spain, and I resolved to risk the dangers of a voyage thither. I followed the sun through the whole length of the Mediterranean Sea. What Muslîm ever travelled so far? Here again, I, with my wide experiences, was on the way to high preferment. A man of brilliant understanding was needed. The Christians were pressing hard on the Faithful. I went to the Kaliph and told him of the power of the African Moors. 'We are all of one faith,' said I. 'Behold me a Persian from Rey in Irâk, I, too, am of the faith of Muhammâd.' The Kaliph liked my advice, but again jealousies stood in my way, and I was charged with inordinate ambition, with trying to overthrow the Kaliph — I who was as innocent of such ambition as you, Hasan el Tusî, are innocent of wishing to overthrow your master, Malíkshāh! But the charge brought me heavy woes: I was arrested, thrown into a filthy dungeon, and left there to starve or be devoured by rats. Fortunately I had saved several jewels. By means of one I bribed the jailer to let me escape. I shook off the dust of Spain from my sandals, and after long wanderings, whereof to tell would take too long, I once more reached my father's house. He was dead, but his brother, my uncle, who had come into possession of the house, — a debt he said had given him the right,

—had kept for me a certain part of my inheritance. 'Twas a small share; yet my father had been rich. He explained that losses had overtaken him, and that after he had helped the old man out of his difficulties this was all that was left. . . . But we are all in the hands of Allâh! I was even in the midst of talking over affairs with my uncle when all our arrangements were rendered at once nugatory; my uncle and his house, which had been my father's, and the little bag of gold which represented all my worldly possessions, were transferred into hands accustomed to reap where others had sowed. An incursion of Kurds swept through Rey like a mountain tornado. The bāzâr was pillaged and set on fire; the chief men and their families were seized and bound. The children were dashed against the stones and their blood ran through the streets. Resistance was in vain; my uncle—may Allâh cool his resting-place—was compelled to show where his treasures where hidden. He at first refused to speak a word, but when they threatened to kill him on the spot, he fell on the ground and begged for his life. I caught one glimpse of the costly cups and jewels that I recognized as having been my father's pride—they were all swept into the saddle-bags of the barbarians, and my bag of gold was snatched from me. My uncle and I, whom he had undoubtedly robbed, were reduced to an equality of misery. We were driven on foot at a pace that tested even my endurance and soon used up my uncle's strength, but though he fell more than once, he was given no respite till we reached our first halt. Here sentinels were posted and a division of the spoils was made. The miscreants were of three different tribes. I never saw my uncle again: he went by lot to one village, I to another. If I had harbored any resentment against the poor man, I felt that he was now punished. I could even pity him, torn away from his family whom he would never see again, and doomed to live a few years or only months, doing the degrading work of a slave in a Kurdish village.

"My prospects were not better, but I was young and gifted with some cunning; I had been in even worse situations. I called on Allâh the All-Merciful, and faced my lot."

"But how did you escape?" asked Nizâmu'l-Mulk, who had followed this tale with keen interest, though his skeptical mind was ever alert to detect the improbabilities.

"'Tis the old story: by woman man fell and by woman man is sometimes restored to liberty. I was taken by the brother of the sheikh of the mountain village. At first I was watched very closely; a billet of wood was fastened to my leg; you can see even now the scars made by the knots!"

There was no question as to the scars. Hasan

ben Sabah bared his ankles and displayed the marks made by cruel thongs.

"But I made no complaint, because I saw it was useless to complain. I knew that other captives had softened the frozen soil of their lot, not by the continual rain of their tears, but by their zeal in the service of their masters. I resolved to be cheerful and good-tempered, I who am naturally testy and gloomy; I smiled at their blows; I learned that one can wholly control one's moods. I quickly mastered their language. Allâh akbár! God is great! He gives his servants power over many things. The wife of the sheikh cast a favorable eye at me. I remembered the story of Yusûf, and Zuleikhâ, the Egyptian Mace-bearer's wife. I resolved to be wiser than even the great Yusûf. She was a young Circassian. She persuaded the sheikh to take me from his brother. The Circassian was very wise in her behavior; the sheikh never suspected her motive. Nor did I, by a sign or a look, betray to a soul that I read the woman's heart. She alone knew, and we sometimes had a moment's speech. When it was seen that I was apparently contented, and made no attempt to escape, when I made myself useful by reason of the many things I had learned, gradually the bondage was made lighter for me. I loved horses, and could manage them; I had the gift of taming even the most unruly. One day I rode without a saddle a stallion that my master had captured from some Fārsî merchant. He was young, and as yet untrained; fiery and full of the spirit of Shaitân. I offered to tame him and make a useful creature of him. I was given the chance. I taught that horse, which I named Thawah, to be as obedient as a ship to its helm. But me he looked on as his master. By a pressure of my hand, he would turn to right or left, or stop as rigidly as if carved from granite.

"Byrādár jân! [Brother of my soul!] how I came to love that horse! And he loved me no less. One day when the sheikh had gone on some expedition, to plunder some caravan, he had wanted to ride Thawah, and bade me saddle him; but though I knew I should be made to eat many sticks, I managed to loose him and let him go, and as the sheikh was in haste, he forgot his wrath and took his ordinary horse. Then I knew my opportunity was come. I could speak a few words of Cherkess, and I bade Leila, the Circassian, meet me with a supply of provisions, and some of her husband's gems, the hiding-place of which she knew. Nor was she loth to do my bidding. I had ever a masterful way with women; they seem to dread my eye, and yet to follow its glance. When the sheikh and most of the young men had gone, I went out and easily caught Thawah. A Kurd, who was especially appointed to watch me, evidently suspected that something was wrong. He endeavored to stop me. I enticed him behind a knoll, and before he had time to give an alarm, I had pierced his heart with a dagger that Leila procured for me. Then I laid him down as if he were asleep in the sun, and no one suspected.

"Leila met me as I had bade. I knew there was no time to be lost. Swinging her on the saddle behind me I whispered into Thawah's ear, and we were off. Never as long as breath sucks through my nostrils shall I forget that wild ride. I could only judge by the sun whither we were going! We might any moment stumble on the sheikh and his men. Then what a fate would have been ours! Death by torture! I knew that Thawah could bear us both safely, that he would even doubly loaded outstrip any horse that my master possessed. But by a miracle, if we were pursued we never knew it. But what was I to do with Leila? She had deserted her husband to follow my fortunes, and where was I to find my fortune? My own city was sacked and destroyed; my home and all its small possessions were gone. What more natural than to think of Nishāpûr, the gem of Khurāsân? Nishāpûr where I had been educated? What more natural than that I should remember our schoolmate, Omar al Khayyâmi, who might tell me more than what I was already beginning to hear of the fame of the Nizâmu'l-Mulk, the supporter of the Realm? Accordingly, a day or two ago I reached Nishāpûr, but alas, in what wretched poverty! how unfit to be seen by the Eye of Science! Nevertheless I went boldly to his residence, which I found by diligent inquiry. I should not have known the city; it has trebled in population since our day. That gracious lady, the mother of Omar, remembered me, though her eyes were not so keen as once they were. She remembered my voice. She offered me hospitality; her son she said had gone to meet the Wazîr to the Sultân Malíkshāh, and would not return for several days. I left Leila there. I came as I was, in the garb of a pilgrim, which I had assumed to disarm suspicion. I resolved to test the promise of the Sultân's minister. Here I am!"

There could be no doubt the man had been through trials; his story of captivity, told by him with animated gesture and variety of intonation, was dramatic enough; nevertheless it had a certain suspicious hollowness, as if he had not been through the experiences himself.

The three old friends had found it pleasant to sit outside of the sarâi in the sun, and sheltered from the fresh wind that had arisen. The farrâsh had brought them rugs and cushions, and they indulged in that pastime dearest to the Persian's heart, — the hearing and telling of stories. The view from their resting-place was different but scarcely less superb than that which they had enjoyed on the plateau of the pass. A soft haze, violet and diaphanous, hung over the valley, lending a poetic glamour to the landscape; the distant mountains seemed farther away and gentler in their outlines; only deeper shadows marked the ravines on their sides. No one would have imagined that only a few leagues to the south lay the great salt desert, the Daryâl Kabîr. A few clouds had gathered in the west, and promised a royal sunset.

Omar's quick ear heard the sound of a silvery laugh quickly repressed. He looked up and caught sight of an exquisite face, a pair of large laughing eyes, a mouth like the bow of Cupid, and — was he right? — the dearest little mole — or was it a dimple? — that ever inspired a Persian poet to song! All that he saw in an instant's glance. Then the veil was drawn, and the three friends saw hurrying by two ladies of the anderûn, as the Persians call the women's quarters. They were attended by two stout eunuchs who at first scowled fiercely at the three men, but when they recognized Nizâmu'l-Mulk they bent low and kissed the ground.

A single arrow from the eye may sometimes by strange chance strike to the heart. Omar, the poet, could not forget that heavenly glimpse. He forgot that the eunuch whom Nizâmu'l-Mulk addressed as Agâ Zālým spoke to one of the ladies as banû, princess. He forgot to look at the sunset, though even now the clouds were beginning to grow golden and the mountain-tops turned a royal purple.

He said to himself, "Who has seen once may see twice." He was a man and a poet. He knew that a fair one, with gazelle eyes and a "cypress form," had, for an instant, looked at him; the electric flash was all-revealing; hopes, fears, desires, joys, that he never suspected lurked in the depths of his soul, were disclosed by it. The place waiting for the ideal was shown to be as empty as a shrine in a temple as yet undedicated; here was the ideal!

Love opens many doors, but more powerful is money, and if Omar had before resolved not to accept, much more to ask, any of the Wazîr, his scruples suddenly vanished. All this revolution was worked in his mind and heart in an instant of time; but he knew the absolute necessity of caution. Just then, too, broke in the sound of the kettle-drums announcing the return of the hunt. So he, with seeming alacrity, followed Nizâmu'l-Mulk and Hasan, as they went to meet the Sultân.

CHAPTER VI.

THE VESTIBULE OF THE ORIENT.

THE next day the Sultân went down to Nishāpûr, though he would have gladly lingered in that paradise of hunting. His experiences with the wild goats and with the gamy boar of the mountain had but kindled his desire; but his nephew told him that it would be better to go down to the city and afterward return if it still pleased him to hunt.

Malíkshāh had every reason to be satisfied with his reception in his Persian capital. It seemed as if all the inhabitants of the city came out to meet him; the air resounded with acclamations. A thousand and one mamelūks rode out in advance, and when they had escorted the train to the gate, they were met by thousands of maidens, each bearing gifts in their hands, and as they walked along they scattered delicious perfumes, the 'itr of roses, musk and aloes, liquid amber and camphor. It was a brilliant scene, and was compared to the meeting of the elect in paradise, where the Rízwan of the Heavenly Gardens shone in celestial beauty. The Sultân, on his part, gave such abundance of alms that every one in Nishāpûr received a gift, and it is said that that year poverty was there unknown.

The city at that time had not far from three hundred thousand inhabitants. Never since its foundation by the great Peshadian Tahmurath had it been so prosperous. Alexander the Great destroyed it, and it had risen from its ruins, only to be destroyed again and again. But at this time it had been enjoying many years of prosperity; its powerful wall, flanked by massive towers, promised permanence of defence. No town in all Irân had a more imposing *arg* or citadel, and the palace where Malíkshāh was lodged was furnished with every comfort that was procurable at that day. The principal bāzâr or market exposed for sale all the products of the East, and not a few of them were manufactured in the city itself.

On one side was the quarter of the potters where Omar especially loved to linger watching the men with their deft hands turn on the revolving wheel the silent forms of clay. How many times it occurred to him that the wet clay thumped by the artisan might well cry out:

"*'Tis thy father's ashes thou torturest thus with thy hands!*"

"*Many are the excellent men whom malicious heaven has turned into wine cups and flagons.*"

Malicious Heaven! What else would he have done with his own clay than to let the potters re-create it into wine jars to be forever filled with the rosy perfumed wine?

To him the jars and pots were all alive, some silent, some speaking, but all full of memories of the happy days when they, too, loved and were loved in turn. The handle of yonder graceful jar was the arm that once twined around the maiden's slender neck! And the pottery of Nishāpûr went to all parts of the East. The pots there forever listened to the porter's "shoulder-knot a-creaking!" —eagerly waited for the long journey to distant scenes.

Here, again, the coppersmiths worked at their noisy trade. The clang of hammers rang all day, and the brass and copper utensils, that shone on the walls of their shops, went by many a caravan to be distributed in the marts of Asia and even Europe. Here, again, steadfastly labored the rug weavers, patiently working out their exquisite prayer rugs and carpets, woven of silk or the softest wool, in the most harmonious colors that the dyers could furnish them withal. Caravans of hundreds of camels were coming and going, bringing in the silks of Gilân or the gold and silver filigree work of India, Batavian sugar and spices from Ceylon. The great bāzâr and, indeed, every smaller market was substantially built, with arched roofs; the streets were paved with marble from the quarries on the mountains, and the great central street running east and west was lined with palaces that would have excited admiration in any city.

Nor was the material side of civilization alone represented; the spiritual and intellectual needs of the people were fully provided for. There were dozens of splendid mosques, with lofty minarets. The domes of the colleges and academies also made a brave showing with their glittering tiles. Here far-famed teachers lavished their learning in expounding what they considered the weighty matters of the law, indoctrinating their pupils with orthodox views and the traditions of the prophets, or disputed with fiery zeal over moot points of the Qurân and the Surahs. Ample libraries were furnished with manuscripts, to which industrious scribes were constantly adding. Hundreds of students, even from distant cities, came there eagerly trying to squeeze every drop of wisdom from the dry books of commentaries.

Omar himself was nominally connected with a darû'l-funûn or university, but, as he had little patience with the system of education that prevailed, and as he was out of sympathy with the other professors who resented his criticisms, he did not like to lecture very frequently; when he did he had a crowded audience, for it was known that he would say many droll and even heretical things.

On the very day before he had gone to meet the Sultân, he had stopped at an old academy or seminary called madrasá, which, having fallen into disrepair, some workmen were restoring to propriety. Omar stood for some time watching the asses that brought the bricks for its restoration. Several students were by his side. One of the asses was unable to push through the court, but stuck in the entrance. Omar went up to the donkey, and addressed it with an impromptu rubâ'ī:

"*Thou hast gone and returned like a child in the game, Ass!*
Disappeared among names is thy once honored name, Ass!
Thy nails grown together a horned hoof became, Ass;
Thy beard down thy back is a tail! Who's to blame, Ass?"

The ass, as if animated and encouraged by these dulcet strains, put forth a final effort, and made his way through the narrow entrance with his load. The scholars expressed their wonder that poetry should have so powerful an effect on the long-eared animal. Omar, with that sly humor characteristic of him, answered their queries, saying:

"The soul entangled in the body of this ass was many years ago in the body of one of the teachers in this seminary; it was, therefore, hard for him to go in; the humiliation of returning in a humbler form was too great for him; but when once he knew that his colleagues recognized him, he was encouraged, and made grateful; so he put forth the additional effort, and made his way in."

Some of the students, catching the humor, repeated the master's innuendo, applying it to the professors, and it was rumored that Omar had called them asses. By such ways men win unpopularity, and Omar was regarded as a freethinker, and even sacrilegious. But little recked he of the bad reputation that he was winning for himself.

When he reached his modest home he found that it was true that Hasan ben Sabah had been there a few days before, accompanied by a veiled woman, whom he had desired to leave with Omar's mother. He was properly and decently dressed, however, and must have procured his pilgrim garb elsewhere, and have purposely disguised his appearance so as to test and prove the friendship of Nizâmu'l-mulk. But the woman had not stayed long with Ziba-khanùm; she had suddenly disappeared, and the poor old lady was greatly exercised for fear some harm had befallen her. It was all very mysterious.

Omar had invited Hasan to make his house his home while he remained in Nishāpûr, but as Nizâmu'l-mulk had given him a similar invitation to take lodgings at the palace in the Arg, he had naturally accepted it, with the wider scope for his ambition that it might give him.

The weather which had been so beautiful had changed. A storm was sweeping down from the mountains, and the heavy rain was beginning to pour along the streets. Omar welcomed it with equanimity, if not joy. He would have no excuse for going out, and he was amusing himself with composing a treatise, called "Needs of Places," dealing with the peculiarities of the four seasons, the prevailing climatic conditions, and the variations in the weather in different countries and different parts of the same country. His keen mind saw that storms and droughts seemed to follow the lines of natural laws, and he believed that by a system of signals one might foretell the approach of bad weather or the end of rains.

The house in which he lived with his aged mother was like most Persian houses. It was four square, of sun-dried brick, protected from the storms by blue tiles made by Selim ibn Ibrāhîm, the potter. The centre room was covered with a dome; at each corner were apartments. From the outside little could be judged of the inhabitants; and inside, the furnishings were what would be called scanty in a modern house. But in spite of limited means, the rugs or carpets of Birjând spread on the floors were of beautiful designs and harmonious colors, and Omar had not haunted the coppersmiths' quarter in vain. The ceilings were painted in conventional designs.

His mother prided herself on her housewifery, and if the Sultân himself had entered at any moment, he would have found perfect order, and simple but elegant fare.

Back of the house was a garden stocked with fruits, for which Khurāsân was famous, — the mango and jujube, the pipal and apricot, while a tall date-palm lifted on high its graceful head, bending caressingly and, as it were, lovingly over the house that it seemed to protect. Red-legged rooks found shelter there, and he was especially fond of the pigeon, the wood-pigeon, whose pathetic cry forever asking the question, "Where? Where? — *Ku? Ku?*" — was a reminder that Nishāpûr, which had been laid in ruins so many times, might again become as desolate as the Takht-i-Jamshîd, those imposing relics of the departed glory of the ancient kings — and that other races of pigeons would ask, and ask in vain, "Where, where are they who once dwelt happy mid all the splendor now vanished?"

Nishāpûr was well supplied with water. Down from the mountain-sides flowed a hundred cooling streams; and across the plain led upwards of ten thousand irrigating canals, and the water was brought into the city so that every garden was watered. Flowers bloomed in incredible abundance, and Omar's garden was one mass of gorgeous roses, double roses, white and pink and red as the lips of a Khurāsân maid. Omar was especially proud of the bush that bore a great yellow rose with its scarlet heart. When it was in bloom it was to him an undying poem.

While the rain was falling musically in the paved court, and was dripping from every leaf in his thirsty garden and filling the central tank to repletion, Omar himself, content, if not wholly calm, made ready to compose his famous treatise. But he was destined to be disturbed. A messenger from the palace brought word that the Sultân Malíkshāh desired Omar's presence. "A dark and gloomy day," said the note, "requires the Sun of Poesy to shine in the Sultân's palace."

Omar returned word that he would put the neck of humility into the noose of obedience and would follow the messenger.

The thought occurred to him, that perchance he might once more catch a glimpse of the lovely princess or princess's attendant — he cared little which. Fate again was kind, — or, if by infusing still more of the intoxicating poison of desire, — one would better say unkind to him! As he crossed the great hall of Attendance, he came face to face with the same two ladies. Again it was only a glimpse, but he saw that she was tall and fair, lovely as polished ivory, with dusky, musky ringlets, blushes like the rich pomegranate flower, eyes as soft as the narcissus, but overflowing with merriment, eyelashes like the raven's jetty plumage, brows like a bow, a mouth all sweetness; and as with one quick glance she drew her veil across her face, he noticed that her fingers were tapering and delicate, the nails slightly tinged with henna, the hand as beautiful as a butterfly's wing. What struck him particularly was a sort of appealing look in her eyes which for a moment shaded the sunlight of their smile. Poor Omar, the trouble that had interfered with consecutive thought when applied to the problems of weather would grow into a sort of delirium if many times more that fascinating maiden should cross thy path!

The Sultân, confined to the palace, or rather preferring not to stir out in such a pouring rain, had resolved to atone for the disappointment by a splendid entertainment within doors. If the dinner at the hunting-sarâi had been appetizing, prepared on the hill-top as it was, what could be said of the feast that the Sultân spread for his guests in the city, where every luxury of the season was ready at hand? And when the dozens of courses perfectly served were accomplished, the Sultân rising, announced that he had several proclamations to make: one was that Nizâmu'l-Mulk's friend, Hasan ben Sabah, at the Wazîr's request, was appointed to the responsible and lucrative position of mace-bearer; the other was that Omar al Khayyâmi was henceforth to consider himself malikuâsh-shuher' or poet-laureate, and also court astronomer, with an annual pension of twelve hundred golden mithkals from the treasury of Nishāpûr.

And Malíkshāh, with charming grace, recalled the example of the great poet Firdausî, author of the Shâh-nāmá, or Book of Kings, and like Omar, a son or a sun of Khurāsân, and how he, on promise of a gold dirham a line, wrote sixty thousand lines, and the Sultân, the great Māhmûd, sent him silver instead of gold. But after Firdausî, through whom Sultân Māhmûd would be forever remembered, leaving a bitter and biting epigram, fled, and had been wandering for years in poverty and wretchedness, the Sultân repented and sent him the sixty thousand golden dirhams, and many gifts beside. But it was too late. As the caravan bearing the costly gifts from the Sultân to the poet entered one gate of his native Tûs, the procession bearing his body went forth through the other to lay it in the tomb on the mountain-side. But his daughter took the gold, and erected to her father a noble monument that bears down to remote posterity the expiation of the Sultân.

"But we, O Omar al Khayyâmi, do not wait until you are dead, — may Allâh remove far hence that day! — to give you this mark of our appreciation of you as a poet, and as the very eye of science."

And Omar, even as he heard these flattering words, saw the living vision of the unknown maiden, who twice had by miracle crossed his path, and he welcomed the golden mithkals as the key to the door of his happiness.

The feast was followed by an exhibition of dancing girls. Dressed in diaphanous silks of Mosûl, the clinging folds of which patterned themselves to every grace of curve and mould of beauty, with bare feet and ankles, they bent and swayed to the voluptuous tinkling of the lutes played by the cleverest musicians of the East. Through intricate evolutions they now acted in mute pantomime the gracious love story of Lailî, the beautiful Arab girl, who stole off to the desert to meet her lordly lover, Kais Majnûn, — a story afterwards exquisitely told by Omar's gifted pupil, Nizâmi, — or gave a dramatic representation of an assaulted harâm ; now they intermingled, bending and glowing like a bed of flowers before the caressing wind, now marching and countermarching till the eye was almost satiated with following so many entrancing forms, cypress-graceful, their high breasts rounded like the cup of Jamshîd, their faces wreathed with smiles of pleasure in their art, and the appreciation of the august assemblage.

Then when these maidens beautiful as the Hûr promised the faithful in paradise had finished their evolutions, the chief story-teller was called. He told them first some of the fables of Anwâri Suhali, and then the story of the two angels, Hârut and Mârut.

"Hârut and Mârut," he said, — only he told the story with quaint repetitions, and with fervor of glowing fancy, — "were two of God's chief angels. And one day a dispute arose between Allâh and the angels, as to the reason of sin and disobedience being in the world. And Hârut and Mârut came down to earth to find the reason for man's sin, to learn if it were, as Allâh said, the passion and lust that tempt poor man. Before they came to earth, God taught them the great and ineffable name which not even the archangels knew, because, knowing it, they would be equal with God, and able to create. But to Hârut and Mârut, Allâh himself taught the ineffable name. And to earth came Hârut and Mârut; they came first to Bab-El, the Gate of God, the Sublime Porte of the East, Babylon the mighty. And they there studied man, and the works of man; man in his pride, and man in his glory, and man in his sin. And Zuhrâ, the sweetest singer of the East, heard of Hârut and Mârut, and she came to them, even as Balkis, the Queen of Saba, came to Suleymân, and she was desirous of learning the ineffable name. And she sang for them, and not even in paradise had they heard such singing. And they fell in love with her, for particularly susceptible to the charms of earthly women were of aforetime the emissaries from the angels. She put wine before them, wine which Muhammád our prophet called the mother of iniquities. They drank of the intoxicating child of the vine, and their desire for her waxed ever greater; they forgot their errand from on high; they killed Zuhrâ's husband, and then Zuhrâ, when she had heard from Hârut and Mârut the ineffable name washed and changed her raiment, and going forth from the court of her home, and standing by the water-pool, she uttered the ineffable name, and by the power thereof she ascended to the sky, where she merged her splendid beauty with the star Zuhrâ, which star when the storm shall clear we shall see hanging over the western mountains like a golden lamp. But Allâh knew that Hârut and Mârut had committed the terrible sin. He called them back, and before all the angels he charged them with unfaithfulness to their trust, and when they confessed that they had sinned even as mortals sin, by reason of lust and passion, he condemned them to be suspended head down in a pit near Bab-El, the Gate of God. There they forever remain unless Allâh relent. They blame each the other for the woe that is theirs. And men bold enough have visited them in the pit near Bab-El, and have learned magic of them; and it was from Mujâhid, who saw them, that he who told me this tale learned that Hârut and Mârut, bound with iron bonds, still hang in the pit head down, and wait for the judgment day, hoping then to be released from their penance."

One story always leads to or suggests another, and the great nakkâl of Nishāpûr, Abdallah ben Yusûf told the familiar tale of Ibrāhîm and his handmaid Hagar, and how Hagar bore him a son — his wife Sarah being barren — and the boy's name was Ishma-El, the beard of God. But Sarah was jealous. And Ibrāhím, willing to escape the reproaches of Sarah, his wife, went to Sham and built the great city of Makka. But he left Hagar in the wilderness with her son. And when she had used up all of her food, and the milk in her breasts dried and there was nothing for her baby boy, she called on Allâh, and Allâh sent Jibrāîl (Gabrael), called Zarosh or the messenger, and Jibrāîl bade her go to the mountain Safa and she would find food. Seven times she went between Safa and its opposite mountain Marvah, and her soul was heavy in her bosom, and she despaired and would have laid herself down and perished, but at last she found the sacred spring Zam-zam, which proved to her a well of healing and consolation. And once again Jibrāîl came to her and blessed her for her faith and constancy, and told her that her son Ishmael would found a great people, and that from his descendants would arise the greatest of the prophets, who would lead all peoples to the Ka'aba of his father Ibrāhîm. And once a year Ibrāhîm came to visit Hagar in the wilderness and brought her costly gifts on his camel, Zark. And to this day pious pilgrims go seven times from Safa to Marvah and from Marvah to Safa, and try to find the sacred stream Zam-zam, the water of which, said Jibrâîl, would never cease to flow.

And the thought of the desert suggested to the Sultân's story-teller a terrible story of the ghūl of the desert who dwells in the Dashti Nâummed, or desert of despair, and who lures travellers on by the strange weird music of the Reg rawân, or singing sand, which as the wind plays on it gives forth notes like distant drums and lutes. Then arises before his eyes the sihrâb, the "magic waters," the mirage; splendid palaces seem to beckon to him; the forms of seductive maidens stand under the crimson-flowered Judas-tree; but it is all delusion; suddenly arises the sand storm; 'tis the wings of the ghūl, and the poor victim blinded, perishing of thirst and starvation, falls, never to rise again.

> "*The fountain is far off in the desolate wilderness:*
> *Because lest the demon deceive thee with the mirage.*"

And thus story led to story, and again Omar was called on to give the august audience one of his poems, but he rose and, laying his hand on his heart, said that since the unequalled ruler of the world, the defender of the faith, had mentioned that renowned poet, Abul Kasim Mansur Firdausî, he would repeat a few lines from the Shâh-nāmá, the epic of kings, the Persian of yore, and in a voice thrilling with passion and power he cited those magnificent lines:

"*Paradārî mîkunad dar Kasr-i-Kaisar' ankabût—*
The spider weaves her web in the Cæsar's palace,
The owl stands sentinel on the watch-tower of Afrâsiab."

The dramatic fire and expression which he threw into those sonorous lines, the grace with which he declaimed them, the modesty which led him to substitute the verses of the great national poet for his own, made a profoundly favorable impression on all present.

What would Omar have thought had he known that behind a Chinese screen of many folds were gathered several ladies of the imperial household, and that most eagerly listening to every word that fell from his eloquent lips was the maiden who had already cast her undying spell upon him?

Just as he finished repeating the lines, the lofty room, where they were seated cross-legged on the softest carpets that ever looms produced, was illuminated by a golden radiance. The storm had passed, the clouds had broken, and the glorious sun sinking toward the western mountains sent forth his parting salutation to the world. The rays seemed to crown the noble-looking poet as with a jewelled halo. His face was still glowing with the enthusiasm of the inspiration. It seemed as if that royal sun of Persia, so long worshipped on those mountain-sides and on that very plain, had consciously wished to make an apotheosis of the poet and to show his appreciation of poesy so perfectly in consonance with his own dethronement from the land of Khurāsân.

As Omar, having made his salâm to Malíkshāh, and said a few words of farewell to Nizâmu'l-Mulk, agreeing to spend the next day with him, was about to leave the palace, the Agâ Zālým, intercepting his path apparently by accident, thrust into his hand a tiny slip of parchment. Realizing that it contained some important secret that should not be detected, he waited until he was out of sight of the palace before he dared open it and read.

But his prescient soul told him that it was a missive from the unknown maiden. He trembled with eagerness. He hastened his steps, and when he was sure that he was secure from observation he unfolded the precious little scroll.

It was written in Greek!

CHAPTER VII.

AN AMBITIOUS SCHEMER.

THE Wazîr Nizâmu'l-Mulk had fulfilled the promise made a score of years before. He had presented Hasan ben Sabah to the Sultan, and, with a word of recommendation, procured his appointment to the lucrative and important position of mace-bearer, with the promise that he should be made īshík-ākāsí-bāshi, or Chief Lord of the Threshold. The Wazîr gave him also a heavy purse of gold, and, as he had already provided him with suitable raiment, he would have, indeed, been churlish and ungrateful had he found fault with his treatment.

But Hasan ben Sabah was an inordinately selfish and ambitious man. He had prepared himself during his long residence in Egypt with a training that he intended should make him a power in the Oriental world. He was profoundly learned. He told Malíkshāh:

"From my childhood, even from the age of seven, my whole endeavor has been to get knowledge."

Although the Sultân had come to Nishāpûr for the summer season, which is particularly delightful on that lofty mountain-surrounded plateau, the climate of which, if variable, is regarded as the finest in the world, he had no intention of relaxing the cares of state. Many important problems faced him; the sway of his dynasty was to be spread through Tāberistân, and, if possible, his banner was to be carried even into Syria, Karman, and the farthest provinces of Asia Minor. He had many plans to lay and great preparations to make. He welcomed the eager willingness of Hasan to take hold without delay, and he resolved to make use of a man who spoke so many languages and had seen so much of the world.

Some of Hasan's story had been true. During ten years of semi-obscurity he had travelled far, and had gone even to Egypt and Spain. His father had died as he said; but not in his own house, nor had he met with losses. His father had suffered from the repute of being a heretic, a Motasâl; but he bribed Abu Muslîm, the governor of the province, though a Sunnite, and proud of his orthodoxy, to vouch for him, and the bribe was not small. He afterwards wearied of life and retired to a monastery, where he died at a good old age.

The part of the story that he told his two friends about being carried into slavery had also a foundation of truth; but he displaced it in its chronological order. It must have been sixteen years before, for the veiled figure, whom he had brought to Omar's house and left there as his wife, was in reality his son, Ostad-ben-Hasan, a youth of sixteen, of remarkable keenness of intellect, though without beauty of person. Children of mixed nationalities are apt to inherit peculiar gifts, and Ostad's mother was a Circassian, whom Hasan had met and carried off in somewhat the way that he described. Ostad was completely under his father's influence, and obeyed him implicitly in everything. Just why he had disguised him as a woman, and introduced him into Omar's house, would, perhaps, have been hard to say; and how was he to explain to his two friends the disappearance of Leila without exciting their suspicions? This was a problem that he had to face. But his plan had been all laid beforehand. Ostad was directed to steal quietly out of Omar's house and to go to a certain caravanserai which his father indicated, and wait there until he should send for him. His plan, in case he was appointed to office as he confidently expected, was to introduce him into court, not as his son, but as his page. The supposed disappearance of Leila would afford sufficient excuse for him not to enter into the festivities that he felt would delay his purpose.

Everything so far was working as he had anticipated. He was placed in a position near the Sultân, and he had no doubt that by his usual astuteness he would soon master the internal machinery of the empire, and find out what would be the course of external politics in Asia, if not in Europe. He knew well that great events were likely to happen, that the Christian world, alarmed at the spread of Muhammadanism, might at any time strike at the Oriental powers; and that, on the other hand, "The Sword of Allâh" would never rest till the victorious hosts of the Prophet were firmly intrenched in the capitals of Europe.

'Tis a great thing to live at the end of a century; great to live at the end or at the beginning of an epoch. Time has its great moments, when, as it were, its alarum-bell sounds the hour; it has its grand climacterics as in human lives, coming in rhythmic order; revolutions occur at the end of centuries; minds above the ordinary feel instinctively that these seismic disturbances of history are impending. Hasan was one of these men. He realized, dimly, perhaps, since the collated facts of history were fewer then than they are now, that the world was on the verge of a crisis; something told him that he, too, was destined to have a share in the work; but just what he did not yet foresee. He had not a little of the prophetic insight, too, and there was a constant call within him to go forth and preach a new gospel, of which he should be the central sun.

He felt that the first step had been taken when the Wazîr received him so generously; another when he was washed and clad; another when he was bowing low and kissing the ground before the Sultân; and having thus begun he had already gone so far that he had a room in the palace and was already counted as one of the Counsellors. The second day had not gone before he had quietly procured the presence of his son Ostad, whom he lodged near him. Ostad was a slender stripling, with the quietest and most unobtrusive manners possible. He was grave beyond his years. Never did the suggestion of a smile light up the cold depths of his melancholy eye or curve the corners of his compressed lips. What strange experiences had so early quenched the charming, playful spirits of youth? What dark horizon lowered before him, so that sunshine seemed forever absent from his brow shaded by thick masses of coal black hair? Was it his father's oppressive personality that dominated him? It would have been hard to tell what strains of fierce and untamed blood ran in his veins or what hereditary influences swayed his mysterious soul. He was the embodiment of obedience: his father had but to look, and the quick intuition of Ostad leaped on the task as a tiger leaps on the prey. His was one of those mathematical minds that reach abstruse conclusions as directly as lightning leaps from magnet to magnet.

He rarely spoke, having learned reticence from his father, who had trained him sternly and severely. In spite of his youthfulness he was wiser in most practical affairs than many a graybeard. Hasan knew that he was as true to him as steel, devoted to his interests body and soul. He took his place in the Sultân's household as naturally as if he had lived at court all his life. When asked as to his page, Hasan simply gave his name as Ostad ibn 'Ali al-Kufai, an Arab boy that had followed him and proved a faithful servant.

Nizâmu'l-Mulk meeting Hasan early the next morning, invited him to go with him to Omar's summer-house by the river-side, but Hasan politely declined, saying that as it was his first day in his new office he thought it best not to go pleasuring. The Wazîr replied that there was no special business that required such diligence, but that he must consult his own convenience.

Hasan perceived that he had made a mistake in declining the invitation, but it was not for him, having put his hand to the plow, to turn away. He merely said:

"Nay, O mighty Regulator of the Realm, I would fain go with you, but, having journeyed far since the night of the new moon, rest is to me even more precious than the communion of friendship. Another day will I go to our friend Omar's pavilion and inhale the perfume of budding roses. But to-day I crave indulgence of the friendship that I prize."

This was a plausible excuse, and Nizâmu'l-Mulk accepted it frankly. Nevertheless, he said to himself with the shrewdness that was a part of his character :

"Even from the first day I must guard well against surprises. Hasan is deep like a well ; but the truth does not lurk in the depths of that well. He claimed. I have paid the claim. Let me not forget the camel and the Arab's tent."

And aloud he said :

"*Astahfyru' llâh!* God forbid that I should add a feather to your burden of weariness. To-morrow will be another day and the week that begins with Jak shamba ends with Shamba, — seven days with but one day lost to pleasure! Allâh bless your new office and you and yours!"

Then the two men parted. Hasan went in search of his son, and Nizâmu'l-Mulk, mounting his horse, directed his way to the abode of the astronomer.

CHAPTER VIII.

A POET'S EDUCATION.

WE have said that Nishāpûr contained several excellent libraries. Among the manuscripts there preserved — a few years afterwards, alas! destined to be burned, torn, and destroyed, by the Turkish tribes that sacked the great city — there were many Greek scrolls that had been brought into Persia and strangely deposited there, just as a stream in the mountains brings down the golden grains and sweeps them into some sink-hole in its rocky bed. The knowledge of the Greek language was not common in Irân, but occasionally an adventurous Hellên made his way over the mountains either as an ambassador from the Greek Emperor or more frequently as a hostage or even as a slave. It was owing to the somewhat impudent remark of an envoy from Konstantinos, that Malíkshāh that very year had built the castle of Shāhdurr or King's Pearl on the summit of an almost inaccessible crag. For the two were out hunting not far from Isfahân, and the Sultân's favorite dog made his way to an incredible height.

The Greek ambassador seeing it, remarked that in his country such a spot would have been chosen for a castle. And Malíkshâh immediately ordered his pearl of castles to be built there.

Omar Khayyâm had been fortunate enough to become acquainted with an educated Greek, and with him had explored the riches of the manuscripts. With him he had read Xenophon's ever-fascinating story of the expedition of the Ten Thousand when Kurush tried to wrest the kingdom from Artaksathra, and so narrowly failed of changing the destinies of Asia. He had read one or two of the now forever lost plays of Aristophanes, and the missing play of Alkmaion of Euripides. He had read Aristotle, whose philosophy had charmed him, and Plato, the prose poet of Attica; but most of all had he been influenced by a fragment of Epicurus, which claims that the gods made up of atoms lived apart from the world, exercising no influence on the destinies of men, who were the blind and helpless children of fate, their greatest good consisting in the happiness they are able to snatch from the passing moment.

There, too, had he found Euclid's immortal treatise, and one of his most pleasing tasks, undertaken solely for his own pleasure, was the composition of an algebra that should reduce to simpler terms the propositions established by the great Alexandrean mathematician. And perhaps we ought to mention that there was also saved most mysteriously, and undoubtedly because none of the Muhammadan priests knew its tenor, a fragment of the Septuagint. It contained intact the Greek translation of the Koheleth, and there Omar read such passages as these:

"*What profit hath a man of all his labor which he taketh under the sun?*

"*One generation passeth away, and another generation cometh; but the earth abideth forever.*

"*The thing that hath been, it is that which shall be; and that which is done is that which shall be done. . .*

"*There is no remembrance of former things; neither shall there be any remembrance of things that are to come to those that shall come after.*

"*There is nothing better for a man than that he should eat and drink, and that he should make his soul enjoy good in his labor.*

"*Be not righteous over much; neither make thyself over wise. Why shouldst thou destroy thyself?*

"*As is the good, so is the sinner; and he that sweareth as he that feareth an oath. This is an evil among all things that are done under the sun, that there is one event unto all.*

"*Go thy way, eat thy bread with joy, and drink thy wine with a merry heart. . . . Let thy garments be always white, and let thy head lack no ointment . . .*

for there is no work, nor device, nor knowledge, nor wisdom, in the grave whither thou goest."

These words of Hebrew doubt lingered in Omar's mind, and many were the quatrains which he wrote embodying the same or similar thoughts. It was impossible for him, being thus brought into contact with certain phases of Hellenic philosophy, to remain satisfied with the narrow, bigoted religion of the prophet. Outwardly he may, for the sake of example, or from sheer indolence, not caring to give up the habits of his boyhood, have conformed with the rites and ceremonies of the Muhammadan ritual; but he never hesitated to express his opinion that one creed was as good as another. Church and Ka'aba, rosary and cross, pagoda and synagogue and masjíd were all the same to him.

"Seek not the Ka'aba," he sang, "rather seek a heart."

And in spite of all Muhammád's prohibitions he praised wine, the ruby wine of Mugh; he declared that simply because a drunken Arab once cut the girth of Hamzah's steed, — Hamzah, an insignificant relative of the prophet, — Muhammád called drink a vice.

Of course, such outspoken heresies did not fail to bring him into disrepute, but his wit was an armor that protected him. Besides, though he sang of the pleasures of drunkenness, he was never seen intoxicated, and though he sometimes sang the lyric praises of the cypress-slender minister of wine, and gave it to be understood that his chief delight in life was to carouse with loose women, fair as the Hûr promised as companions of the faithful in paradise, it is safe to say that he was not so black as he painted himself.

One episode in his life had done much to make him understood by his fellow citizens. A certain doctor of the law was particularly severe on Omar's heresies, and left unused no occasion to slur at his irregularities. Omar happened to hear of it. Now, this Hālím came secretly every day before sunrise to Omar's house, to read and study philosophy with him. Omar gave no sign that he knew anything of his learned pupil's duplicity. One morning, however, he kept him longer than usual. Suddenly there was heard in the street a tremendous blaring of trumpets and beating of drums. Omar and his critic went to the door, the one wondering, the other knowing what was its cause. When all the people had gathered in the street, Omar raised his hand, and the musicians, instructed beforehand, ceased their din. Then Omar, good humor beaming from his handsome face, exclaimed, at the top of his voice:

"Men of Nishāpûr, behold your teacher! He comes every morning secretly to me and studies philosophy and science with me. But you know well how he speaks of me behind my back. If I am really the heretic and law-breaker that he tells you I am, why does he come to study with me? And if he knows that I am not a man to be feared, why then does he abuse his teacher?"

The Hālím, abashed at being thus publicly exposed, slunk away, and thereafter left Omar his morning hour free for other and more congenial duties. If there was any one thing that Omar detested with all his honest heart it was hypocrisy, and the city often was stirred to laughter by some audacious quatrain floating about and holding up the learned ulemâ or the hypocritical priests of Islâm to scorn.

The Greek note that he received he was able, thanks to his studies in Hellenic lore, to decipher, and for the most part to understand. It ran to this effect:

"*O Poet—*

"*I overheard thy poem, and I, being Greek, though having lived long years in Persia, am bolder than it would become a maiden of Irân to be. I would fain hear more of thy verses. Also I would gladly return to my own land. But I see no way to compass it. I know I may trust thy face, even as thou mayest trust the Agâ Zālým. If thou wilt sometime let me ask thy advice, when next thou comest wear a yellow rose or one of the pink-streaked wild poppies of Shirâz and leave the rest to me. If the seed I sow fall on stony ground in thy heart, heed me not, and forget that I wrote to thee.*"

The note was signed Agapê.

Omar was dumbfounded; how should the beautiful Greek girl know that he could read Greek? Why should she have selected him to aid her in escaping from the Court? Might it not be a plot to ruin him? Then he remembered the look of mute appeal that he had detected in her eyes the second time they met. He had not understood it then. Now the mystery of it appealed to all the romantic instincts of his heart; for eight and forty hours he had been haunted by those beautiful eyes. But the first time he saw her they were full of merriment, and her laughter, as he had overheard it, was sweeter and clearer than the tinkle of crystalline waters in a basin of mother of pearl. How was that gayety to be reconciled with the homesickness that breathed through her note, and evidently drove her to such a risky step?

These questions were impossible to answer, but he resolved to follow the adventure to the end and see what would come of it. The flavor of danger was not its least attraction. He was restless, and his mind wandered from his mathematical work; he could not sleep, and when the night was far spent he went out and looked at the sky, now swept clear of every cloud. A meteor leaped suddenly from the zenith down in a long curve toward the mountains, behind which it disappeared leaving an evanescent trail of light. He laughed as he thought that the superstitious muazzîn on the minaret would predict misfortune for some one. Did it forebode disaster for him, or for the generous Sultân? Day was approaching. The strange phenomenon of the Subh-i-nakhûst or False Dawn was clearly defined on the eastern sky, — white against dark like a wolf's tail. Into Omar's mind came that beautiful quatrain, where he compares true love with insincere:

> "*A lover takes nor rest, nor peace, nor food, nor sleep*
> *Through year and month and night and day.*"

And when he had composed that, he composed another which he vowed should be presented to the beautiful woman he loved:

> "*The breath of the early Spring in the face of the Rose is sweet;*
> *The Face of my Love in the shade of the garden-close is sweet;*
> *Naught thou canst say of the day that has faded away is sweet;*
> *Be happy; speak not of the past, for to-day as it glows is sweet!*"[1]

He could hardly wait for the day, and yet he knew that he should not see Agapê for another four and twenty hours. It had been arranged that he and Nizâmu'l-Mulk were to pass the morning together at a favorite būstân or garden on the banks of the river not far from Nishāpûr. This spot had been imitated from the Zinda-rûd at Isfahân, which, as every one

[1] In the mutakārib meter.

knows, is, or was, the loveliest river in Persia, flowing amid gardens and palaces. Here there were no palaces, but the bulbúl sang with all the passion of a soul that loves and can never express all the height and depth of its longing. The fragrance of the roses was forever wafted on the soft breeze, and the murmur of the river, as it flowed down to lose itself in the desert, was soft, like a perpetual flowing music. Omar always spent many hours in the warm season under the shade of a pretty arched summer-house or pavilion overlooking the river and the poppy fields beyond. It belonged to a sort of tavern or refectory, the proprietor of which was a genuine Parsî, who prided himself on his descent from the old sect of the Fire Worshippers. He liked the poet-astronomer, and also gave him of his best cheer when he came there for a day's outing. When Omar heard the intimation that the Wazîr would like to accompany him thither, he sent word to the mai-farúsh or inn-keeper that a party would be there that day, and asked him to save his pavilion for him, and have his best entertainment and his most skilful sākî or cup-bearer and his best lute-player at his service.

CHAPTER IX.

A DAY IN THE BŪSTÂN.

THE sun had hardly dried the raindrops from the roses when Nizâmu'l-Mulk appeared. He was accompanied by a single rider, who bestrode a horse which would not have attracted attention where horses were compared with the Arabian standard. He was dressed in a garb which suggested a disguise, but even before he reached the house Omar thought he recognized something familiar about his person. And as the two dismounted, and, leaving the horses with a zin-dal, entered the court, Omar realized that it was the Sultân himself who had come to visit him incognito. It was a favorite entertainment of Malíkshāh to assume a disguise and go out into the city. All wise monarchs have had this desire to mingle with their subjects, to hear the truth from uncourtly lips, to see for themselves how life goes among the great masses of the citizens; sometimes, to be sure, to carry on petty intrigues. Malíkshāh had then come to visit Omar in his comparatively humble home. Etiquette would have required that the host should not appear to penetrate the disguise, but the Sultân had come to unbend and to lay aside for a little the cares of state. So when he was free from danger of espionage he threw the hampering cords of conventionality aside and was as charming a companion as could be found.

He proposed to spend the day with Omar and the Wazîr and to accompany him to the summer-pavilion; but first he was interested to see how Omar lived; he wanted to make the acquaintance of the aged Zibâ-khānúm, to whom he addressed kindly words of interest, such as win a woman's heart, however young or old she be, and then he wanted to see Omar's garden, and particularly his mathematical appliances. He was delighted with a water-clock which measured time with no small degree of accuracy, and he was interested in a kind of orrery, constructed by Omar himself, and representing the celestial sphere, the signs of the zodiac, and the revolutions of the planets. Then there was a sort of arch in one corner, with a perforated top like a dome, and the sun's rays, falling through the apertures, struck on certain lines on the pavement which indicated in degrees and minutes the altitude of the sun, and thus the period of the year. All these contrivances were, of course, primitive and crude, but they proved a certain mechanical turn, and served their purpose.

Malíkshāh asked various intelligent questions which Omar answered with modesty and clearness, and showed that in his knowledge of astronomy he was far ahead of the science of his time. He spoke with some scorn of the barbarous and inaccurate calendar which was in general use, and was supposed to date back to Jamshíd, and was cumbersome and inaccurate. He also gave his reasons for believing that the earth was round. The Sultân listened with the keenest interest, and before they left the house he had promised that Omar should have a well-equipped observatory on the hill where the hunting-sarâi was situated, and every instrument that the best brass-makers of Irân could, under his direction, construct. He also, then and there, resolved that he would distinguish his reign by a revision of the calendar, and entrust the task to no one else but Omar; of this, however, he said nothing at that time, as he would have to consult his counsellors as to the effect of such a far-reaching change.

Meantime Zibâ-khānúm had prepared a delicious sherbet, and a neat little sharbat-dâr or waiter brought it to the guests as they sat in the shady garden, where the water tinkled in the fountain and the fishes splashed in the quadrangular tank.

Meantime a servant from the palace had brought another horse for Omar, and then, at the suggestion of Malíkshāh, the three men mounted and rode slowly through the city and out the Southern gate, the Dar-î-Janûb. Outside the walls men were still plowing with cumbrous wooden plows. The air was full of fragrance, with thousands of fruit-trees in bloom. The sunlight glinted gayly on the water courses and on the fresh-washed foliage of the vineyards and orchards. Years of uninterrupted prosperity had shown what the valley could do in the way of productiveness; it was one beautiful garden in which were produced all the fruits that the appetite of man might crave. A little farther on the Sultân, who was of a practical nature in spite of his love of poetry, was interested in the operations of a windmill, made of two parallel walls of sun-dried bricks, and fitting into a cross-beam was the revolving post furnished with wings and fastened at the bottom to a round mill-stone. When the wind blew it rushed into this trap and caused the mill-stone to grind. The Sultân insisted on stopping to examine it thoroughly, and after he had questioned the miller he tossed him a gold coin and rode away, saying, "Allâh keep you, body and soul, in his protection."

After riding for an hour they reached the būstân, which was their goal. In the eyes of the faithful it was an unholy place, because wine flowed freely there. It was mainly visited by those that justified themselves on the ground that they were Sûfis, and therefore freed from the strict interpretation of the prophet's command. In later years the doctrine of the Sûfis underwent great changes, growing onerously complicated, so that even the poems of Sa'adi and Hâfiz are twisted out of their natural meaning, and interpreted, word by word and line by line, into absurd and far-fetched esoteric meaning. But at this time the Sûfis were hardly more than free-thinkers. To be sure they had their scheme of four stages through which any one was supposed to pass ere he reached hakikât, or the absolute truth and the divine union with divinity. But many, then as now, were content, having passed through the first stage, which required the disciples to live in accordance with the holy law, and to observe all the rites and ceremonies, such as are useful for the great mass of humanity, to remain in the second stage, called the path (harikât). Persons who have arrived at this fortunate stage may abandon religious forms and ceremonies, and, though nominally great purity, virtue, and fortitude are required, the license permitted by the disciple's conscience easily degenerates into self-indulgence.

The true Sûfi is an optimist, regards everything as good and divinely ordained for his pleasure; to him religion and infidelity are equally indifferent; the lawful and the unlawful are alike; he eats what is set before him, asking no questions; his women go unveiled, and the drinking of wine is as Omar said:

"*Drink wine, for this is the life eternal,—this is the season of roses, and wine, and joyous companions; be happy for an instant, for this, this is life!*"

And even as he now rode along with the Sultân and the Nizâmu'l-Mulk, he was thinking out the quatrain that runs something like this in humble prose:

"*In the time of roses—the fasl-i-gul,—on the river's brink, on the grassy edge of the garden, drink wine with one, two, three choice companions, and a few young maidens fair as the Hûr of Paradise!*"

Little did the sharâb-furûsh who kept the tavern that Omar liked to patronize imagine that the two men in simple dress, and accompanied by only one servant, were the two chief officers of the Seljûk Sultanate—even the Sultân himself and his famous Wazîr! He would have stared with his little round eyes and gone and whispered the news to his other guests and thenceforth boasted, all his life long, of the honor that had been done him. He suspected naught, though he was not a little awed at the dignity of the three guests, and he gave them his best pavilion, which was furnished with a luxurious divân and soft cushions of Shirâz silk. There they took their places, and the graceful sākî soon brought them cups brimming full of the ruddiest wine that ever glowed, ruby-like, in the spring sun. Before them flashed the rippling waves of the river curled by the fragrant breeze; over their heads waved the branches of the plane-trees; beyond on the other bank a poppy field, all aglow with myriad shades of yellow and crimson, had the appearance of a gorgeous carpet. The charming picture was framed in an exquisite arch of what one might call Moorish design; the birds were singing as if their hearts were full.

A farrâsh came and spread a beautiful prayer-rug on the tessellated pavement, and just outside a lute-player took up her position, and touched the strings with long, slender fingers, breathing forth the tenderest strains that were ever heard. Then a single dancer, swaying like a lily, and with bare feet and slender, graceful ankles, came forth, and, waving her bare round arms, began a series of pantomimic impersonations, unlike anything which the place had ever seen before.

Omar was electrified. He could not believe his eyes, and yet he could not be mistaken; the fair rakkâs was none other than Agapê, the mysterious Greek maiden, the beautiful idol of his heart. He knew by her eyes that she had recognized him. But how came she there? That was a question he asked himself and could not answer. If she had managed by her own Greek cunning to escape from the anderûn, and had dared, with unparalleled audacity, to run the risk of recognition by Malíkshāh and Nizâmu'l-Mulk, what would she not dare to do? He actually trembled to think of the consequences. But neither the Sultân nor his Wazîr seemed to see anything unusual in the phenomenon! Malíkshāh, as he sipped the liquid ruby of the wine, looked languidly on at the dance, which was perfectly free from improper suggestion or voluptuous display, enjoyed the graceful spectacle, which was so harmoniously related to the beauty of the day, the perfume of the roses, which now and then dropped their blood-red petals, the cloudless sky seen through the foliage of the plane-trees, and the sparkle of the clear river, and he said:

"Ya Allâh! the maiden dances with grace, and she is beautiful. Had I my jîka here she should have the diamond that fastens it to my crown."

"Balî! Yea, verily," said the Wazîr with a touch of irony, "she deserves the Sultân's favorite diamond, the daryâ-i-nûr (Sea of Light), and what would friend Omar give her?" he asked, turning to the poet, who had eyes for nothing, for no one else.

"He would give her one of his rubāiyât!" exclaimed the Sultân. "Come, O my prince of poets, pronounce a quatrain which shall bring the color to the maiden's brow."

Omar, as if inspired, looked into Agapê's lovely eyes, and in a low and trembling voice repeated that quatrain, which eight hundred years later sang itself to music in an English garden-close:

> "*A Book of Verses underneath the Bough,*
> *A Jug of Wine, a Loaf of Bread—and Thou*
> *Beside me singing in the Wilderness,*
> *Oh, Wilderness were Paradise now.*"

But in the original there was a somewhat audacious allusion to the Sultân, to the effect that if he and the fair one were in the desert together, it were a joy which the power of the Sultân could not diminish or bound! But the Sultân cared not for that; he was delighted:

"Barîk Allâh! Praise God," he cried, "that we have a poet so ready with verses! Now give us one on the day and the hour!"

Again, Omar, as it were inspired by the face of the lovely Greek girl, broke forth with this improvisation in the typical metre of the rubâ'ï:

> "*How pleasant is this day; neither too hot nor too cold!*
> *The rain washed the dust and the roses' heart has consoled;*
> *The Bul-búl in Pahlavî tells the bright yellow rose:*
> *'O drink of the red wine! ere the sweet day shall grow old.'*"

The Greek maiden with graceful imperiousness seized the wine-jug from the waiting sāqi, who frowned at first until she smiled on him, when he, too, smiled, and she filled the cups of the three friends.

"Give her a question in mathematics," cried Nizâmu'l-Mulk, who, warmed and made good-natured by the generous wine so strange to his lips, was entering with all his heart into the spirit of the occasion, and was disposed to treat her as his equal for the time being, — and indeed by birth, she, though now an exile, was more than his equal. "Give her a problem in your favorite algebra!"

Omar looked at Malíkshāh as if to see what he would say, but the Sultân gently nodded.

Then Omar, beckoning to Agapê to come nearer, and as she came, feasting his eyes on her beauty, — to him she was the very pearl of women, — gently took her hand and said:

"Well, fair dancer, since I must, I will give thee a problem to answer. Tell me this: Out of a swarm of golden bees one-fifth part flew to a kadâmba blossom; one-third lighted on a silíndhra-flower; three times the difference betwixt those numbers fled to the bending branch of a síngit-tree, very fragrant, bending over a glassy stream. The bee that remained hovered about the mouth of a lovely maiden, taking her to be a rose. Tell me, charming dancer, the number of bees!"

"In āsân nîst! This is not easy!" she murmured in pretty Pahlavî showing the trace of her Greek accent. "But methinks the number of bees will be the same as the number of poems which I could wish to listen to in a long summer's day from the lips of the sweetest poet of Nishāpûr!"

"Crown the Poet of Nishāpûr! Crown him with roses!" cried the Sultân, and he pointed to a rose-tree in full bloom.

Agapê, flushed with pleasure, went, and gathering a great armful of royal blossoms deftly wove them into a wreath which, when it was completed so that no thorn might prick his brow, she gracefully laid on his thick waving hair.

Then she hastily withdrew, and, as she vanished round the carved pillar that stood beside the arched entrance, Omar imagined he saw the burly form of the Agâ Zālým, and he was still more mystified.

CHAPTER X.

THREE FRIENDS AT PLAY.

By this time it was near the hour of noon prayer. The three men had not come to carouse. In spite of Omar's somewhat impudent and sacrilegious quatrains about the virtue of drunkenness, he was really temperate. He knew the dangers of overindulgence in any luxury. He enjoyed it the more that it was forbidden, but he did not care to abuse his liberty.

The three friends, for such they might certainly be called, were now weary of inaction. After the call to prayer had been heeded, and they had knelt toward the East, they got up for a stroll among the sweet-scented paths of the būstân. As they went the Sultân said:

"Rest and relaxation are good for the mind as well as for the body. We have rested; we have spent the morning in idleness; I have now many things to think and talk about. First I would speak of Hasan ben Sabah."

Instead of speaking, however, he paused for a moment, and looked down at the river, which was wider there, and somewhat choked with tamarisk. Some boys along the shore were playing with a raft which they had constructed of bulrushes, and bound together with tamarisk. They had showed no small ingenuity in their device; it was large enough to hold two of them, and these two were paddling about trying to get into the clearer channel. Several other boys on the bank were shouting directions to the two; the merry ring of their laughter came cheerily on the soft breeze. Far beyond, the mountains raised their jagged heads; the plain was swarming with industries. Such prosperity gave the Sultân cause for thought.

"Your Kizzil Bâsh," said he, addressing Omar, and calling the Persians by their quaint old name, which means Red Heads — "your Red Heads are a singularly prosperous and happy people. The plain — how many watercourses and canals has it?"

"It is watered by twelve thousand karez streams, and twelve larger courses; it has an abundance of ābambârs or water cisterns that keep the water against the drought caused by the 'One Hundred and Forty Days Wind,' — these are a farsâkh or two apart. If you will raise your august eyes you will see here and there across the plain the domes that cover them. 'Tis irrigation makes the land so fertile, and the climate so delightful in summer."

Omar with his quick wit saw what these questions

portended. He was sorry to be even the remote cause of putting on the thumbscrews of taxation.

"But to return to Hasan ben Sabah: he seems to be a man of mark. I had him with me last evening. A profoundly learned and acute mind; but he has no small opinion of himself and his abilities. Almost his first remark was that Nishāpûr, for a city so large and prosperous, paid too little revenue into the imperial treasury. What think you thereof, O Nizâmu'l-Mulk — you, who think of everything?"

"Nishāpûr has fortunately escaped from any recent raid," said the Wazîr. "It has had its share of misfortunes; but it is happily situated, and soon recovers from whatever blow is struck. Behold it from this knoll; you might think that it had stood for ages. And yet, less than fifty years ago it was levelled to the ground, and many of its inhabitants were carried into Afghānistân. The mountains give excellent shelter to raiders. It behooves a wise ruler to keep them well guarded."

"Nevertheless, methinks the fair city might stand a little more pressure. How are the mines? There are mines, are there not?"

Malíkshāh had received only the day before the report of the manager of the great turquoise mines of Abû Ishâk. He had brought him several magnificent specimens of that superb gem, there called fīrūzá.

"The mountains are full of minerals," said Omar. "Lead and copper, antimony and iron, marble and soapstone; a wise manager would fill the Sultân's treasury without overtaxing the merchants of the city."

"Hasan ben Sabah last night hinted that lack of management kept low the tide of receipts," continued the Sultân. "He said if he were Treasurer of the Kingdom he would bring great returns from so rich a province."

"O illustrious Commander of the Faithful," said the Wazîr, "why not commission the able Hasan to make out the budget as he would if he were Treasurer of the Realm? Give him six weeks to do it in."

"A capital suggestion! If he succeeds in accomplishing his task we will reward him; if his conceit cause him to fail, no harm will have been done. He is a man of energy and ability. Surely our visit to our beautiful city of Nishāpûr has been prolific of great profit. Not soon again shall I have such another day of hunting as that in the Park! Did you see the fortunate stroke I made with the boar-spear?"

And without either pausing to hear the Wazîr's answer or remembering that he had been called away from the boar-hunt, he went on recalling the enthusiasm of that exciting moment when the boar, having been maddened by his wounds, suddenly turned and charged the Sultân.

"I can see him now," said Malíkshāh. "How fierce and fiery-blood-shot were his wicked eyes! His jaws were dripping with bloody foam. On he came! Ibrāhîm Niyâl shouted to me, but I was on my guard. I set my spear, and he rushed against it with such violence that it went through his heart and broke short off! If I could only have kept his massive head. No such boar has been seen on the mountain-side for many long years, they all told me, and I can well believe it! But let us return for the midday refection."

They went back to the pavilion and found that everything had been ordered, and a delicious repast of sweets and fruits was quickly brought for their delectation. Then after they had chased away the eager appetite their walk had given them, a new entertainment in the performances of an Indian juggler was given. Wonderful were the tricks which he performed with no apparent aid, either from disguise or assistant. But for Omar, the rose-lover, what could have been more delightful and surprising than to see a pot of gorgeous, crimson roses, hundreds on a single little tree, apparently materialize out of thin air before his eyes? One moment and there was the empty, cold, and lifeless earth in the vessel; the next came the sprouting green of the first rose-leaf; then each time that the juggler lifted the silken turban that he used as a veil, the rose-tree was nearer its quickly attained perfection. When it was fully grown he brought it to his amazed spectators and let them pick the fragrant blooms.

He did another thing scarcely less marvellous. He took out a long, slender silken cord, and handed it to the Wazîr to examine. The Sultân also wanted to handle it; he remarked that it would make an excellent kemend or lassoo, wherewith to take the gur-kher or wild ass of the mountain.

Then the juggler took the cord, and with a strange whirling motion sent it straight up into the air. It hung there as if fastened to some nail or beam; but where he stood was under the open sky; no nail or beam, or even the branch of a tree, supported that mysterious cord. He called a small boy who looked like a Chinese, and muttering some gibberish pointed to the top of the cord, which seemed to be out of sight. The boy began to climb the rope, hand over hand, whirling slightly, but not kicking his legs. In a moment or two he vanished from sight. Then the juggler called or pretended to call to him: "Come down, come down." But when no answer responded, taking a keen sword in his mouth, he, too, climbed up the cord and disappeared. A few moments later an amputated leg fell to the ground; then came another, followed by an arm; and when the limbs had all been flung down from the invisible country, or plateau, or place in the cloudless blue, down came the headless trunk, with the sword thrust through its heart. Finally the impassive Indian himself came down the rope, bringing the boy's head in one hand.

It was a terrible spectacle even to men like Malíkshāh, used to bloodshed. His impulse was to summon a farrâsh and have the apparent murderer haled to justice. But before he had a chance to speak, the juggler had thrown his silken veil over the ground where the remains lay scattered, and when he pulled it off again, there lay the boy whole as before, who leaped to his feet, with a grin on his ugly phiz, and bowed low before his illustrious patrons.

Omar ordered a bowl of wine to be taken to the waiting Indian, who, when he had finished his display, knelt and kissed the ground before them. Nizâmu'l-Mulk tossed him a purse full of gold, and again he bowed to the ground. Then, when he had gone, the talk became serious again. The Wazîr had in mind a plan to revise the system of education in the schools and universities, and the occasion now offered to talk it over with the Sultân. He knew that in Omar he should find a powerful ally, and he was not disappointed. Omar spoke with eloquence regarding the stupid conventional system in vogue. He gave many amusing instances of the ignorance and lack of common sense shown by the teachers, and, at the Sultân's request, he developed at some length the wider and more liberal curriculum that he wanted to see adopted.

"Students come here to Nishāpûr," said Omar, "hungry for knowledge. They are fed on dry husks. The professors, who are under no supervision, sit on their heels, leaning lazily back against a pillar, and talk to them about the traditions. They fill their minds with dull and stupid genealogies; they interpret the poems of Muhammád in their own idiotic fashion, contrary to all common sense, and, what is worse, they attack others who try to give the meat of the word, instead of the indigestible shells."

"What would you do about it?" asked the Wazîr, anxious to draw Omar out, and noticing with delight that the Sultân was becoming deeply interested.

"I would put all the universities and academies under State control," said Omar. "I would weed out the dull, incompetent, and bigoted teachers; I would put in their places young men specially trained in the sciences; I would have courses given in mathematics and astronomy, as well as in the interpretation of the Surahs; I would have the art of poetry taught by zealous and capable rhetoricians. The wide realm of history should be opened to survey. I would not banish religion, but instead of unprofitable discussions of unimportant details, wasting precious energies, as now, I would substitute liberal studies."

Omar's fine face glowed with enthusiasm, and his eloquent tongue poured forth convincing arguments.

Nizâmu'l-Mulk felt very much as Omar did, and he, too, was anxious to make an entire change in the system.

The result of the talk was that the Sultân agreed to everything, and the Wazîr, aided by Omar, drew up a scheme for the revision of the universities. In this respect the afternoon at the būstân bore most important fruit. Not only at Nishāpûr was the new impulse felt from that time forward, but new universities were founded in various parts of the Sultanate. Particularly famous became the one established at Bagdâd by Nizâmu'l-Mulk. It was called after the Wazîr, and lasted for several hundred years; though, in the course of time, the instruction which it furnished became too conventional again.

In this lofty discussion, in which the Sultân bore his part, the afternoon wore away; the sun was now declining; the shadows of the sycamores began to stretch longer and longer across the river banks, and the nightingales were tuning up their evening song in the clumps of the garden. Ever more and more beautiful grew the afternoon light, and the far-off mountains turned rose color, and glowed like heaps of gems. The river, now freed from the caresses of the wind, grew glassy, and reflected every tree and bush and reed, its surface only now and then broken for an instant by the dipping wing of a swallow, or the fall of some insect, or the answering leap of a fish. It was pleasant lingering as the evening dewy coolness descended, and, as they rode slowly back to the city, they talked cheerfully of various things, the pleasure of their day's outing, the marvel of the juggler's performance, which savored of the supernatural, so that the suspicious element in Malíkshāh's spirit still impelled him to send and have the man arrested. Not even Omar could find an explanation for the miracle. The science of hypnotism had not then been invented, although the thing itself, under various disguises, had been in the world for thousands of years. They had still more to say regarding Ḥasan's appointment and the possibilities that he might evoke from his new position, and ever and again they recurred to the new plans for education.

As they reached the gate the darkness fell; but in the western sky, suddenly emerging from behind a drifting cloud that had faded from crimson to gray, flashed the radiant sickle of the new moon, seeming to reap the sky and gather in the harvest of light.

"Give us one more rubâ'ī, O Prince of Improvisers," cried the Sultân, and Omar, thinking regretfully and longingly of the Grecian maiden, spoke, quietly, the exquisite quatrain that plays so charmingly on the three meanings of *mâh:*

> *"Since on thy face the morrow may not shine*
> *Make jocund now this passionate heart of thine!*
> *The Moon shall seek us long when we are gone,—*
> *Then in this moonlight, O my Moon, drink wine."*

"Ever-ready!" cried the Wazîr, with pride in his friend's accomplishment, "we will accompany you to your door and leave you there."

"My aged mother would delight to have you rest once more under our humble roof," said Omar, looking at the Sultân. "I make no doubt that she has, against our return, a kid stewed in its mother's milk."

And even as he said these words they came in sight of Omar's dwelling, and there, looking down the street with her aged eyes, stood Zibâ-khānúm watching for her son's home-coming; and when the three horses stopped she raised her voice and begged them to come in, saying, in her pleasant, friendly tone:

"*Hosh āmdâdīd, safâ āwúrdīd!*—You are welcome, you have brought joy with you!" And she added her entreaties to Omar's that they should come in once more.

CHAPTER XI.

THE KEEN EYE AND THE HUNGRY PURSE.

THE Sultân imagined that he had been successful in eluding observation as he slipped out through a secret gate in the back of the Arg, known only to his nephew, Nizâmu'l-Mulk, and one or two trusted officers. But he did not elude the observation of Hasan ben Sabah. Hasan managed to discover, also, who was the single servant who followed the two rulers as they rode to Omar's house. He, himself, had no intention of following, or of sending a spy to bring him an account of what should take place. But he resolved to exert the influence of his compelling eye, possibly strengthened by the magic of gold, to induce the zin-dal to tell what he saw, where the Sultân went, and what he did. Hasan had great power with his deep-set eyes. Few men could withstand the fire of their direct gaze; bent on any one in anger or scorn it seemed to sear the very soul. This went far to explain the marvellous influence that he wielded over his followers. Once under its hypnotizing control, a man was never knewn to disobey his commands, even though they sent him to certain death.

Hitherto in his experience of short-lived eminence he had failed in tact, or had showed his hand too soon. His ambition was insatiable and could not wait to be fed. But through years of vicissitude, he had learned a measure of wisdom. He had an able assistant in his silent, wise, and crafty son. He now knew how to keep his peace, to bide his time, to seize the occasion. Or at least, so he confidently told himself. He thought that he could read Malíkshāh like a scroll; he could easily insinuate doubts regarding Nizâmu'l-Mulk and undermine his influence, and, in time, bring about his downfall and secure his place.

When Malíkshâh the next day summoned him to a conference and confided to him that he was not satisfied with the revenues accruing from the province of Khurāsân, and especially from the city and plain of Nishāpûr, Hasan ben Sabah fell in with this line of reasoning. He said:

"If the Commander of the Faithful will bear with me I will tell him that only yesterday, while he was absent from the palace, I, endeavoring to become wonted to my duties, saw the under-secretary of the bureau of mines secrete in the fold of his jubbâ an emerald." . . .

The Sultân, though generally good-natured, was

quick tempered, and could not endure any malfeasance. Without waiting to hear further he exclaimed:

"Have that hawk of a clerk brought here instantly. Allâh akbár! God is great! What right has he to be thieving my jewels?"

A servant hastened out and brought in the trembling culprit.

"Tell me, son of a burning father, what right thou hast to secrete my turquoises and emeralds? Is it that I employ thee to rob me? No excuses. Call the nazîr, have him bring the bastinado block and the rods. Have four farrâsh-hâ instantly."

The trembling wretch, who had possibly stolen more than one of the Sultân's gems, turned pale and tried to open his mouth and speak. In an incredibly short time the nazîr or inspector had come, followed by four farrâsh-hâ, who brought with them the falak or block into which the clerk's legs were thrust. With nooses fastened to the man two of the farrâsh-hâ held him firmly, and the others began to raise their willow rods to inflict the terrible punishment. Then the poor fellow found a voice and in a pitable tone, full of tears, he screamed:

"By the grave of thy father, pardon, pardon! I have sinned, I and my father and my mother before me. I know not what I have done, but I promise never to do it again."

The Sultân had a quick sense of humor and this desperate confusion of thought pacified him.

"Wâ-īstíd, step back," he said to the farrâsh-hâ, who were waiting only for the signal to begin the flailing of the clerk's soles.

"This time I will pardon thee, though I intended thou shouldst eat a hundred sticks. But if I hear again that thou hast stolen, I will send thee to the city of non-existence. Let him up."

The attendants unfastened their nooses, removed his feet from the block, and lifted the young man to his feet. He was as white as spun flax, but in a trembling voice he kissed the ground at the Sultân's feet. "Pure art thou, O God, and worthy of praise, and blessed is thy name, and exalted thy glory," he exclaimed, quoting from the Qurân.

"Thou hast had a narrow escape," said the Sultân.

"My beard is in thy hands," replied the other.

Here the Sultân himself could hardly refrain from laughing, because the man, though he used the traditional phrase, had no sign of a beard.

The man was then dismissed, and the Sultân, restored to good humor, proceeded to the business which had been so incontinently interrupted. Hasan ben Sabah could scarcely conceal his impatience at such weakness on Malíkshāh's part. He would have had the farrâsh end the whole matter by tightening a shawl or a rope around the young man's neck. Clerks were easy to supply; the loss of one, especially of a dishonest one, would not be felt. However he was not sorry to discover a new weakness in the Sultân. Every weakness would be to him additional strength.

"I have decided," said Malíkshāh, "to entrust to you the drawing up of a scheme for increasing the revenues of this our province of Khurāsân. You have been pleased to criticise the apparent feebleness of the golden stream that flows from this rich city into our treasury. If, through malfeasance, any part is diverted from me, 'tis for you to stop the leak. If you can, without too great pressure, so as not to cause too great discontent, increase its annual amount, make it plain in your report, and if it seem practicable, not only shall it be tried but you shall have the honor of putting it into execution. Every faculty shall be given into your hands for making investigations. Will six weeks be sufficient for your purposes? You will have to visit the mines in the mountains; you will have to determine carefully how much increase the merchants in the city will endure; you will have to learn the state of the various industries in the city and in the whole province. Six weeks, methinks, is scarcely sufficient time to do all this and make out the budget."

"In the name of God the merciful, the compassionate! verily thou dost honor thy humble servant.

The fate of every man God has bound about his neck. O exalted one! I will use all diligence to fulfil thy commands. But I feel so confident that I can master the situation that all I ask is four weeks; from moon till moon will be sufficient time. Indeed I have already made a beginning —"

And Hasan ben Sabah began to detail to the amazed Sultân the receipts from the turquoise mines of Nishāpûr during the year preceding and showed conclusively what they should have been. He could not refrain from a slightly ill-natured remark reflecting on the Wazîr, and hinting that if he had been in control no such niggardly outcome should have resulted from mines so rich in gems.

So the affair was arranged. The proper farmân or order was issued and Hasan was made nominal Lord-Treasurer of the Province. With characteristic zeal he set about his work. He went out every day and assiduously visited the bāzârs and the various manufactures of the city. He found how many pots each potter made and how large were his profits. He discovered who owned the mulberry groves and how many silk spinners were at work and how much the cost and profit on that beautiful industry were. He got a list of all the taverns and caravansaries and the numbers of their visitors. With incredible celerity he gathered a thousand details of the industries of the city and the province, of the prosperous villages along the plain and of the caravans that came in daily across the great trade-ways leading to India and the West.

Nizâmu'l-Mulk with some little suspicion followed his movements. He held under seeming inattention the key to every department of power. His eyes were in every place; he had perfectly trusty spies who brought him ample reports of all that was going on. He foresaw that there would not be room for both him and Hasan at Malíkshāh's Court, but he was in no hurry to precipitate any open rivalry or out and out enmity. But he meant to have the whip-hand over his old schoolmate, and it was not long before a discovery which he made gave him a feeling of security. He no longer had any apprehension that Hasan by his ability or by his skill in intrigue could permanently injure him. He resolved to let the skein tangle itself to the last knot before he would interfere.

The secret was that Hasan was taking bribes from many of the merchants and wealthier artisans. It was no coarse bribe-taking, but a delicate acceptance of more or less valuable considerations. The offer of a bag of gold outright was indeed openly rejected with every appearance of indignation: but the quiet transfer of a jewel or of a little piece of land accompanied by an apparent deed of purchase made it easy for the transaction to seem legitimate: Hasan ben Sabah each time remained the gainer and each time let the imposition of the tax fall less heavily on the victim.

Thus Yusûf al Zar-gár, the great gold-beater who performed such marvels with his hammer and his graver, took Hasan ben Sabah over his establishment supposing that Hasan was a prospective purchaser, and with great good will showed him the stores of exquisitely engraved plate that he had made for the trade with Damascus. Hasan took his breath away when he told him that he would be obliged to double his taxes, but he reduced them materially on Yusûf's promise to duplicate a certain cup set with rubies and diamonds in alternation making an elaborate sentence from the Qurân. A famous horse-dealer sent him a noble Arabian steed of purest breed, and Hasan in consequence turned the screw only once and a half instead of twice. So it was with hundreds of the taxpayers of the city. They knew that it was their misfortune to attract the attention of the Treasury and that they must diminish their profits by a forced levy; they were ready to keep on the good side of so reasonable a man as the new Lord-Treasurer by flattering his vanity or making his life easier. Bribe-taking was so common that they expected nothing else, and Hasan's indignant repudiation of the open offer made his gracious acceptance of a more elegantly directed gift seem like a favor.

One morning he came to the establishment of a carpet-weaver.

"Alâ yâ ayyuhâ!" he said, to attract the attention of the proprietor, who came forward bowing humbly, evidently thinking that the great lord who had stopped at his door was some patron.

"You are Adâm Abdullâh, the rug-maker?"

"For so my father — Allâh rest his soul — named me."

"You have a large and flourishing trade?"

"Allâh has been kind to me."

"Can you show me your assortment?"

"Ba-chashm! Willingly! If your honor will do me the grace to come under my unworthy roof!"

Hasan accepted the invitation and, while pretending to ask questions for personal information, and giving the dealer hopes that he would indulge in a handsome order, not only made a mental inventory of the rug-maker's establishment, but learned from him enough to justify him in extorting a large increase in the yearly tax.

Hasan had ordered laid aside for him a magnificent prayer-rug, woven of the softest silk and with gold fringes, the design graceful and harmonious, soft to the touch and almost imperishable. He went through the usual comedy of purchase, gradually beating the dealer down from the first exaggerated price until at last it approached somewhat nearly to the value of the article. Thereby he gauged pretty accurately the craftiness of Adâm Abdullâh. Then only did he show the poor man his hand. When the rug-maker learned that it was the newly appointed nāzîr-i-mālīyyȧ, he fell on his knees before him and kissed the hem of his coat, protesting:

"By the soul of my forefathers! Be indulgent, O most exalted! Even now the taxes are more than I can pay. I have had to sacrifice my father's little patrimony and the savings that I had hoped to leave to my only son. O increase not thy demands! Be easy and I will give thee a receipted bill for the prayer-rug. It is thine! And it cost me a year's profits!"

Hasan pretended that even such a piece of munificence would not affect his duty to his august master. But nevertheless he gave Adâm Abdullâh the address to which it might be sent, and eased his mind a little by telling him he would take his case under advisement. There would certainly be some increase, but not enough to make him lose an hour's blessed sleep.

Hasan was too wise to store in Nishāpûr the precious things that flowed into his possession; he had them sent to a certain address, and when a sufficiently large package of carpets and furs and brazen dishes, and the exquisite filigree work of the silversmiths, and costly pieces of pottery, and no small store of jewels had been collected, he sent them all to his wise and firm friend Abulfasl, of Isfahân, with whom he knew they would be safe. This was managed so dexterously that Nizâmu'l-Mulk failed to trace them.

But to all appearance Hasan ben Sabah was a most industrious and faithful servant to the Sultân. He was at his work early and late. He almost invariably refused all invitations to join in the pleasures of the Court. He could not be pursuaded to go hunting. He declared that he had more important game to chase than wild asses. Malíkshāh, who occasionally invited him to drink the tea of China with him, was considerate enough not to ask him to go to Omar's pavilion, though a word would have been an order. Nor did he seem to care to mingle with his old schoolmates, in their pleasant excursions, or in their hours of friendly talk either in Omar's garden or on the mountain, where, by the Sultân's orders, the new observatory was fast becoming a reality. He always had an excuse ready, and he told them frankly that with him so much of life had passed fruitlessly, he was anxious, now that he had a chance, to make the most of it; moreover, he felt that he should be the death's-head at the feast; the cast of his mind had become gloomy, and laughter to him was like the crackling of thorns under a pot.

It was the truth; Hasan ben Sabah was a fanatic. Deep down in his heart were germinating the seeds of what may have been madness, and was surely black ambition. Could he himself have told what the next months and years would bring him to? Could he himself realize in any degree the trend of the dark current that was even now beginning to seize him in its grasp, and hurry him onward like a flood? Could he have had thus early any definite plan to displace his benefactor and friend, if possible, and, perhaps, having got the reins of power into his hand, to place himself on the throne of the Seljûk Sultâns? Was even that a clearly rounded scheme?

CHAPTER XII.

POET AND MAIDEN.

THE next time that Omar went to the palace he wore a single yellow rose. He had little expectation that it would be noticed or bring a response. He knew that he was running no small risk in entering into an intrigue with any woman of the Sultân's household, even though it were not one of the Sultân's wives. But the fact that Agapê had appeared at the pavilion, before the Sultân and Nizâmu'l-Mulk, and had caused no remark, emboldened him, and he resolved to put his happiness or fortune in the Greek girl's hands. He at least would do his part.

That afternoon the Sultân gave a great feast to which the notabilities of the city were invited. It was a long and tedious affair; Omar was not sorry to be present, but being a sensible man, he cared far more for the small and choice supper, where conversation might be general or mutual, where there was sufficient familiarity of acquaintance for the jest or the poem to be appreciated by all. He felt lost and insignificant among so many, — men bearing long titles, and proud of the insignia of office. But before the feast was over a hādím or waiter passing innocently by managed to convey him a little scroll. It made his heart throb, and he found means to read it while all the other guests were watching the antics of a juggler, who was enlivening the space of waiting between courses by performing wonderful tricks with balls and knives.

It was very short. It was, as before, written in Greek, and asked him to be at the pavilion the following afternoon. "Do not fear for me," it said, "I shall find the means to come."

He sat there as if in a dream. The attendants passed back and forth, the musicians played, the dancers danced, a bear-tamer exhibited some wonderfully trained animals, but Omar sat thinking only what might happen on the morrow. What he would have done had the Sultân suddenly called on him for one of his rubāiyât would be hard to say. He would probably have been covered with confusion, and obliged to ask indulgence. He managed to make his escape early and went home, but not to study or write. He remembered how the beautiful Greek girl praised his poems, and he resolved to have several ready for her in case — but how absurd it was to deem it possible for her to meet him. He almost laughed at the idea. How could she escape from the hundreds of watchful eyes, from the eunuchs alert to detect any irregularity? And he shuddered at the thought that she might be caught and brought back. He had heard some of the tragedies that had taken place behind the pardah, or veil of the anderûn. But then he knew that she was a Greek, and some of the wiliness of the crafty Odysseus was undoubtedly hers.

The night was splendid; the moon rode high and sent down her golden beams, making the city, with its domes and minarets and its embattled walls, like a vision of loveliness. Omar could never resist the beauty of "the heavenly bowl," which, adorned with brilliant jewels, arched above his head. Only the greater stars kept the moon company; he knew them all as no one else among the thousands of inhabitants of that big city knew them. He gazed at the twinkling points that outlined the Great Bear — the dúbb-y akbár — and at the calm radiance of náhid, or Venus. How little he knew of all that mysterious population. He murmured:

"The stars that adorn the Heavens for a measureless sum of Time,
They come and they go, and again they come with Time;
In the skirt of Heaven, and under the womb of the earth,
Are creatures that while Allâh lives will speak and grow dumb with Time."

He imagined the Milky Way — the tarîqu'l-labbāná — was a great caravan route down which passed the souls of the millions of hapless sons of men, and this splendid quatrain came following close on the other:

> "*One moment in Annihilation's Waste,*
> *One moment of the Well of Life to taste —*
> *The Stars are setting, and the Caravan*
> *Draws to the Dawn of Nothing — Oh, make haste!*" [1]

He wondered how far the astrologers, of whom he so often made sport, were right in calculating the influences of the planets on those who were born under them. Was he, himself, born under a happy star? He, the poet, the star-gazer, had now only one wish:

> "*Ay! woe to the man who in passion's joy has no part!*
> *To the man if the spell cast by love works no cheer on his heart!*
> *Each day that thou spendest on earth unwitting of love,*
> *Remember how wasteful of precious moments thou art.*"

A deep sense of his insignificance came over him; yet it was not exactly depression. Those same stars had seen Kaî Khosrû on his throne; they had looked down on the great ruins of the Takht-i-Jamshîd where were the silent figures of kings hewn out of the living rock; they had seen all the generations of men — all the blooming maidens, like the houris of paradise — perish, and go back into the dust. The very

[1] E. FitzGerald's paraphrase.

tulips to which he compared the face of his love — the lālá rukh — were made up of the dust that had once been tulip-faced girls:

> "*We must perish in the path of love,*
> *We must perish in the talons of Fate,*
> *Ay! sweet-faced Sákí, sit not idle!*
> *Bring me water, for dust I shall be.*"

One after another the pathetic graceful quatrains rose into his mind, all tinged with the melancholy of the lovely night:

> "*Every crimson rose and tulip that beside the roadside springs*
> *Tells the story of the spilling of the blood of mighty kings;*
> *Every lovely violet growing from the bosom of the earth,*
> *Is the beauty-mole of some fair maiden that the poet sings.*"

And as if in answer to his thoughts, he heard the distant voice of a night owl echoing his plaint of the swift flight of time, the paltry state of world-famous kings, the fleeting nature of moles, — for he remembered with a touch of whimsical amusement how the merry maidens of Irân in order to win favor with the men — for with the Persians the mole is a crowning touch of beauty — sometimes create artificial moles with the oxide of antimony, or with zarb-chub and charcoal. Yes, the owl was a fitting chorus for his monologue; he heard it and listened; a dark cloud swallowed up the moon; the night air grew chilly; he shivered, and went to his sleeping-room.

Never did morning seem longer to a busy scientific man: his mathematical problems would not solve themselves; the quatrains that he had composed the night before seemed stale, flat, and unprofitable; his little garden failed to please him; even the sweet note of the wood-pigeon repeating its everlasting question of "where? where?" — "*ku? ku?*" grew tiresome and monotonous.

All diseases taken late in life are apt to go hard; so it is with love. The young man may — he not always does — recover easily from its first or second attack; but the man of middle age who has hitherto escaped or who has even had mild and harmless lesions is an almost hopeless victim. In his case it is apt to be accompanied by delirium. In all cases it leads to more or less permanent blindness: no defects in the object adored are visible; all is enveloped in a glamour. Work becomes an impossibility: reason vanishes, and the most sensible of men have been known to do and say the most imbecile things. Prosaic individuals who have never been moved by Poesy's divine voice are suddenly seen trying to find impossible rhymes; men with voices like a raven's, plume their feathers and imagine that they are singing, and that all that listen are amazed at the beauty of their song. But the poet? Omar himself sang that love had taken him unaware, that he was verily distraught for love. "My heart is in such a blaze that there is no telling which is heart and which is blaze!"

The Sultân, with his nephew Ibrāhîm Niyâl, with Nizâmu'l-Mulk and a number of the principal personages of the Court and town, had gone to see the Nishāpûr turquoise mines. Omar heard of the projected expedition and avoided being invited. It required considerable skill, for it was known that he was an authority regarding gems, his little book entitled "Mîzân-ul-hukm; or, The Scales of Wisdom," which was a treatise dealing with the problem of testing the value of objects set with precious stones without removing the jewels, had gained him no small reputation, and he was constantly called on to decide vexed questions in dispute among the jewellers. Quite alone, he therefore proceeded to his favorite resort, all the time pondering the probabilities of Agapê's keeping her promise. Of course he was there ridiculously early; the sun had not reached the zenith when he established himself on the divân, and with the unusual solace of a little of that famous Indian herb called *bang*, gave himself up to the strange day-dreams that it engendered.

Never before had the būstân seemed so lovely to him; the season advancing even a few days had developed the foliage and clothed the trees and vines with richer green. The soft breeze scattered the petals of the flowers. This almost petulant rudeness of the zephyrs moved Omar to his usual mode of expression:

> "*Lo, the skirt of the rose has been torn by the breeze,*
> *And the bulbúl delights in the beauty he sees,*
> *Oh, sit in the shade of the rose, for the wind*
> *Has scattered the rose-dust of thousands like these.*"

And when a moment later another gust swept into his arched doorway a little whirlpool of mingled blossoms, like an impromptu came the words of this melodious rubâ'ī:

> "*Narcissus-blossoms from the skies are raining!*
> *Into the garden blooms richest dyes are raining!*
> *I pour the red wine in a lily cup*
> *As violet clouds the jasmin I prize are raining!*"

Suddenly a shadow fell across the arched doorway. He had no need to look up; his eyes were all the time fixed with expectation on the picture that it framed, — the river flowing softly-murmuring by, the rose-branches swaying in the soft air, the occasional flight of a bird singing as it flew. But —

Now the one thing that the picture lacked was present. The miracle that he had longed for, had hoped for, and yet had not believed possible, was accomplished. Paradise had its Eve at last! This Eve was dressed in the Fārsī costume and of course had her face hidden by the usual veil. But Omar needed no interpreter except his own heart to tell him who the slender, graceful maiden was.

She came in, gliding like a shadow.

"Poet of the rose-twined lyre!" she exclaimed, "I have escaped from the jaws of the lion! I trembled lest you should not have read my note aright!"

Omar rose and went to meet the maiden.

"The moon should not hide her face behind a cloud," he replied. "Sweet is the voice of the nightingale and we care not whether we see him or not. But when I hear thy voice, clearer than the song of a brook, then my heart must be gratified. I beg thee, lay aside thy cumbering veil. Let the sweet moon of thy face shine on me."

The Greek maiden was willing enough to comply with his demand. But first she showed the native coquetry of a woman's nature. She pretended to hesitate. He insisted and with his own hands seized the end and began to unwind the gauzy material.

When this pretty little battle was over and the victory remained with him, he took her by the hand and led her to the cushioned divân and enthroned her there. Then at his summons came the sharbat-dâr and brought a simple but delicious refection, beginning with the sweets that maidens like. Nor did she, being Greek, disdain sipping daintily the sweet-scented date-wine from a graceful cup shaped like a water-lily.

Omar had made sure of being undisturbed. There

was nothing that troubled his mind, unless it were the fear lest the maiden's absence should be discovered. But when he suggested that possibility she laughed at him with that silvery laugh that had at first rung in accord with hidden harmonies of his heart.

"Were I a dull-witted Circassian slave," she said, "there might be cause for fear, or even one of those Chinese maids with their black hair and almond eyes a-squint, — stupid dummies, though the Persians do consider them models of beauty. But an eye-flash of wit is worth all the rest. So trust to me."

"But how did you get away and how did you come?" queried Omar, with all the inquisitiveness of his sex.

"I walked out and came in a palankin, — as a court-lady should do," said Agapê.

"But did no one attempt to prevent you?"

"Why should any one attempt to prevent me? Besides I had a special order from Nizâmu'l-Mulk; and all the Court has gone to the turquoise mountain. I had been here before; I knew the way."

"Mysterious Agapê!" exclaimed Omar, with a man's admiration of a clever woman who has accomplished a miracle and makes no account of it. "I was never more surprised than when I saw you dancing — dancing in this very pavilion! Unless indeed I may confess to being more surprised that you have answered the dearest wish of my soul and come to be with me here alone. Do you know I was jealous of even the two who with me saw your graceful motions as you swayed like a flower that day, and told in gesture and look the story of the fair Shakh-i-Nabât and the Jinnî. I would fain have had you then all to myself. How favored I am!"

And once more Omar spoke with softest inflections that exquisite quatrain:

"*I desire a sack of ruby wine and a dīwân of verses, and half a loaf, to keep the soul in the body, and to sit with thee, apart from all the world. Ah, that is better than the empire of the Sultân.*"

"Now I have my wish," he added, with a caressing look.

"And you have given me something better than a loaf of bread," said Agapê.

"What is that?" asked Omar, pretending to be obtuse. "The date-wine?"

"Nay, the poem. That I shall never forget. It is sweeter than our Platon's, for he sang:

"'*Seat thyself 'neath this high-branched pine-tree that murmurs while the zephyrs sigh through its needles, and near the lapsing stream my pipe shall bring sweet sleep to thy soothed eyelids.*'"

She cited it in Greek and he wondered how she could have remembered it. She had to repeat it, and yet again, before he caught all its meaning, for it is one thing to read a language however well, and another to understand it when spoken. But the Greek and the Persian are not so alien as are the Persian and the Arabic. Greek and Persian are sister and brother: Persian and Arabic are husband and wife, — united and yet not akin.

"But the line that you repeated called for '*the book of verses underneath the bough.*' I claim the promise of the poems. We are underneath the bough."

Here now entered the coquetry of genius. The poet and singer, even when they greatly desired to show off their accomplishments, let themselves be urged. It is the expression of a subtle and intoxicating self-flattery.

"You do not care to hear my rough verses," urged Omar. "What is there in them?"

"Our Greek poems are sweet, but they do not so appeal to the ear. I love the graceful, swinging rhythm, the double and triple rhymes, falling like the rippling waves of my native Ægean."

"Tell me about your native Ægean," said Omar.

"When you have repeated to me a dīwân of your poems, then I will."

So at last persuaded by her pleading, dark-brown eyes, and her rosy lips so enticingly lifted, he began, and first he repeated the quatrain that he had composed the night before about the rose-bed that marked the red blood of mighty kings, and the violet arising from the cheek of a beautiful maiden:

> "*Har zha ke gul-i u lâl-i zari bũdast*
> *Az sarkhyi zhun-i shar-yari bũdast:*
> *Har shagi bunassha kaz zamin mî ruid*
> *Khãlast ke bar rukh-i nagari bũdast.*"

"Nay, but that is too melancholy!" exclaimed Agapê. "It makes my blood run cold! I love light, and color, and beauty, and cheerfulness."

"Then tell me how you like this one:

> "'*With my rose-blooming Love my very soul is united!*
> *My hand with the flask and the brimming bowl is united!*
> *Ay! Every part of my earthly lot I will joy in*
> *Ere my every part with the One Great Whole is united.*'"[1]

"I like them all, but I like the joyous ones the best. I know that life is full of shadows and terrible things, and I am often homesick, but for all that when I see the sunlight glinting on the river and the poppies swaying in the sweet-scented breeze, and the swallows darting through the azure and playing hide-and-seek with the clouds, then my heart beats with rapture, and I, too, could fly away and forget every care!"

Then she insisted on hearing some more, and he chose some of his cheerfulest ones; but as he told her, most of them were composed before he had seen

[1] Somewhat altered from the translation of John Payne.

her, and she made him promise to write her a little book of them. But he would not promise before she had agreed to give him a kiss for every verse, — the būsá-dusti, he called it, — and, like a crafty tradesman, he wished half of them paid in advance!

"'Hold fast this ready money, and let go that promise-to-pay!'" he quoted from one of his own quatrains. And they compromised by four kisses for the four lines of the following impromptu:

> "*Arise! give wine! What do we need to say?*
> *Thy sweet young mouth fills all my need to-day!*
> *Give wine as rosy as thy rosy cheeks!*
> *Thy tangled curls repentance plead to-day!*"

Then when that little debt was gallantly paid — did we not say that love makes even wise men ridiculous, and did not the great Sultân Suleymân declare that past all comprehension is the way of a man with a maid? — Omar suggested that it was time for him to hear the story of Agapê's life. Was he not dying with desire to know how she, a Greek maiden, happened to be in the Court of Malíkshāh? How had he been able to curb his curiosity so long? Here already the sun was beginning to slant towards the western mountains, and the shadows were growing long.

"But my story is not long or very interesting," said Agapê.

"How could anything that concerns thee fail to

be interesting?" exclaimed Omar, in protest, and he looked so serious out of his handsome eyes that Agapê laughed merrily.

"But can we not go down nearer the river?" asked the girl. Omar took her by the hand — he was not too old to be thrilled by its touch — and they sauntered slowly down through the būstân to a little clump of arghāvân-trees still glorious with their crimson buds just bursting into bloom. Here there was waiting for them a rustic seat wide enough for two, for any seat is wide enough for two that will hold one, when the two are lovers. The birds were singing with all their hearts; the wind had died down; the river was so glassy that every tree and reed on the opposite bank had its counterpart in the world of reflections. Not far away a lute player was strumming gaily, and in a peach orchard at the left of the poppy field the nightingale was essaying the first flights of his passionate song. Such days, such hours, such moments, come rarely, and perhaps only once in a man's experience. As Omar looked at the lovely girl, whose liquid eyes answered his deepest thought, whose fragrant, intoxicating breath caressed his brown beard, who nestled so confidingly into the shelter of his arm, he could hardly believe that it was not all a dream, and as they sat there under the declining day, Agapê, in her pretty, broken Palahvî, told him the story of her life.

CHAPTER XIII.

AGAPÊ'S STORY.

"HAVE you ever seen the sea?" she asked first.

"No, but I have seen the desert," replied Omar.

"Oh, but the beauty of the sea!" exclaimed Agapê.

"Oh, but the beauty of the desert!" interrupted Omar.

"Your desert is covered with salt, and not a tree grows in it."

"Your sea is nothing but salt water, and not a flower grows in it."

"Ah! but it is blue, like a turquoise, and the soft wind curls the waves and makes them break into white, like liquid marble."

"Yes, and over the desert plays the sihrâb, — the magic water, and how fascinating it is to watch it: now there are cities with walls and domes, now it is like a pond, and it changes all the time. Oh, the desert is beautiful!"

"But no desert can equal the beauty of the Gulf

of Corinth or the Ægean Sea! And now I will tell you. I was born by the sea; I was born at Athens," said Agapê, "and my very earliest recollections are of Athens. Oh, Poet of poets, had you lived in Hellas instead of in Irân! Oh, I can shut my eyes now and see the Akropolis with its dream of beauty, — the temples glowing in the sunlight."

She suited the action to the word, and Omar seized the opportunity to touch gently with his lips the blue-veined eyelids quivering with the thought of what her inner vision saw.

She opened her eyes, as if she had just wakened from sleep, and went on:

"Once, they say, all Persia came to Athens, and the king, though his forces overran the whole country, took such delight in the temple of Athene and the marble sculptures that adorn it, that he would not allow his soldiers to harm a single statue. I don't know; I only know that I was born under its very shadow, and that as a little girl I used to look up and see those marble columns, and the lovely images, glowing under a sky brighter even than this lovely sky. And when I was older I used sometimes to climb up the steep hill and sit on the steps and look down on the city at my feet, and off to the mountains and across to the violet sea. Oh, the thought of it makes me sick with longing!"

The bright diamond-like tear came into her beautiful eyes, but instantly the sun of her smile shone through them, and, as it were, turned them into rainbows. She said, "But there I had no poet to tell my story to; and I had no story to tell."

And Omar's heart was gladdened by the music of her laugh.

"My father," she went on to say, "was the protokometes or hereditary chief of a little district, and they used to call me 'the princess.' We lived in comfort, and my father, who was fond of our ancient books, taught me also to love Homer. Oh, I could repeat by heart all the lovely story of our great hero Odysseus, coming from the island of Kalypso and visiting the land of the Phaiakians, — I heard you the other afternoon telling the story of Byzun and Manîjeh. Oh, and the garden was like this:

"'Roses blooming, sparkling fountains murmuring, the earth rich with many-colored flowers, musk floating on the breeze, hyacinths and lilies perfuming the air, the bright pheasant strutting stately along, the bulbúl warbling from the cypresses —'"

"Yes," interrupted Omar, "and here is 'the love-inspiring maiden, her lips sweet with smiles, her cheeks like roses.'"

"I cannot tell my story in a straightforward way if you interrupt me so," said Agapê, laughing again, for she herself saw that she had been wandering from the path of her story. "But, as I was saying, I came to love Homer —"

"If you would only say that you came to love Omar," said the poet, with an Oriental's excessive fondness for playing on words.

Agapê's look was sufficient answer to that, and would have satisfied the most exacting lover.

"My mother died when I was young," continued the girl, "and I was more to my father than many daughters, for I had no brothers and only one little flower of a sister. I wonder where she is now! . . . We lived in Athens till I was sixteen; no, till I had seen seventeen winters, —"

"Seventeen summers," interrupted Omar; but Agapê smiled and went on:

"And then my father took me to the little village where he needed to look after his property. It was across the violet sea that we sailed, and how I wish that you, O Poet of poets, might take that voyage —"

"With you?" asked Omar.

"Yes, with me," said Agapê, enthusiastically. "I would point out to you the islands like gems, the mountains rising into that exquisite turquoise sky —"

"Lovelier than yonder mountains?" asked Omar, lifting her hand and pointing with it and his to the distant snow-clad peaks turning into purple glories under the level rays of the sun.

"Yes, because they rise out of the sea! There is Olympos, where they say the gods used to live, — I love to read about them in our poems, — and you are the only Persian that can read them or understand them! . . . Well, we crossed the Ægean in a little vessel and we landed at Smyrna, and then we had to ride many days before we came to my father's village. Since he had been there last great changes had taken place. The men of your religion — "

"Not of mine, sweetheart, because I could have no religion but yours," said Omar.

"I am a Christian," said Agapê, simply, "or at least I was — "

"Then, so am I!" said Omar. "If you were a Fire Worshipper, then I too would be a Fire Worshipper."

"What was I saying? Oh, yes, our village had become Muhammadan. Most of the former inhabitants had been carried off or killed. We found one poor old man who told us how it had all happened. It was dreadful. Then my father resolved to go to Byzantium and try to get the emperor to send an army and regain that district. But before he had a chance to make his arrangements we were taken prisoners and sent to Bagdâd. The Sultân Alp Arslân happened to be there at the time. He was not discourteous to us. When my father told him how he happened to be taken prisoner, the Sultân gave him leave to return to Greece to secure a ransom; but he obliged him to leave me as a hostage. That was four years ago, and shortly after Alp Arslân was killed and the present Sultân came to the throne."

"Have you never in all this time heard from your father?"

"Never a word! Sometimes I think he must be dead! It is our Greek nature, you know, to be hopeful and to see the sun behind the clouds, and yet often and more often, oh, how often, when I am alone, I weep for him and for my beloved Athens. I have been kindly treated. I have been almost free. Malíkshāh has scarcely noticed me, but Nizâmu'l-Mulk has been like a father to me. He has taken the deepest interest in me, and pitied me. But I must get away, I must get away, for I am *not* free. I must go and find my father — if he is alive!"

There was a tremor in her voice which betokened that the fountain of tears was opening, but suddenly the mercurial little creature caught a glimpse of the sunset, and with the Greek love for color she forgot her sorrow, as she was constantly forgetting it. And the sunset reminded her that she must not linger another minute.

"There," said she, "I have told you my story, and I told you that there was not much to tell. The greatest event of my life was —"

But she did not finish the sentence. She left

Omar to complete it, and he was Persian and keen enough to do so.

"In the days of Māhmûd," said he, "there were seven great poets, and the greatest of them all was Hasan, who was called the Poet of Paradise, — Firdausî. And Firdausî tells of love at sight. The daughter of Gureng, King of Zabulistân, found Jemshýd sitting in a garden in the city of Rustemdâr in the spring season when the roses were in bloom, just as they are in bloom to-day. She thought he was a warrior of Irân, with wide shoulders and well-girt loins, his face pale as the pomegranate, looking like light in darkness, and she gave him to drink of the ruby wine, and when he hesitated to come in she said: 'Why dost thou hesitate? I am permitted by my father to do as I please; my heart is my own.' And the moment he looked into her lovely face, his heart was enamored of her. And he complied, and she took him by the hand and led him into the beautiful garden, moving along with dignified and graceful step, as moves the mountain partridge through the meadow, her long hair falling even to her feet, and filling the air with the sweet odor of musk. . . . Thus Omar at sight of the fair Agapê was at once entangled in the meshes of Love. And Agapê?"

"Agapê, like the daughter of Gureng, also saw the stranger at the very first with the eyes of Love, because he was a poet. . . . But see! the sun is already setting. I must hasten back."

"But you will come again? Come to-morrow? When shall I take thee to my mother's house? Remember the daughter of Gureng took Jemshýd for her spouse, and Rustem, with equal good fortune, won Tamîneh. Do you remember how she stood before him, brighter than the moon, her eyes sparkling with a heavenly light, with cypress form and waving curls, her eyebrows like a bended bow, her curls snares for his heart, her cheek glowing like the rose and lily, earrings in her delicate ears, and her lips like honey, while sparkling pearls gleamed in her rosebud mouth, full of fragrance she stood before him, just as you, pearl of women, in your haste to leave me, are now standing in front of me, while I hold your two little hands, and kiss first one and then the other?"

"But really I must go," she said. "Yes, I will come to-morrow, and we will plan what we can do."

"But how will you go?" he asked. "It is not safe for you to go alone."

"I shall not go alone," she replied. "The Agâ Zālým is waiting for me with a palankin. Remember that you are to give me the dīwân of verses."

"And remember that you are to pay me for them. Give me another instalment of the payment."

"Then repeat one more rubâ'ī."

Omar thought for a moment, and in his passionate voice repeated the poem beginning, *Bar rui gúl,* changing only one or two words to make it suit the occasion :

"On the face of the Rose the cloud-veil remaineth still;
In the depth of my heart the wine-thirst complaineth still.
Do not depart yet, why should sleep call thee?
Give me wine, sweetheart, for the Daylight reigneth still."

CHAPTER XIV.

THE JEALOUS PRIESTS.

In all religions, in every age, the priests, as a class, have claimed their privileges with the greatest jealousy. Accustomed to the belief, carefully cultivated, if not in their own souls, at least in the souls of the exoteric, that they are in possession of the only channels of communication between God and man, and that they have the power of wielding the very thunderbolts of the Almighty, they guard, and always have guarded, with fiery zeal this prerogative. Witness the power wielded by the Hebrew priests and Levites, the hierarchic web woven by the priestly caste in ancient Egypt, the despotism of the old Latin *flamines*, the long arm extended by the popes. Not less grasping were the Mollâhs, or priests of Islâm. Many times the "Shadow of God" — Sayâ-i Hodâ, as the Sultân was called — was made to feel their hand. Many times they dared cross or bend the imperial will.

Hasan ben Sabah well understood the working of this secret politic, and having been himself trained in the strictest sect of the faith, he resolved to profit by it.

We have seen that he knew of the Sultân's expedition with Nizâmu'l-Mulk and Omar Khayyâm. His informant did not succeed in witnessing the irregular entertainment, especially the wine-drinking which the two rulers had indulged in. But Hasan knew of Omar's reputation, and had no doubt that the unlawful was practised then and there. The fact of the existence of the tavern — called kherabat or ruins, because, on the establishment of Islâm as the state religion, the wine-houses were generally concealed from official knowledge in the long-neglected atásh-kadâh or fire-temple of the old Parsis. He resolved to show his hand. It happened that the chief of the Qurân Readers, the so-called Proof of Islâm, Abu'l Hasan Al-Ghazzâli, was at that time in Nishāpûr, attracted by the presence of the Court. At the first possible opportunity Hasan ben Sabah took counsel with Al-Ghazzâli to shut up the tavern where Omar was so fond of tasting the "rivers of wine, delight of the drinkers," as Muhammád called it.

"Is it not a shame, O Proof of Islâm," said Hasan ben Sabah, putting on a pharisaical look of horror, "that the laws of Muhammád are violated even under the walls of the city?"

"What is your meaning, Ba-sakar-i?"

"My meaning is that within less than a farsâkh

from this spot stands a tavern where wine is openly sold. I have it on the best authority that the Hakîm Omar, called the Tentmaker, goes frequently there and boasts of his debaucheries!"

"Omar Khayyâm is the shame of Islâm; had I my way I would give him the bastinado. A rubâ'î composed by him, and now going the rounds, shows him shameless. In it he exults in the fact that though he is over thirty he has not as yet taken unto himself a wife; and that for a Muslîm is a disgrace."

"But he is in high favor with 'the Shadow of God!' It will not do to touch him; except indirectly."

"How may that be done?"

"Complain to the Sultân that his tavern is a sink of iniquity and oblige him to order the muhtesîb to raze it to the ground."

"It shall be done and that immediately."

This conversation took place shortly after the Sultân had returned from his visit to the turquoise mines of Abû Ishâk, where he had enjoyed a most exciting chase of the wild ass. He was, therefore, in the height of good humor when, as he was seated on his throne, — a gift from a rajah of northern India, — ebony carved it was, and cunningly inlaid with exquisite designs, — when Al-Ghazzâli with an expression of appalling sternness on his face drew near and stood like a prophet before him. He was a man of striking appearance, with snow-white beard and long, flowing locks, dressed in the snow-white dress of his order. A rumor ran through the assembly and then deep silence followed.

"Speak! O Mirror of the Truth! What would you have?"

"Tâhlil lâ illâha illallâ hu! There is no God but God!" exclaimed the Chief Reader, piously. "I am credibly informed that the law of Muhammád is broken in this city, which, now that the Shadow of God is here, should be the Suburb of Paradise."

"'Ṭis a grave charge, O Light of the Faith! Be more specific! What is the law that is broken? Tell me, and by Allâh, the guilty man shall not escape!"

"On the bank of the river that flows south of the city there is a notorious tavern where the forbidden wine flows freely. I demand that the tavern be destroyed."

"How know you of this tavern, Keen Eye of the Law?"

"Ask the Hakîm Omar al Khayyâmi, who has the reputation of frequenting that unhallowed haunt."

All eyes were turned on Omar, who, putting his hands to his breast, bowed low, and without showing the least discomposure said, in his soothing, delightfully melodious voice:

"Yes, verily, and Yahmid, alhamdu lillâh — Praise

be to God! I have on the end of my tongue a poem that answers the reproach of our learned Proof of Islâm. Shall I repeat it?"

The Sultân gave his assent and Omar with a twinkle of fun in his eye repeated the quatrain beginning:

"*Mai mihurâm u mahālāfân az chap u râst.*"

"Wine I eat, and enemies from left and right
Say, 'Drink not wine, for 'tis Religion's foe.'
When I learned that wine was Religion's foe,
'By Allah,' (said I), 'let me eat the blood of
the enemy since that is lawful.'"[1]

Al-Ghazzâli turned pale with rage and was strongly tempted to show his indignation by spitting; but dared not in the very presence of the Sultân. He muttered beneath his breath such words as mulhýd, heretic, and zindîk, blasphemer. He could not forget how, when last he met Omar, Sanjar's great Wazîr Abd-ur-Razzâk had called Omar *the* authority on the Qurân, and that when there had been a disagreement concerning a certain reading of the text, Omar, being asked his opinion, enumerated the various readings and explained the grounds for each, men-

[1] Why, be this juice the growth of God, who dare
Blaspheme the twisted tendril as a snare?
A blessing, we should use it, should we not?
And if a curse,— why then, who set it there?
— Edward FitzGerald's paraphrase.

tioning, also, the exceptional readings, and expressing his preference for the very one that he, himself, the Chief of Qurân Readers, had rejected. And he had done it all so eloquently that every one who heard him was convinced. Al-Ghazzâli could not forgive him for such insulting superiority and now hoped for his revenge. And here was the scoffer replying to his complaints with a poem which actually quoted the Qurân in favor of wine-drinking because, forsooth, Muhammád had ordered his followers to destroy their enemies. Moreover, as usual, Omar's wit had carried with him all who heard him and there was danger that the irregularity would continue unabated.

He therefore bent on Omar a scowling face and then, turning to the Sultân, said:

"In Musulmân-i durúst nîst! Surely he is no genuine Musulman! O Commander of the Faithful, surely such flippancy is out of place! The Faithful complain at the scandal, and in the name of our faith I solemnly demand that the offending blot be wiped out."

Such an appeal could not go unheeded. Malík-shāh immediately ordered the muhtesîb, who had charge of the policing of the city, and whose duty it was to eradicate houses of ill fame and taverns, to be summoned.

The man came trembling; perhaps he was conscious that he had been derelict in his duties ; certain sums of money that had found their way into his pocket as hush-money for permitting the weeds of sin to flourish unrooted in the garden of his oversight may have troubled him.

But the Sultân, intent simply on satisfying Al-Ghazzâli, for he knew that even he, the Shadow of Allâh, could not afford to offend the Mollâhs, bade him take a body of men and destroy the offending tavern.

Omar, who heard with amazement and pain the order permitting such a piece of tyranny, was casting about in his mind how he could send a word of warning to his friend Al-Hammar, the jolly proprietor of the tavern. He would have himself gone, but it was impossible. He would have protested, but he knew that any formal protest could only stir up his enemies, the pietists, to greater animosity. But he felt that Malíkshāh was placed in a peculiarly trying position, having himself, as it were, accepted poor Al-Hammar's hospitality.

The Sultân shortly after this trying episode dismissed his Court, retaining only his Wazîr. As Omar was about departing with a feeling of indignation in his heart, a page called him back. The Sultân wished to speak privately with him.

"I read your thoughts in your face, my Prince of Poets," said Malíkshāh, when they were out of hearing of the rest. "I am full of regret for this hard necessity, but there is no real harm done. I have already sent a trusty messenger to warn your friend; and after a little he will build his tavern better than before. I will see to it that his loss is more than made good. I do not forget the good cheer that we enjoyed."

This assurance somewhat cheered Omar, but what concerned him most was the interruption that this destruction of his favorite tavern might cause in his pleasant intercourse with his little Greek princess. She had promised to come the next day, but he himself had been prevented; a special messenger from Nizâmu'l-Mulk had summoned him as an expert to the turquoise mines, and he had of course been obliged to depart immediately, as there was urgency in the call. He had been gone two days, — days which would have been full of the keenest enjoyment had it not been for that foolish fever in his blood.

The next day after the return of the Court, Malík-shāh insisted on his going with him and a small party to hunt the *hubarâ* or spotted bustard, which requires two kinds of hawks, that used in chasing the wild ass and another that will attack the hubarâ as it flies along. This was the most delightful sport that Omar had ever enjoyed; for, as he told Agapê, there was for him a great fascination about the desert, and who could not feel the zest of sitting on a beautiful, intelligent horse and watching the well-trained hawks spy out their prey miles away and with almost human endeavor fly to meet it, and to win the victory over a creature so many times its size, quickness being more than a match for strength? The exhilaration of the swift dash across the level plain; the pleasure of congenial company, — all this had tended to make Omar for the time being forget the misfortune of being unable to keep his appointment with Agapê. It was impossible for him to send her any word! Would she forgive him? What had happened? Had she gone there and imagined him recreant? All the pleasures of the mountain-side, the glorious views that he as a poet could not fail to appreciate, the excitement of the chase, and the friendly words of the Sultân could not wholly banish the anxiety that swelled his heart when he thought of what he had lost.

The day that Hasan ben Sabah had chosen for his insidious attack was Friday, the Muhammadan Sabbath, and Omar knew that it would be impossible for Agapê to meet him that day. He himself would have had no hesitation in going there on Friday any more than any other day: did he not write —

"*Friday and Saturday in our religion are one; worship Allâh! be no day worshipper; and if thou hast drunken on Monday, drink also on Friday?*"

But Omar was a true Oriental and a Fatalist.

When in his passionate infatuation for Agapê he had composed the quatrain —

> "*From science and piety flee — for so it is best!*
> *Twine thy fingers in the curls of thy love, for so it is best.*
> *Ere Destiny spill thy blood on the ground*
> *Pour into the cup the blood of the flask, for so it is best*" —

he did not really renounce his philosophy, though for the moment he was nearly carried away. He therefore tried to calm his perturbation and wait developments, knowing that the Sultân would keep his word.

His three days' absence from Agapê had had one important effect on him. He had begun to wonder if after all it would be best for him to take the girl as his wife. It would make an absolute change in all his life; he had for years resisted his mother's plea that he should marry, he had good-naturedly laughed when she told him that it was contrary to his duty as a good Muhammadan to live in the unmarried state. He always replied that he was not a good Muhammadan, and why should he now, having withheld so long, rush on like a heedless youth, put his head into the noose of marriage, and bring to his house a gay young girl of alien race and religion?

It was a serious question and doubts began to assail him. Through the veil of these misgivings he saw his love just as passionate, just as youthful, just as beautiful as it had been three days before. It was a strange mental state, as if his mind were divided into two compartments by the clinging woven curtain of doubt and as if himself a disinterested observer were enabled to look into both and compare them. On the one side stood Agapê, so beautiful, so fond, so sprightly in conversation, so well-educated, so different from any woman he had ever seen before; on the other his studies, his freedom, his bachelor wont.

Moreover, if he took her as his wife, she would have to conform to the marriage customs of Persia; it might be permitted him, as it was, to set himself above the law, and to endure the criticisms of his stricter neighbors; but even he sometimes found the aloofness of his father's friends a trial, as is shown by the poem where he says:

"*Ai, Heart, for a time seek not the company of the love-sick;*
Cease for a time to engross thyself with the commerce of love.
Frequent the thresholds of the Darwishân;
Perhaps then thou mayest be accepted by the Elect (mabulî)."

But as a general thing he cared nothing for the bitter remarks of the Faithful, the hypocritical reproaches of the Mollâhs, who, he knew perfectly well, not only envied him, but in many cases secretly practised what he openly avowed.

"*Follow not the Sunnât* (*that is the Traditions of Muhammdd*), *leave the Divine Ordinances alone. Share with another the mouthful thou possessest;*

Slander not another; seek not to afflict another's heart;
I promise thee the world to come! — Bring wine!"

Such was his elastic and liberal creed, and as we have said, the wine of which he sang the delights in so many melodious rhymes, was not merely the "daughter of the grape," or the intoxicating-juice of the date-palm, famous for a thousand years, but it stood for all the good things of life, which the fanatic and hypocritical would forbid others to enjoy.

All this delectable license, which might go so far as intoxication and kalendarism, and every infraction of the law, if he wished, — and that is all that his most audacious quatrains signify, — was permissible to him. But he realized very well that the wife who once went behind the bronze-barred gate of his house would have to be his prisoner, as it were: the Qurân compelled each husband to be the head of a petty despotism; would not the graceful, free-born creature pine away in the prison of the high-walled house? It was a tremendous responsibility, and the more he thought about it, the more he desired the girl, and the less he desired her as his wife. He expressed the thought in the rubâ'I:

"*Be wise, for the means of life are uncertain;*
In (fancied) security sit not, for the sword of Fate is keen!
If Fortune put almond-sweets in thy very mouth
Beware! Swallow them not, for poison is mingled therein."[1]

[1] E. Heron-Allen's version.

He knew that the girl would give herself to him soul and body; at least her every action whispered that to his heart. But Omar was too true and too noble a man to take advantage of the beautiful gift of Agapê's love. Stirred as he had been to the inmost being by her presence, by the intoxication of her loveliness, by the touch of her hand, and the ravishing sweetness of her wine-like lips, he had also a natural delicacy, as modern as his philosophy; she was as safe with him as she would have been with her brother. He was even now just as anxious as ever to see her again, but mingled with this desire was the cooler thought that perhaps, if he did not, it might not be the worst thing that would happen to either of them. She was enough of an inspiration to him in any circumstances, and he composed for her the dīwân or book of verses that he had promised. Some of them are still extant, though now arranged in all manuscripts in the strange alphabetic sequence conventional with Persian scribes. One can read in them the odd mixture of passionate love and calculating philosophy that occupied his thoughts all those spring and summer days when Agapê was with the Court at Nishāpûr. For instance in these, selected at random:

"O thou, of all creation the chosen part to me;
O goodlier than eyesight, and soul and heart to me!

There's naught than life more precious, O idol mine; and yet
An hundred times more precious than life thou art to me!

"Since she, for whose sweet sake my heart afire 's become,
Captive herself elsewhere to anguish dire 's become,
Ah! whither shall I look for healing of my pain,
Since she, my leach, herself sick with desire 's become.

"If the ruby-lipped fair in this bosom of mine is,
Khizr's water outvied by the juice of the wine is;
But thou Zuhreh be minstrel, and Jesus be mate,
If the heart 's not in presence, no gladness in wine is."
— *Translation of John Payne.*

"Last night upon the river bank we lay,
I with my wine-cup and a maiden gay,
So bright it shone, like pearl within its shell,
The watchman cried, 'Behold the break of day!'"
— *Translation of Whinfield.*

CHAPTER XV.

A PRESENTIMENT OF ILL.

AGAPÊ did not go to the būstân on the day following her visit there with Omar. The messenger that had summoned Omar to the turquoise mines had previously stopped at the Arg to deliver a message and to get fresh horses. A chance word which he dropped as to his purpose in coming was reported in the anderûn, and Agapê therefore got her warning and stayed sensibly at home. She however resolved, woman-like, to torment her poet a little, and so he heard nothing from her and saw her not for several days. She received through Agâ Zālým the little scroll containing the rubā'iyât, and though she was delighted she still gave no sign. Omar naturally thought that she was offended; he still supposed that she had gone to the meeting-place and failed to find him. At last, not liking to trust writing a note, he bethought him of sending her a single quatrain. He copied delicately on a bit of parchment these lines:

"*Joy, for loss of thee, all is turned to sorrow;*
For the tristful heart is no glad to-morrow:
With thee the world's bitter I was wont to sweeten;
'Gainst thy loss's bitter, sweet whence shall I borrow?" [1]

And in answer to this came the long-expected note saying that she would meet him on the second day following as before. And now the Sultân's order had put an end to that! Had it? Omar suddenly recollected that the warning had probably reached Al-Hammar in time and that in any event the muhtesîb would not destroy the garden. So the next afternoon he went early to the būstân. Al-Hammar met him with a rueful countenance and related in a style as flowery as ever Persian employed, how on the previous afternoon a mysterious warning had come to him that the Mollâhs had complained of him and that he had best hide all signs of wine-selling. He had deemed it advisable to heed the warning and had safely conveyed the jars of precious wine and the beautiful cups into a place of safety and had waited with a clear conscience whatever might happen. He had hardly completed the task when the muhtesîb and his minions appeared; but as they could find no witnesses or any proof of irregularity they had satisfied themselves with simply knocking down the old fire temple that had stood there for no one knows how many generations.

[1] Version of John Payne.

"Shall I have no wine then, this afternoon?" asked Omar. "I will do the best that I can for the crown of poets," replied Al-Hammar, "but all the sākîs have run away, fearing lest they should have to walk the sky with the soles of their feet."

Omar laughed at this graphic way of expressing the attitude of the bastinado.

"I will see that a jar is brought to your pavilion. And may I ask if you expect *her?* For of all the tulip-cheeked maidens that breathe the rose-scented air she is the pearl."

"Truly thou art an admirable judge," said Omar with another laugh. "But fail not with a jar of thy very best wine and — how about sweets?"

"I will send in for *her* a patty of dates and almonds; not such an one has been seen since the Parsîs emigrated."

Like many another man, Omar, remembering his irresolution, recognized his folly in playing with the dangerous fire of love; but he had confidence in himself that he could stop ere it reached a conflagration. He went to his pavilion and happily found it untouched. All his anxiety had been for naught; the uncompromising Al-Ghazzâli had been foiled and again life smiled, even as the day itself smiled. Smiled? It would rather be called a laughing day; everything was full of cheer; the air was soft and yet bracing; the breeze tossed the leaves of all the trees and sent bright butterflies whirling away as if it were chasing rose-leaves. The little waves on the river laughed aloud with glee. Omar sat on a thick felt by the arched door and drank in all the beauty of the scene. He thought of the delight in store for him if Agapê should come; at the same time there mingled with his anticipation the doubt as to the outcome of it all. As usual with him his thought took the form of a rubâ'ī: one with rhymes at the beginning as well as at the end:

> "*Old am I, yet my love for thee has led me to the snare;*
> *How comes it else that in my hand the cup of wine I bear?*
> *My mistress has destroyed the vow that I to Reason sware;*
> *And passing days have rent the robe I sewed with patient care.*"

He had hardly completed the last rhyme when his heart and eyes at once told him that Agapê was there once more. Once again there was the graceful little coquettish battle over the veil which Omar soon carried by assault. Again the diplomatic parley over the terms of surrender and the payment of the indemnity: in other words the fulfilment of the bargain for the rubā'iyât. And Omar, who only a few short days before was contentedly counting the stars and calculating the revolutions of the planets, was now, like a schoolboy, counting the kisses that Agapê let him give and take. How strange life is and man!

Even with the girl's sweet breath in his nostrils his heart was saying:

> *"Blame me not if I act like a fool,*
> *For once more am I intoxicated with the wine of love."*

Al-Hammar showed himself a master of circumstances: what would the Mollâhs have said if they had chanced to surprise their enemy as he sat in the rose-scented pavilion with the beautiful maiden contary to the Qurân unveiled and—horror of horrors!—occasionally sipping the musk-scented wine and nibbling daintily at the deliciously broiled partridge that the tavern-keeper sent in after they had enjoyed the date-and-almond confection? Again the swift-winged hours flew over their heads and the summer wind died down and the sunset splendors lighted up the sky and clothed the stern distant mountains in the purple robes of royalty. The moon was full that night and Agapê, trusting to her Greek cunning, yielded to Omar's entreaties to remain till it should pour its silvery flood through the valley.

And as they sat there floating down on the swift current of time in the light bark of love Omar asked Agapê if she could be content to live the shut-in life of a Farsî woman; if they were married there could be no more delightful meetings by the river; the conventions would be too strong for even them to overcome them.

"But why not come with me to Athens?" asked Agapê.

"I could not leave my old mother," said Omar. "Besides, how could we live in Athens?"

"No, I should not like to live as the Persian women do," said Agapê, "but let us not think any more of these disagreeable things; it is enough for to-night to be alive and hear the nightingale sing. Listen!"

"This is what it seems to say to me," whispered Omar:

"'*Khayyâm, if thou'rt drunken with wine, be content!*[1]
If thou with thy tulip-cheeked love dost recline, be content!
Since out of the world into naught thou wilt soon pass away,
Imagine non-being already is thine! Be content!'"

"That is another melancholy quatrain, O my poet," exclaimed Agapê.

"But is not the nightingale melancholy, Agapê? Listen to the long-drawn cadences, so full of passion and of sadness. Infinite passion, infinite pain! It is the song of a soul that was once a loving woman and who was separated from her love!"

"Oh, but I love it," exclaimed Agapê. "No, I will shut my eyes to the trouble that may come to-morrow, that will come to-night when I must return to my slavery!"

"Agapê, I too love the beauty of it all! See the

[1] *Hush-bash*, literally, "pleasant or beautiful be."

full moon just rising over the mountain-tops, how huge, and round; that moon, Agapê, will look down into this garden when we are dust! Our feet tread on the dust of lovers like ourselves. See, I cast a cup of wine on the dust! Perhaps it will soak down and bring comfort to the lovers whose dust mingles with the rose-leaves of a thousand years!"

Sometimes there comes to one even in the midst of joy the presentiment of approaching misfortune. Agapê knew that such a presentiment was lurking in her inmost heart. She tried to explain it to herself by attributing it to the cadences of the nightingale which, perched on a neighboring rose-bush, was still pouring out his whole soul, to the melancholy turn that Omar's poem had given to her thoughts, to the soft languor of the evening. She had come with the full intention of telling Omar how precarious her position at Court was growing to be. She had hinted at something of the sort in her first note to him, which she had written with an inspiration born of despair. But she saw as well as Omar saw that she could never be content, dearly as she loved him, to immure herself "behind the veil."

To tell the truth, Agapê, like Omar himself, was in advance of her own day. Her peculiar education, under the direct care of her father, had given her insight into many things which were hidden from the women of her own country, and still more so from the women of Persia. There are always such women, there have always been such men, and generally they have suffered in consequence. They may have had a philosophy to help them withstand the sorrows of their isolation, but it was none the less real. This exceptional understanding on the part of Agapê was what attracted Omar to her, no less than her exceptional beauty. This exceptional beauty was of a type that fortunately did not appeal to the passions of the Sultân, who, as we have said, belonged to the Seljûk Turks, and, though a man of unusual breadth of view, nevertheless, or perhaps in consequence thereof, conformed in his appreciation of female charms to the ideal generally worshipped by the Turanian race: a good broad back and what Browning calls "the breast's superb abundance, where a man might base his head;" in other words, obesity attracted him more than the slender, graceful Greek type of which Agapê was such a perfect example. That explains why, though she had been at his Court so long, he had scarcely noticed her, and why he had filled the regulation quota of his wives with women of another kind.

But Agapê was tired of remaining as a hostage and she had made up her mind that she would go back to Athens and seek her father, if he were still living. This desire had been growing in her heart long before Malíkshāh left Marv; it was an almost impossible undertaking for a young maiden, delicate and beautiful as she was, to make that terrible journey, even if she could have escaped from the anderûn. The Agâ Zālým, who was especially appointed to serve her as well as watch over her, she had succeeded in winning as her faithful slave; he would do anything for her, within reason, and that explains how she was able to meet Omar. Zālým was not far away, and as long as she did not try to escape entirely she was comparatively free.

When she first saw Omar, the passionate love at first sight which the Persian poets from Firdausî down are ever singing, took possession of her heart. When she found that the poet was the friend of Nizâmu'l-Mulk and the favorite of Malíkshāh, a wild hope seized her that at last she might escape: she even went so far as to plan the way of it. But when Nizâmu'l-Mulk asked her to come to Omar's favorite garden and dance for them, she entered into the spirit of the thing, as she always did. She was a true Greek, fond of new things, gay and merry, with all sorts of ideas rioting in her pretty head, — and having found the way there once, it was easy to go again. Meantime, she, like Omar, had thought over all the inconveniences of actual marriage and she resolved to see what time would bring forth. Perhaps she might persuade him, if he loved her as she thought he did, to dress her as a servant and thus make with her the long journey to Byzantium, if necessary.

She knew well enough that she could not long keep up the clandestine meetings with Omar at the būstân. It might be done twice, but the prying eyes of the hangers-on would soon detect it. It occurred to her to ask Omar to intercede for her with Nizâm-u'l-Mulk, but it was a delicate business: a stranger, even though he were a friend, could hardly interfere with such matters without causing suspicion; and unless Omar was really to take her as his wife, that was impracticable.

It may have been this uncertainty that caused the shadow to grow deeper over Agapê's mind till she could hardly throw it off. It was like the little cloud that gathers round the moon at midnight. A few moments before the moon is shining in untroubled splendor; then the light halo clings to the beautiful orb and saddens the light; before many minutes have past, the moon is quite hidden; a cool wind blows and a feeling of depression seems to pass over the whole landscape; within an hour the rain begins to fall. So it was with Agapê.

She suddenly sprang up, threw her arms around Omar's neck, and burst into a flood of tears. Now if there is any one thing that disturbs the equanimity of a man's spirits it is to have a woman, the woman whom he loves, weeping bitterly. Omar was wholly unused to such a phenomenon, but he gathered the girl into his arms and tried to soothe her as he would have soothed a trembling nightingale. He patted her cheek and smoothed her curly hair; he kissed away the tears and asked in a caressing voice what was the matter.

"Oh, I want my father! And I want to see the moonlight dimpling the sea!" she sobbed. "And I thought that you would take me away,—away to Athens, anywhere away from the desert and from Persia!"

Then a frightened look came into her eyes and she said in a lower voice:

"Oh, I have felt all the evening that something terrible is going to happen! It seems to me as if this were our last evening together! I don't want to go from thee and yet I must. It is too late; I must go!"

Omar could feel how her little heart was beating, fluttering as from the effect of fright. Again he tried to soothe her:

He said: "Agapê, my idol, my darling, my lālá rukh, do not weep; I will do anything for thee. I will take thee to my house, and when my aged mother is no more, then I will go with thee to the ends of the earth. My bright-eyed Agapê! trust me! And now cheer up! See, the little cloud has gone from the face of the moon: it shines again in all her glory. And remember, Agapê,

"HE GATHERED THE GIRL INTO HIS ARMS."

"Do not allow sorrow to embrace thee,
Nor an idle grief to occupy thy days, for
Thou hast no power over the morrow,
And anxiety over the morrow is useless to thee."[1]

The sweet rhythm and the fall of the rhymes of these couplets, dast rasi qarda nîst and marda nîst, fell like music on Agapê's ear.

"You are strong and wise; I am weak and foolish," she said, "and it is impossible that you should love me!"

"Nay, not impossible, for it is true!" said Omar.

"But I hear Agâ Zālým's whistle. He is getting anxious; he will be cross. I must go. Even now we may not be able to pass the gate."

"Then one more kiss and two and seven, for seven is a sacred number—and when wilt thou come again?"

"As soon as may be. But oh, I feel that we may never meet again!"

"Do not worry, Agapê."

The next instant she was gone.

[1] Translation of E. Heron Allen.

CHAPTER XVI.

HASAN THE TEMPTER.

THE monotony of female wearing apparel in the East is favorable to intrigue. Hidden completely in a loose indigo-dyed chuddar, and closely veiled, with loose, baggy pantaloons, one woman differs from another not in glory, but in size or height. But nothing escaped the watchful attention of Hasan ben Sabah. He was attracted by Agapê's graceful gait, which her costume could not wholly disguise. There seemed to lurk some mystery about her and he determined to penetrate it. He saw that Agâ Zālým must know about her and at the first opportunity he addressed the tall eunuch.

"Who is the woman?" he asked, fixing his keen, compelling eye on Zālým's.

"She is the hostage," replied Zalým, evasively, yet truthfully.

"What hostage?"

"The Princess Agapê."

"Did I not see her on the mountain?"

"It would be presuming in me to tell you what you saw on the mountain."

With this Agâ Zālým was turning away; but Hasan was not a man to be so baffled.

"Wait!" he said.

The eunuch turned back.

"I saw her come in."

"Shak nîst — no doubt."

"Are the ladies of the anderûn in the habit of wandering about the city at all hours?"

"Khodâ mî-danad u bas — God only knows."

Hasan began to grow angry.

"Nar ja kî parî vash-î'st, dîv-î bâ û'st — wherever a Peri-like beauty is there also is a devil," he muttered, "and I believe you are the devil that accompanies that hostage of yours. There is something wrong about it."

The Agâ Zālým delayed no longer, but went away muttering under his breath. He intended to submit to no impertinent inquisition into his affairs.

But Hasan was made only the more curious by Zālým's replies. He bade his son keep a sharp watch on the movements of the Agâ, and if he should see him accompany a woman who went out otherwise alone, he was quietly and secretly to follow them and report where they went.

It so happened therefore that Ostad-ben-Hasan had followed Agapê to the būstân, and though he had not been a witness to the meeting of Omar and the girl, he had lingered round the garden long enough to see Omar follow her back to the city. He was therefore able to give his father a tolerable idea of the intrigue, for such Hasan ben Sabah supposed it to be. He was selfish enough to think that what was good enough for the poet was good enough for the mace-bearer and treasurer, and he was malicious enough to take pleasure in trying to forestall his old friend. But first he thought he would find what he might learn from Omar himself. He regarded it as perfectly possible that by flattery and an appearance of disinterested friendship he might lead Omar to confide in him.

Accordingly the next morning he directed his steps to the poet's home. He found Omar in his little garden, busy with certain calculations in regard to an eclipse of the moon. The poet-astronomer caught sight of Hasan ben Sabah and hastened to meet him.

"This is indeed an honor and a surprise!" he exclaimed. "Since the mysterious disappearance of your Circassian whom you left in my mother's care, I had supposed my house stood in disgrace with you."

"That Circassian woman was ungrateful to me!" said Hasan, with a lowering brow. "After all I had done for her and the risks I had run, she deserted me at the first opportunity. Do you know the doom that Allâh prepares for such ingrates?"

"Nay," said Omar, "Allâh has never taken me into his counsels, but I will give you a poem that expresses my feelings in regard to all such matters:

"*To make but few friends in this life, I advise.*
Hold aloof from the men of your time and be wise.
The man thou art bound to by closest of ties
Is the foe when wisdom uncloseth thine eyes."[1]

"I should not have supposed," remarked Hasan, "that a poet who was always so fond of beauty and of society, should become so pessimistic."

"You are mistaken," said Omar, "I am not a pessimist. I simply look on life as it is. I am happy; I am content. Pessimists are not happy. I make no complaint, so long as I can get my occasional cup of wine."

"But are you not afraid of losing paradise by disobeying the commands of the Prophet?"

"No, why should I be? Allâh is all-merciful; mercy is not for those who do not sin; but for those

[1] Another version, which almost reproduces the quadruple rhymes dûst, tagûst, tarûst, and ûst, might read this way:

"To make but few friends as thou livest is best;
Hold aloof from the men of thy time is my hest;
The one whom thou takest most close to thy breast
Is proven thy foe when he's put to the test."

Literally, "when thou openest the eyes of wisdom."

that break the law, else would not Allâh be merciful. Besides, at the very beginning, nay, before creation it was written that I should drink and Allâh knew that I should drink; if such was Allâh's wisdom I should turn it into folly by not drinking."

"You are blasphemous," exclaimed Hasan.

"Not so," replied Omar, laughing slightly; "what says Muhammád's great throne verse: '*There is no God beside Him, the Living, the Immovable! He is never a prey to slumber nor to sleep. Whatever is in the heavens, and whatever is in the earth is His. Who shall plead with Him, save by His leave? He knoweth what was before us and what shall come after us, and we may not grasp His knowledge, save what He willeth.*' Besides, if wine is good in paradise, why is it not even better now? For we are here and we may not be in paradise. Muhammád, as you know, promised that we should recline, — only a few of us, mind you, — adorned with bracelets of gold and clad in green garments of fine brocade, should recline on inlaid couches, while immortal damsels with eyes like pearls should move among us with cups and jars and flowing wine! But as I shall ever say: 'Give me the present money; you may have the promise to pay.'

"I know not whether He who made me destined me for heaven or hell, but I am happy if I have a mouthful of food, and my sweetheart and a cup of wine on the green bank, near the river. You may have heaven for all me! Besides, I am convinced that though wine is forbidden, it depends on who drinks it and how much one drinks and with whom one drinks; so I should like to know who should drink wine if not the philosopher? Now won't you have a cup of wine?"

Hasan shook his head.

Omar, who was fond of shocking the ultra-pious, went on:

"I have given orders that when I die my corpse is to be bathed in wine and I am to be buried in a coffin made of the vine, and I have written a rubâ'ī — nay, I have written a whole dīwân of rubā'iyât in praise of wine. Perhaps you would like to hear some of them if you will not drink with me."

Omar, without waiting for Hasan's assent, began to repeat some of those delicious quatrains in which he rings the changes on the blessings of drunkenness, the pleasure of wine, that destroys all the sorrows of life, the dregs of a single draught being better than the whole heavenly vault, a cup of wine worth more than a hundred hearts and faiths, a single draught more than the empire of China (memleket Chin), and ending with the rubâ'ī where he wishes to be buried near the tavern, that the fumes from his body like pure spirit may intoxicate the boon companions as they pass.

When he had finished Hasan ben Sabah with a sneering smile said:

"They are very smooth and cleverly rhymed; but I will make a prediction; you may shock the sentiment of the Faithful as much as you will; but the time will come when, if these ribald verses survive, they will do no harm; because the Sûfis, who even now interpret Firdausî to suit themselves, will find that you mean by wine, the Spirit of God, and by drunkenness the intoxication of union with the One Spirit that fills the universe."

There was a subtle flavor of flattery in Hasan's words, and Omar felt it. He laughed.

"Thou hast spilt my rose-red wine on the ground, Rabbi," he said, quoting from one of the protesting quatrains.

"But tell me, most learned Omar, why, when you praise the delight of sitting at the edge of the desert or beside the flowing stream, with an idol fairer than the Hûr of paradise, tell me, how is it that you have not — "

Hasan hesitated, thinking how best to put his impertinent question, and Omar, seeing his drift, anticipated him:

"Again I have the best of authority for praising the pleasures of the garden and the flowing stream and the fair maid. What says our sacred book? 'For him that feareth the majesty of his Lord shall be two gardens with o'erarching trees and with two flowing wells, therein palm and pomegranate, and the best and comeliest maids, with flashing eyes, dwelling in tents, man nor Jinnî hath not touched them, and they recline on green cushions and beautiful carpets.'"

Hasan found that he was not making much progress toward the knowledge that he wished to obtain. He persisted in his matrimonial drift.

"Now that the Sultân has enriched you, there should be no reason for you not to marry. You remember what Muhammád said: 'Marry, those of you who are single. . . . And let those who cannot find a match live in chastity, till Allâh of his bounty shall enrich them.'"

"Why should you care, O Hasan ben Sabah, whether I marry or not?"

"Because I, as your old friend, am concerned to see you out of the right path."

"You are very kind; but how would marriage put me in the right path? If I should marry, my studies would be interrupted. My mother suffices to keep my house; I have no need of a wife."

"But think of the dangers that you run. Have you not been carousing under the roof of that now ruined atásh kadâh? How about the hostage?"

Hasan asked this question in a lower but intense voice, and watched its effect on Omar. Of course it was a tentative attack. But Omar was not to be surprised. He realized too thoroughly that Agapê's happiness, her very life depended perhaps on his self-possession. He saw that he must be wary. How much did Hasan really know? Had misfortune befallen Agapê on her return to the Arg? Had she been found out? All these questions rushed through his mind even while, with the greatest apparent coolness, he was looking Hasan square in the eye.

"Whether I carouse or do not carouse at the tavern, — what is that to you? Do you follow Al-Ghazzâli in his persecutions? What had Al-Hammar done to him?"

"So then you know the tavern-keeper?"

"Know the jovial Al-Hammar? Of course I do, and if you had been wise enough to join Nizâmu'l-Mulk and me the other afternoon, you, too, would have learned to value his reflections. No one in Nishāpûr can compare with him."

Hasan could not fail to perceive that it was hopeless to win Omar's confidence. He had thought himself wiser than he was; his great fault, lack of tact, he saw still stood in his way. He suddenly rose from the felt on which he had been sitting, and looking at the sun, declared that he must not longer stay; he had many things to do.

"I have already accomplished my task," he said,

somewhat boastfully. "'Tis only three weeks since the Sultân commissioned me to make out the budget; it is all done."

"Mâ sh' Allâh!" exclaimed Omar, with a slight intonation of irony. "Such energy was never before known in the history of the world. Not even Isfendiyar, son of Gushtâsp, of whose exploits we read in the Shâh-nāmá, accomplished so much in so short a time. It was only yesterday that the great Sultân issued his decree, and gave you the power. The Heft-khân will henceforth become the Bist-khân, — the seven labors, the thousand labors. Verily, I bow before you, greatest of men!"

It was evident that Hasan took Omar's sarcasm as genuine flattery.

"Omar," he said, "I have always admired your perspicacity. I want you now to listen to me. I am on the path to greater things than you can dream of. When I was in Egypt, I was taught to read the future. By turning my eyes inward, and holding my breath a moment, I can see what happens beyonds the mountains. And I see the future, dimly as yet, dimly, but each time with greater clearness. I see myself a great monarch, thousands at my call. God is great, and I am his servant. I feel certain that he will lift me to a supreme position. Omar, join me, and with your intellect we can yet put an end to this race of stupid Turks.

We are Persians, and our race is as superior to theirs as the sun is superior to Saturn, or as the Himalyas are superior to Sinai! Give me your hand, with me you will go far. I will disclose to you my plan. You will see how satisfactory it is. And I know that I shall succeed. Shall I show you how I can see what is beyond your ken? I can teach you to do the same. You shut your eyes, thus! Then shut your mouth, and press your tongue against the roof of your mouth, hold your breath; occupy your heart with the idea of Allâh most merciful. Pronounce lâ upwards; pronounce ilâha to the right on the pine cone; that is the point of the heart; then, keep saying mentally, *la ilâha illa' llâh.* Now I will do it for you, that you may see that I speak the truth."

Omar scarcely knew what to make of such a rigmarole; but he watched Hasan with curiosity mingled with a strange sort of contempt. Nevertheless what followed was strange enough. Hasan, who had shut his eyes and grown suddenly silent, now lost all the color from his face; his muscles seemed to grow rigid; Omar thought he had fainted.

Suddenly in a changed voice he began once more to speak rapidly, and with impassioned eloquence.

"Allâh most bountiful, Allâh most compassionate, to thee alone be all the glory! Thy hand has lifted me and sustained me. Through thee I am what I am! Now once more heed my prayer! Send thine angel to enlighten me! Already I hear the rush of his eagle wings! His voice rings in my ears! Speak! What is thy message? Speak."

Hasan started as if into a listening attitude; then, in a moment, he went on:

"I understand; thy servant thanks thee for the message. He will obey."

Then addressing Omar, he said:

"Ask any question that thou wilt; I am permitted to answer it."

Omar, supposing the whole thing was a sort of comedy, although there was something uncanny about it, said:

"Well, most mysterious of friends, tell me, is the world round?"

To his amazement, Hasan's reply exactly coincided with his own conjecture:

"Yea, verily the world is round and the time shall come when the doctrines of Islâm shall he heard by those the soles of whose feet are flat to ours."

"What is going on at the palace?" asked Omar, with a sort of fascination drawn to imagine that he might hear something even of Agapê.

"I see a fair maiden in the anderûn; she weeps, and calls for her father. What she speaks is not Persian. It is the hostage!"

"Tell me more of her," exclaimed Omar, forgetting prudence.

"She sits apart from the others; the tall Agâ Zālým stands near her. Ah! and methinks I see afar, yes, very far away, beyond the mountains, a man who looks in this direction; yes, it is her father. He has been long ill, but he is preparing to come to her. Oh, it is far away in another city, where I see no masjíd, no minarets, and no tiled houses, but white marble buildings."

Omar felt the cold chills run down his back; it seemed impossible that Hasan could be making up such a story, and yet there seemed to be so little in what he said.

"I see my own castle," Hasan went on, suddenly changing entirely the trend of his discourse; "'tis high up on the mountain-side. I am king there; I hold such state as these Seljûks never dreamed of. They pay tribute to me."

There was more of the same sort, sometimes rambling and disconnected, but evidently the fruit that grew on the tree of internal sight. Then he grew silent. He raised his hand to his eyes for a moment, rubbed them as if awakening from a long sleep, opened them and came out of the strange state in which he had been.

"Where am I? What has happened?" he asked, excitedly, as if he were alarmed. "Oh, is it you,

Omar al Khayyâmi? I have had such strange dreams, but I cannot remember them. What were we talking about? Oh, yes, about my success with the budget. I feel within my heart that I shall rise high. Did I say anything about — but the time is not yet ripe. Wait! Wait! When I am ready, then you will join me. Now I must go."

Hasan, whose color had by this time returned, though he still looked sallow, as if he had been ill, rose to take his leave. Omar begged him to have a glass of wine.

"Never! Never! I follow all the ordinances and you will see whether you or I rise the higher. Allâh will reward those who deny themselves."

Now the truth of the matter was that Hasan just before he had gone to Omar's had taken some of that insidious drug, the Indian hemp, and possibly to the influence of that was due the extraordinary performance that had so mystified Omar. Hasan was addicted to hashish, and under its inspiration he was able to accomplish many strenuous undertakings. He now, as he went away, found it expedient to drop a hint regarding the hostage. He was still anxious to know how far Omar had progressed in his acquaintance with the girl.

So he said, as it were flying a winged arrow at Omar: "I have more than trebled the Sultân's revenues from the Province; and I can see ways of cutting down the expenses. He has now at a charge the keeping of the Greek hostage ; if her ransom does not soon come, she is to be sold as a slave. I mean to buy her."

As he said this he gazed piercingly at Omar, who clenched his fists but said nothing. Could Hasan distinguish the least tremor in the poet's beautiful face, could he read as in a book the thoughts in his mind ? With a laugh he passed out under the arched doorway, exclaiming as he went :

"Shumâ salāmât bashîd!" which was equivalent to "Peace go be with you."

CHAPTER XVII.

A SKILFUL SERVANT.

OMAR was at first alarmed at what Hasan had said regarding the possibility of selling Agapê as a slave. Yet as he thought it over it seemed to him an improbable thing: surely Nizâmu'l-Mulk, of whom she had spoken so affectionately, would not permit it. But on the other hand, Hasan had seen Agapê and his remark about securing her if she were sold, indicated that he had some peculiar interest in her. Omar had no confidence in him and felt that it was advisable to be on his guard and, if necessary, to get Agapê out of his reach. He asked himself if it would not be well to go to Nizâmu'l-Mulk, tell him exactly how affairs were situated, and ask his advice. He knew that the Wazîr was his firm friend, was the soul of honor and generosity, and would do what was right. But first he would talk with Agapê and let her decide his action.

Having come to this conclusion, he calmly took up his customary work, making use of all his philosophy to put aside his anxious and pleasant thoughts of the Greek girl.

Hasan mounted his horse and rode back to the palace, communing with himself and perfectly satisfied with his course. Though he had not surprised Omar into any disclosure he felt certain that the poet was having an intrigue with the woman they called "the hostage." It was contrary to his nature to look on and see others enjoying what he would himself enjoy. Thus he was working as far as he could to undermine the Wazîr, and he actually pictured to his own mind the possibilities of his taking Nizâmu'l-Mulk's place and thus approach one step nearer to that throne that in his inordinate self-confidence and conceit he felt so able to fill. It was a favorite mental exercise of his to plan what he would do, not if, but when he should be Shāhinshâh. He had no patience with what he called the weaknesses of rulers: he would not yield to the pleadings of mercy, the man who proved unfaithful to his duties, or who was not obedient to his least command, should die. Hasan often remarked that the office was greater than the man, that if one man did not suit there was another; the world is full of men and the loss of one or a dozen or a thousand is of no consequence. Hasan had seen a hundred perish from the effects of an earthquake and he argued that if Allâh killed them off like flies, a sultân or king was justified in ridding himself of any number of incompetent or indolent or dangerous subjects.

"When I am Shāhinshâh," he said as he rode along past the bāzâr the secrets of which he had so successfully penetrated, and the dealers of which cursed him under their breath as they saw him ride by, haughty and stern, with his fierce mustachios curling under his hooked nose, and his eyes glowing in their cavernous sockets. "When I am Shāhinshâh, these dogs of merchants shall not make the profits they do now: I will have the lion's share. There is Ahmad, the potter: he tried to hide from me his transactions. I soon brought him to terms. The threat of a generous application of the willow wands was a wholesome medicine; but the fact is better than the promise — "

"To whom are you giving the advantage of your observations?" said a clear voice breaking in on his monologue. "I could not wholly hear, though you were talking aloud."

Hasan looked around with a strange expression of mistrust, hatred, and annoyance changing like lightning into one of apparent affability as he saw the smiling Wazîr coming up behind him.

Self-communion is sometimes wise, but it is safer to indulge in it only with closed lips. Hasan understood this, and was vexed with himself for having been so careless. "I am just come from paying a visit to our poet, Omar the Tentmaker," he said, truthfully; "and I was repeating one of his quatrains," he added. "What skill he has in managing the difficult metres. But I could wish his cast of thought were not so pessimistic."

"Pessimistic? Omar is no pessimist. He is a philosopher."

"Is not this pessimistic?" and Hasan cited the rubâ'ī, in which man is advised not to blame the heavens for his misfortunes for the reason that it as impotently moves as you or I.

"Nay, that is fatalism."

"Or this;" and Hasan, showing surprising familiarity with Omar's work, repeated the rubâ'ī where he wishes he had not been born, — one of the few which are stained by a smooch of Oriental coarseness.

"There is merely the expression of a passing mood," said Nizâmu'l-Mulk. "Because a man utters a pessimistic thought, it does not necessarily follow that the whole trend of his philosophy is pessimistic. What serenity and philosophy, for instance, there are in these lines:

"'*The fears of death from our illusions rise*
For death is but the door to Paradise,
The breath of Jesus hath revived my soul,
The tales of everlasting death are lies.'[1]

[1] Translation of John Leslie Garner.

"Omar accepts the world as it is. It is surely not a wholly cheerful place even for us who get most from it. But I know no one so serene, so contented, so fortified against all trials. I have heard of the Hebrew Shaykh Job, whom Allâh gave over to Shaitân to torment, and who suffered the loss of all his cattle and horses and children, and was afflicted with boils: Omar would have borne all these tribulations with equal serenity, taking them only as his share of the misfortunes meant for man's discipline. And success he would endure no less triumphantly. When Shaitân failed to extort a complaint from Job, as a compensation, Allâh doubled all his possessions."

"Perhaps Shaitân did not take his wives," remarked Hasan, maliciously. Then, suddenly, by a natural connection of thought, it occurred to him that he might learn from Nizâmu'l-Mulk regarding Agapê. He resolved to lead up to it as shrewdly as possible.

"I am ready to lay the budget before the Sultân," he said. "Speaking of Job's possessions reminds me of it. I trust he will be satisfied. I have vastly increased the possibility of revenue, and not added materially to the burdens of the people."

Just as he said that, Nizâmu'l-Mulk overheard some one in the street remarking to a neighbor, "There goes that son of a burning father! Curse him, he has taken the sandals from our feet to shoe his horse with!"

But Hasan went on: "The Shadow of God can surely no longer complain of the stream running low. It will reach the brim of the banks. I have also seen opportunities to reduce expenses with no loss of comfort. I would keep on with the pension given to Omar, but there are too many grooms and too many pages at Court. Half might be spared. Then, there is the money spent for the support of the hostage —"

He paused as if for the full effect of his words to be felt.

"The hostage? Oh, you mean Agapê, the Greek princess. That need not concern you," replied Nizâmu'l-Mulk, with some asperity in his tone. "The prince, her father, was deprived of his village, and when he went to Athens, to secure ransom for himself, the Sultân Alp Arslân entrusted her to me, to hold as a hostage. She shall not be disturbed or interfered with in any way."

"Why does not the prince, her father, send to redeem her?"

"I am not in his counsels," said the Wazîr.

"Our poet, Omar, methinks, has cast on her the eyes of longing."

"Why do you think so?"

"He has met her at the pavilion, by the river.

Allâh be praised, wine no more flows there as it did."

Now, of course Nizâmu'l-Mulk knew perfectly well that Omar had met Agapê at the būstân, but how did Hasan know?

"So your duties as mace-bearer included spying on the Greek maiden?" he asked, pointedly.

That was a turn Hasan might have expected.

"Nay," he swore, "by Allâh I have not spied on her."

"How, then, did you know? Did Omar boast of his conquest?"

Hasan would have given half his tongue to recall the unfortunate remark. He knew not what refuge of lies or truth to escape to, yet in an instant he bethought him:

"Agapê herself told me."

By this time they had reached the outer gate of the citadel, and there was no opportunity for further speech. Hasan, inwardly chuckling at his cleverness, turned gravely to Nizâmu'l-Mulk and asked him to inform the Sultân that he had completed the task of making out the budget, and would be glad to lay the details before him.

It was certainly a remarkable work, and when Hasan the next day was called to an audience with Malíkshāh and unfolded before him and the Wazîr the various methods he had evolved for increasing the revenue, when he explained with perfect lucidity and succinctness the resources of the Province, and made it evident that not a corner had been left unexamined, the two men were filled with admiration at the administrative talent displayed, and at the unexampled diligence which had not only outlined but even elaborated a vast system of taxation within a period of scarcely three and twenty days. Moreover they could not discover that there was any undue pressure on farmer or potter, brass worker or silk weaver, rug-maker or jeweller. Only Nizâmu'l-Mulk and Hasan himself knew how the apparent fairness was somewhat heavily discounted by the gifts given in exchange for a partial relenting, and neither of them knew that the other knew; nor had the Wazîr an idea of the amount that Hasan had received. He would never have been able to accomplish what he did in the course of the years that followed had it not been for the wealth so suddenly acquired.

The immediate result of Hasan's work was that his budget was accepted, and he was given the still more responsible position of actual treasurer, with the duty of putting the new taxes into operation. The Sultân expressed himself as more than pleased with his faithfulness and ability, and drawing from his finger a magnificent ring, set with sapphires surrounding an emerald of perfect color, he gave it to Hasan.

CHAPTER XVIII.

THE SNARING OF A PRETTY BIRD.

THE position of Agapê in the anderûn was exceptional. She had one advantage which, in a certain sense, gave her a superiority even over the Sultân's favorite wife. She was an educated woman, she was quick-witted, and she was wise beyond her years. The women of an Eastern harâm, deprived of outside interests and of much society, lacking any mental training, and not obliged to toil or to spin, naturally find in gossip and intrigue their chief delectation. Jealousies and rivalries are apt to be rampant, and it requires a firm hand on the part of the quadruconjugal husband to keep his flock in order. When Agapê, as a girl of seventeen, had taken her position in the anderûn the Persian or Farsî language was to her wholly unknown; but, as she was gracious in her simple manners, and tried to make friends with the Sultân's wives, as she was evidently anxious to learn to talk with them, she became, in a short time, a universal favorite, and they all took pains to teach her how to express herself, and the diversion which her mistakes caused, the amusement which she herself found in them, and the rapid progress which she made, the stories which she had to tell of her life in a distant land, — all proved a genuine oasis of pleasure in the monotonous desert of their existence.

She was equally at home in the household of the Wazîr, who had not as yet taken advantage of the Prophet's allowance of wives, but was satisfied, and consequently sixteen times happier, with one, — Shirîn Kānúm, a woman of exceptional beauty and intellect. He, also, had found in Agapê a girl unlike any one he had ever before seen. Her life with her father had made a woman of her while still in her teens; she was modest and refined, and yet she could keep her part in a conversation on topics utterly beyond the ken of a Persian woman of thrice her age. She had varied accomplishments. She knew music, she played the lute, and sang exquisite Grecian songs in her pure, high voice; as we have seen, she could dance with all the grace of a hamadryad. She was given more freedom than it was customary to allow Farsî women, and as she was always attended by the gigantic eunuch, Agâ Zālým, she came and went without let or hindrance. Zālým was her devoted slave. His worship of her was touching; great, fierce, ugly barbarian that he was, to her he was as gentle as a trained elephant, and he would have unquestioningly sacrificed his life for her.

Nizâmu'l-Mulk thought it possible that Agapê had told Hasan of meeting Omar at the būstân. Hasan had been at the palace long enough to have seen her, and as she was lively and talkative, she might easily have let slip some intimation of her meeting with Omar; and yet — Of course, he knew nothing of her second and third visit there. The Agâ Zālým was more faithful to Agapê than to him. Agapê had bade him say nothing, and his mouth was sealed.

The Wazîr saw well that something must soon be done with Agapê. The ominous silence of her father seemed to signify that he was dead, and, as his village had been destroyed, there was probably none of her family left to inquire into her fate. She was now a marriageable young woman, and, though portionless, her grace, beauty, and accomplishments, as well as the fact that she was a titled maiden, might make her attractive to some man of distinction.

Hasan's remark connecting her with Omar gave him what seemed the key to the difficulty, If it were true that Omar was pleased with the girl, — and how could he fail to be, after the dainty compliment that she had lavished on him regarding his poems? — surely no better wife could be found for him! The more he thought it over, the more suitable the match seemed to him, and he vowed that if it should come about, he would induce the Sultân himself to confer on Agapê a marriage-portion that would be compatible with her former position.

It need not be imagined that men are above the pleasant diplomacy of matchmaking. Sex has nothing to do with it. It is really an art more absorbing than that of painting: in the one, colors are put together in harmonious combinations; in the other, souls and bodies, dispositions and tastes, are united, and when the contrasts are well relieved, the result is a masterpiece of immortality.

The Wazîr resolved to sound Omar at the first chance; but first he would speak to Malíkshāh about it. He had no doubt that the Sultân would look on it in the same light as he did. So a day or two later, being alone with Malíkshāh, he broached the subject.

"For four years," he said, "the daughter of Prince Kreiton has been living at your Majesty's Court as a hostage. No ransom has come for her, and Hasan ben Sabah suggests that some disposition be made of her. Has your Majesty any desire respecting her?"

"Was it not the Greek girl that danced before me at the poet Omar's pavilion?"

"It was Agapê, the Greek maiden."

"She danced with grace. I remember she also answered Omar's problem with sagacity."

"It had occurred to me that perhaps Omar might

be moved to take her to wife, he being unmarried. From the girl's remark, I judge she would not regard such a fate as cruel. What woman could?"

"I would give my consent."

"But the girl is portionless unless her father be still living, and able to raise the money for her ransom. You remember his village was razed to the ground, and all its inhabitants were—"

Malíkshāh broke in on his sentence:

"Then surely we owe the girl a portion. We grant her ten thousand mithkals of gold. Let it be from the new revenues of Nishāpûr. Hasan ben Sabah shall see that it be paid on the day of her marriage."

This ended the matter and Nizâmu'l-Mulk felt sure of his scheme's success. He felt sure that Omar would gladly take Agapê, and no less sure that Agapê would gladly dwell the rest of her life in Omar's care. He felt a generous delight in being able to put into Omar's possession such an incomparable pearl.

Thus while Omar and Agapê were both trying to shape their destiny and not quite daring to speak openly what after all each desired most earnestly, the higher powers had resolved for them. How unfortunate that Omar did not go straight to the unselfish Wazîr, and tell him exactly how he and Agapê felt and perhaps have asked—as he would have obtained — permission to go to Rūm, as the Persian called the Grecian land, and satisfy Agapê that her father was no longer in the land of the living. But Agapê and Omar both had in their natures a little of the Greek and Persian slyness, which prompted them rather to the clandestine than to the avowed. A surreptitious interview might be prevented or interrupted; but the chances of their meeting, if their plan of meeting was known, were almost null, — or so at least they imagined.

Hasan was all the time maturing his plans. He more than once tried to win the Agâ Zālým over to his interests, but found him incorruptible. Such fidelity was wholly contrary to his experience of the character of eunuchs, who, he knew, were generally mercenary, revengeful, and treacherous. He tried in vain to get speech with Agapê herself; he had great faith in his compelling eye, and no doubt that if once he could bring her under its compulsion she would do as he should will. But Agapê evidently avoided him; her keen instinct seemed to tell her that the tall Persian, with his fanatic face, was an enemy to the joy and brightness which she loved.

But Hasan was more successful with others; he easily bribed the second eunuch of the anderûn to keep him informed of what went on in the women's quarters, and his son was instructed not to fail to follow any woman who should slip out alone or attended. Hasan knew that if Agapê had once met Omar surreptitiously she would surely seize the first opportunity to do so again. His plan was to prevent the meeting if possible, but if impossible, to have a little troop of horsemen waiting to kill the Agâ if necessary, and to seize Agapê and convey her to a house that he had prepared to receive her. He had the ministers all ready to execute his commands; there is no question as to his almost miraculous power in bending the wills of men.

But a much longer time than he anticipated elapsed before Agapê saw her way clear to promise and set an hour for meeting Omar at the pavilion. Omar himself had been occupied in superintending the erection of his new observatory on the hill; the instruments which he had ordered required his personal superintendence, and he had been obliged to be at the coppersmith's every day, lest some mistake should be made in constructing the various instruments which he needed. Then he had to ride more than once to the observatory to see that it was progressing satisfactorily. Then, again, the Sultân and the Wazîr several times arranged to spend an afternoon of relaxation with him, either at the būstân or in the park on the hill. But at last a day came when Malíkshāh and Nizâmu'l-Mulk were to go down to the desert hawking bustards, and Agapê, learning of it in time, found means to send word to Omar, who, on the plea that he must look after his astronomical instruments, excused himself from the pleasure of going with them.

Hasan knew of the meeting planned even before Omar received Agapê's dainty little note. He determined to act instantly. He ordered six men, who he knew would serve him unquestioningly, to ride out, one by one, without attracting suspicion, and to lie in ambush behind one of the round towers that were used on the plain as a house for pigeons, where the guano was collected for agricultural purposes. The path to the river led directly by this building, which was deserted and excellently adapted as a hiding-place or an ambush. They were to let pass without hindrance any man riding or walking alone, but were to seize and overpower the Agâ Zālým, and then take possession of the palankin in which the woman under his escort was carried.

It was a hot day; not a breeze was stirring; the blazing sun poured down from a cloudless sky bluer than a sapphire; the Persian summer had begun.

Omar, unsuspecting of the plot, passed slowly by the tall tower. He paused for a moment in its shadow to watch the doves circling around it, poising on its parapet, marching up and down, their burnished feathers glistening in the sunlight. Then, having rested, he proceeded in the direction of the river, and disappeared from sight.

A little later, riding carelessly along on a mule too small for his long legs, came the Agâ Zālým, immediately preceding a palankin borne by two stout Chinese slaves. A little whistle twice repeated, but scarcely more noticeable than the note of a bird, gave the warning agreed on; suddenly, six armed men dashed out without making any cry; two of them knocked Zalým from his mule, and, quickly binding him, dragged him behind the tower. The others, threatening instant death to the palankin-bearers if they made a sound, halted them. Agapê, for it was she whom they had so successfully stopped, opened the door of the palankin and tried to escape. It took but an instant to recapture her: it was done without violence, for Hasan had cautioned the men to treat the girl gently, and she was put back into the palankin. They admonished her not to open her mouth, and Agapê knew that it was useless to shout for help; for if there were any to aid, they would suppose it was only the forcible cessation of some intrigue, and would not dream of interfering. She knew too well from the gossip of the anderûn how husbands deceived sometimes took their revenge. She, therefore, accepted the inevitable, and waited developments. She had much faith in her own cleverness, and she knew that she must keep her wits about her, if at some favorable juncture she were to escape.

But as the palankin, now under the escort of the four mounted men, made its way back to the city, she turned over in her mind the possible reasons for this outrage. She at first supposed that her visit to the būstân had been detected, and that they were taking her back to the Arg; but when, on passing the gate, the four horsemen compelled the palankin-bearers to turn to the left, and, quickening their pace, to bring her into a part of the city where she had never before been, she realized that some fate, perhaps a thousand times more dreadful than what she had feared, was before her. Her heart sank within her when, at last, the men stopped at a gloomy house, and raising a brass knocker, shaped like a coiled serpent with darting fangs, thumped furiously on the black door. A moment later the door was cautiously opened and admitted all the men; at the same time two grooms appeared and led away their horses.

Agapê was conducted through an inner court furnished with an ill-kept tank, over which leaned a scraggly date-palm; a hideous old woman, whose dark, wrinkled skin could not be hidden by the pretence of the veil that she wore, received the girl, and saying not a word, took her by the hand, the scrawny, claw-like fingers grasping roughly the delicate wrist, and drew her into the anderûn. Agapê tried to question the old woman. She asked why she had been abducted, who had dared to lay hands on her, what they were going to do with her; but the old hag refused to speak, and only shook her head. When Agapê, stamping her foot imperiously, commanded her to answer, the old woman, who had removed her veil, opened her mouth, and Agapê saw to her horror that the repulsive creature was not only toothless but tongueless; her tongue had been torn out years before. The action was an implicit threat, and Agapê understood it so.

Nevertheless the old woman, whose name even Agapê did not know, prepared a dish not unlike pilaf and a bowl of goat's milk, and set it before her. At first she thought she could not eat, — her appetite was stifled, — but as she realized that she might need all the strength she could muster, she forced herself to swallow the food, and found it not ill-flavored.

An hour — two hours passed, and Agapê knew by the changing light that the afternoon was waning. She went with pretended carelessness near the door, but the old woman, whose eyes had been apparently closed, sprang there before her and barred the way.

CHAPTER XIX.

A MIRACULOUS ESCAPE.

WHEN the two men had dragged the Agâ Zālým from his mule, one of them had hit him a violent blow on the head with a club; it had stunned him. After they had placed him on the ground, behind the pigeon-tower, he lay so perfectly motionless that they came to the conclusion that they must have killed him.

"Tamâm shud — he is dead," said one.

"What shall we do with *it?*" asked the other.

"It won't do to leave him here."

"Wait a moment," said the second speaker. "I have it."

He emerged cautiously from the covert, and walking along several hundred paces, came to one of the wells that were a part of the irrigating system of the plain. Having made sure that they were not observed, he went back, and, beckoning to his companion, whispered to him his plan. The other approved it, and they took up the inanimate body of the unfortunate eunuch, and, having brought it to the well, flung it in unceremoniously. Then they started off for the city to report to Hasan and receive their promised reward.

Fortunately the water in the well was not deep, but it was deep enough to break the Agâ Zālým's fall, and it was cold enough to restore him to consciousness. He stood in water up to his shoulders, dazed, dizzy, and absolutely at a loss to know what had happened. He shouted for help, but no one came. He waited shivering; the pain in his head prevented him from any connected thought, but when he found that he was wasting his breath, he desisted from shouting, and tried to climb out. It was a hopeless task; he saw that he was trapped, but as his eyes grew more accustomed to the darkness, he found that the water was pouring down stone-lined channels, leading in several different directions. One seemed to be the feeder of the well and of the others, and into this he climbed without very great difficulty. It was large enough for him to grope through, bent almost double, and though he knew not to what it might lead him, he followed along this kârez, hoping that it would ultimately bring him into higher levels, and thus within reach of the surface. His progress was slow and painful; more than once he felt inclined to give up, — lie down and die. After a long time he reached another well; it was not so deep as the first, and from this also led passages in several directions. Agā Zālým, before he selected one of these, again shouted at the top of his falsetto voice, but still no one came to his aid, and he was unable to climb unaided to the top. Again he had the desperately slow and painful passage through the low, narrow drain; his head was splitting with agony, his body was chilled by his soaked clothing, and the weariness, caused by the unusual exertion, hampered him as if logs were tied to his limbs. It seemed an eternity since he had come to his consciousness, and he was now tormented by the thought that some evil had befallen his beloved charge.

Suddenly he came into one of the ferraniol or reservoirs, of which there were twelve at that time on the Plain of Nishāpûr. This was an extensive excavation, perhaps twelve feet deep; fortunately for him the depth of water was not considerable. A multitude of columns supported a series of arches, over which extended a flooring, covered with soil, and supporting a little peach orchard. A single air-hole let in light and ventilation, and as Zālým happened to come out from the passage into the reservoir almost under this open air-hole, he was able to see where he was. Zālým mustered all his energies and gave one yell.

The effect was startling; his hair, wet as it was, stood on end with horror. His superstitious mind imagined that the whole space, which he could see stretching away into the darkness and distance, was filled with demons mocking him, and, perhaps, ready to tear him pieces. He could hear them gathering behind the pillars, ready to pounce on him. His tongue clove to his throat with terror; but when nothing touched him he yelled again, and again came that blood-curdling pandemonium of sounds. It was really only the manifold echo of his voice, reverberating under the arches, and in the hollows, and against the pillars. This time his cry was heard: the caretaker of the reservoir happened to be not far from the vent hole, and hearing such a strange noise in the depths below him, he put his head down and said:

"What is it?"

When he at last distinguished the cry of "help" he got a ladder and ran it down through the vent-hole; then he himself descended part way and reached his hand to the poor Agâ, who, putting forth his last remaining vestige of energy, managed to climb to the top. No sooner had he reached the surface than he fell senseless. The caretaker, who was a man of sympathetic nature, saw by Zālým's dress, wet and soiled though it was, that he was no ordinary individual, managed to convey the unconscious man to his own house, where he had him properly attended to. He summoned a Hakîm bāshî, as they called the doctor in Irân, and told him the circumstances of the sick man's arrival. The doctor ordered an electuary made of pepper and myrobolans, male orchis, chamomile twigs, pine-seeds, and citron, and ordered it administered in a bolus the size of a walnut every hour till morning. But he added, "Allâh is the curer of all diseases." When the next morning he came again, Zālým was in a high fever and delirious. He was raving about Agapê, calling the name again and again, but, of course, it meant nothing to the attendants. Then he would try to get out of bed, and it required considerable strength to keep him there. The Hakîm bāshî put on a very wise expression, stroked his long beard stained red, and, looking at Zālým, said:

"Verily, his mind is not swinging on its own hinges; he raves like one insane. Now, the proper remedy for insanity is the Mufarrih-i-yākát, which, being properly compounded, contains a solution of turquoise, emerald, chrysolite, carnelian, lapis lazuli, and unpierced pearl; the union of colors and of properties causes a most beneficent and calming effect. But this remedy is excessively costly and difficult to procure. The next best thing is cold water, applied externally and internally. Water absorbs the wild humor and restores the reason."

It was several days before the liberal application of water had its desired effect. When at last the fever abated and the Agâ Zālým came to himself once more, he was as weak as a child. He had not the slightest idea where he was, nor could he remember anything of what had happened. Or, rather, what had actually happened was confused with the dimly remembered dreams that had accompanied his illness. It was a week before he was able to sit up, but after that he recovered rapidly. He could hardly master his impatience to return to the Arg and find what had happened to Agapê.

CHAPTER XX.

AN EMBASSY FROM RŪM.

OMAR was more disappointed than surprised at the absence of Agapê. The marvel to his mind was that she could manage to come at all. He waited two hours beyond the appointed time, and then, relinquishing all hope of seeing her, he drank a lonely glass of wine and leisurely returned to the city.

The next day, at the morning meal, his mother said:

"My son, you know I am wont to dream, and to have strange dreams. Last night I had over and over again a troubled and anxious vision. A young maiden appeared before me, with tears streaming down her face and with clasped hands, and she asked, in a peculiar accent, 'Where is Omar?' She was not like our girls of Irân. And even while I tried to comfort her, rough men seized her and carried her off. Twice she seemed to come to me, and to say, 'Where is Omar? Why does not Omar save me?' and each time she was carried off by the same men. The dream dwells with me, and I can not shake off its influence. It seems to me as if some misfortune were about to strike you."

Omar remembered how only a day or two before his father died his mother had also dreamed a disquieting dream. He remembered also how she had one night dreamed that he, Omar, was dead, and yet he appeared before her and repeated a quatrain so perfect in form and so characteristic of him that he wished he had composed it. It was this:

> "*Oh, Thou, who burn'st in Heart for those who burn*
> *In Hell, whose fires thyself shall feed in turn;*
> *How long be crying, 'Mercy on them, God!'*
> *Why, who art Thou to teach, and He to learn?*"[1]

His mother's dream of a girl with broken accent, in trouble and calling on him for aid, seemed involuntarily to connect itself with Agapê's failure to appear the afternoon before. He could not throw off the incubus of anxiety which each instant weighed heavier on his heart. Instead of going to the brassmaker to see about his new orrery that was to be done that day, he directed his course to the palace, hoping that he might in some way get a word of explanation from Agapê.

At the palace he found great excitement. An embassy from the Emperor at Byzantium had just arrived, and the official meeting was taking place.

[1] Edward Fitzgerald's version.

The gorgeous robes of the impêrial party, which took especial pains to show to the best advantage the wealth and power of the Eastern Empire, the manifold and complicated ceremonies which the etiquette of the Court prescribed, made a scene that was marvellous for its beauty and splendor. The Sultân, blazing with jewels, sat on his ebony throne; at his right hand stood Nizâmu'l-Mulk, more simply clad, but remarkable for his dignity and nobility. Nor was Hasan ben Sabah absent from the distinguished throng; with haughty face and flashing eyes he stood overtopping all but a few of the courtiers.

There were various matters of state importance that had to be discussed by means of interpreters. Then the ambassador remarked that he had in his train the Prince Kreiton who had, four years before, left his daughter, the Princess Agapê, at the Court of the Sultân as a hostage. Various causes — among others a long illness — had (to his great grief) prevented his redeeming her before. The question of the indemnity was to be settled.

The prince, who was now presented to Malíkshāh with due formality, was a pure type of the Greek. His age was not far from fifty, but care and suffering had left traces on his handsome face. He was naturally most eager to see his beloved daughter once more, and had no doubt that the order would be immediately given for her restoration to him. He was ready to pay whatever sum the Sultân should demand.

The Sultân, after consulting with Nizâmu'l-Mulk, replied that he was disposed to remit the ransom of Prince Kreiton in view of the fact that his estates at Koinê had been taken from him; moreover, his daughter, the Princess Agapê, had been an ornament and delight to his Court, and therefore he would give her to her father, as it were, a free gift of friendship and good will. But remembering the talk that he had held with Nizâmu'l-Mulk concerning Agapê and Omar, and not willing to see that pleasant plan broken off, he added:

"Perhaps the Princess Agapê would not be unwilling to remain in Irân; in that case would the Prince Kreiton also be persuaded to become a member of our Court, suitable provision being made for his support?"

This proposition showed the broad and liberal spirit of this Seljûk Turk: to some of his faith the mere sight of a Christian would have been a cause of spitting.

The prince, not knowing exactly what to make of this question, and perhaps a little suspicious, evaded a direct reply, but said he would first talk with his daughter.

Then with a generous delicacy the Sultân ordered

that the prince should be conducted to a khelwát or private room and that Agapê should be taken to him there.

The rest of the day was to be given up to sight-seeing and to a great dinner in the afternoon. The plans were all made in some haste, for the Sultân and his minister being away on their hunting expedition the day before, all the details of the istikbâl had fallen on Ibrāhîm Niyâl, who had performed that important ceremony late the preceding afternoon, and had brought the guests into the city and suitably lodged them at the Arg.

Of course the long absence of Agapê was noticed at the anderûn, and caused some wonder among the women. But as the Agâ Zālým was supposed to be with her, it was taken to be only one of the Greek girl's occasional visits to the wife of the Nizâmu'l-Mulk. But the demand for her to come and meet her father, quickly revealed the fact that she was not in the anderûn, nor had she been in the apartment occupied by the Wazîr and his family. The Agâ Zālým was not to be found. Agapê seemed to have entirely disappeared. So well had she managed her visit to the būstân, not a soul had seen her go out, and the palankin-bearers, who had twice before carried her to the river, were prisoners as well as Agapê. The only person in the Court who could have unlocked the mystery was Hasan ben Sabah. His satanic spirit took a fiendish delight in the success of his enterprise, and in the trouble which he saw was to follow the loss of the hostage.

When the pages returned and informed the Sultân that Agapê was nowhere to be found, consternation reigned. Omar, who had been amazed at the apparition of Agapê's father, had at first supposed that the girl's failure to appear at the pavilion was explained by his unexpected arrival; but now when the rumor ran through the assembly that she had disappeared, he was filled with wild alarm. He felt almost guilty of whatever accident might have befallen her. He knew not what to do, but resolved to confess, as soon as possible, to the Wazîr, how Agapê had promised but failed to meet him at the būstân. He was no coward, and though he had enjoyed the secrecy of the acquaintance, he was not afraid to meet the consequences.

Hasan ben Sabah, his face unusually impassive though stern, managed to whisper into Nizâmu'l-Mulk's ear the suspicion that Omar might know something about Agapê. But the Wazîr, although he remembered well enough what Hasan had once before stated in regard to Omar meeting Agapê at the pavilion, had not the slightest distrust awakened by Hasan's innuendo. Orders were given for a systematic search for her, and the eager father was informed that she was gone out to the bāzâr, but would be sent to him as soon as she returned: that they had summoned her.

But when the messengers and searchers, one by one, returned without finding any trace of her, and when the Agâ Zālým also failed to appear, it was evident to all that something extraordinary had happened. What now should be told Prince Kreiton? It was a most awkward and trying situation, and as the explanations had to be given by means of an interpreter the difficulties were increased. But the marvellous tact of Nizâmu'l-Mulk was here shown. He made the poor prince understand thoroughly that the girl had been treated with perfect kindness, that she had been seen alive, well, and apparently happy, only the day before. One of the women of the anderûn was reported as having heard Agapê declare that she should not wait many more days before she set off for "Rūm," as they called the Western world, in search of her father. So the belief spread that the girl had taken the Agâ Zālým and set forth in the utterly foolhardy errand of crossing a continent, — climbing snow-clad mountains, defying the dangers of fierce, wandering tribes, without money and without defence. The wiser ones doubted; but the father, learning how Agapê had hungered and thirsted to see him once more, convinced himself, against his better judgment, that this was the explanation.

But here Omar at last had a chance to talk confidentially with the Wazîr. He had tried to get word with him, but the duties entailed by the entertainment of the Greek ambassador, and by the distressing disappearance of Agapê, had kept him so busy every moment, that he could not find time to see his friends. When he and Omar were alone, Omar, with perfect frankness, told him how he had twice before met Agapê, at her request, at the būstân, and that he had offered to take her as his wife. He confirmed the story of the girl's intense desire to go to Hellas, and he said she had tried to persuade him to go with her. She was to have met him the very afternoon of her disappearance: he went to the pavilion and waited for her in vain.

"It would have been wiser to confide in me," said Nizâmu'l-Mulk, with a mild reproof in his tone, but he added: "However, you are your own master, and I would not interfere with your wooings. Agapê was free to do as she pleased, and I do not forget that I myself first brought her to you there; though I had no thought of such serious consequences."

In his own mind he coupled Hasan's sneaking hint with a suspicion that the wily treasurer knew something about the matter, but he had no proof of it. The mystery was as yet impenetrable. He decided that he would try to learn from Hasan what he meant by his malicious reference to Omar, and if he really knew anything about it. But Hasan's secretary, his preternaturally solemn son, informed Nizâmu'l-Mulk that "his master, the treasurer, had gone to Resht on business connected with the revenue." There seemed to be no reason to doubt this fact. It was confirmed by others in the Court.

CHAPTER XXI.

THE BIRD IS NOT EASILY TAMED.

HASAN had not gone to Resht. He had come to the conclusion that it was not safe any longer to keep Agapê in Nishāpûr, and he resolved to take her himself to Mashad and put her into trusty hands in that famous city of pilgrimage. It required all his ingenuity to depart from Nishāpûr with his prize without attracting attention to her; for by this time it was known throughout the city that a Greek hostage had disappeared from the palace, and a prize was outstanding for information about her.

Hasan had found Agapê no tractable prisoner. When he went to visit her he learned not a little as to her spirit and her resolution. But, as we have said, he possessed a peculiar power over men and animals, a masterful power that would appear later in Napoleon, for instance, and in modern scientific terms be called "hypnotic." Moreover he was consummately crafty. He made her to understand that she was absolutely in his power; that though she might rave and scream, it would not hurt any one but herself;

no one could or would come to her aid; on the other hand, if she would be reasonable, she would soon be in a place that would make her the envied of all the Orient.

It was the sense of her utter helplessness that finally bent Agapê's will; so that when Hasan brought her the dress of a youthful pilgrim, she, without saying a word, obeyed his command and arrayed herself in it. At midnight she was compelled to set forth with him, and, under the threat of instant death, if she uttered a cry or attempted to escape, she accompanied him through a comparatively unfrequented gate, the keeper of which easily let them pass, supposing from their garb that they were pilgrims bound for the shrine of the holy Imâm Alî, son of Mūsâ. Outside, horses were in waiting, and by morning Hasan and Agapê, accompanied by a little band of men, whom he had brought into the most unquestioning obedience, were miles away from the city on their way to Mashad. It was not strange that dread and terror kept her from uttering a sound. As she rode on in the darkness the scenes of the past few days rose before her like a succession of frightful visions. She saw Hasan as he came in the first evening of her imprisonment: again she felt his frightful eyes fixed on her, and seeming to burn through her very soul. She had tried to hide her face from his gaze, but he compelled her to face him. Then in that deep, powerful, clear voice of his, he had charged her with being Omar's paramour.

"Thou shalt learn," he said, "that the fruit of sin is bitterer than the fruit of the tree Zakkum, that grows from the bottomless pit."

"Who made you my judge?" she had demanded, with her spirit all in flame at the insult. "What right have you to seize me, and confine me in this abominable way?"

And Hasan, whom she knew by sight, laughed with a harsh, grating laugh; it still rang in her ears.

"I make myself your judge, and by the right of power I hold you, and you shall never escape from my clutches. You shall never again lie in the arms of that kabr kāshîda,—that infidel scoffer!"

Again Agapê had started up with indignation with a hot reply, for she, being Greek, had no small store of reproachful terms, but Hasan would not allow her to speak. Suddenly changing his tone, he began to flatter her, promising her that if she would forget that imbecile poet, and would give him instead the treasure of her love, he would wear her like the Sultân's jîka, the very jewel of his crown; for, said he, boastfully, "The reins of fate are in my hands; before I finish my career I shall drive the horses of war up the mountain-side of Fame."

Agapê, young, beautiful, tender, full of grace, was in his clutches, like a nightingale in the claws of a hawk. "You are absolutely mine," he said. "You can no more escape than the new moon can escape from the old moon. You might shriek from now till the day of doom, you are helpless."

Then he had left her for two long days and nights, left her in the silent but ceaseless care of that dreadful, tongueless hag who could not communicate with her except by signs. Not another soul had she seen; she was, as it were, buried. Again and again she tried to devise some means of escape; but each time her fertile brain evolved a scheme, she found herself blocked by the forethought of Hasan, and the vigilance of the old woman.

Then he had appeared once more in the same funest and domineering way, at first trying to coerce her with his fixed and cruel gaze, then working on her passions, — anger, hatred, terror, and, finally, apparently softening and trying the wiles of his smooth and oily flattery.

The arrival of the Grecian embassy and of Agapê's father had put a different face on matters. Hasan knew that he could not long keep up the secrecy of his visits to the girl; suspicion would be awakened, and if Agapê by any means should find her way back to the Court his plans would quickly be dashed. It was one thing to abduct a poor orphan girl, whose disappearance would soon be forgotten; it was another to be proved guilty of having kept in such durance the daughter of the Prince Kreiton, who was in favor with the Emperor at Byzantium, and had produced such a favorable impression on the Sultân that Malíkshāh had invited him to remain at his Court. He had taken the fatal step mainly out of petty spite, but also because he thought the girl beautiful, and he had preferred to have her rather than see his old schoolmate enjoying her favors. He had, therefore, to choose between two alternatives: to take her immediately away, or to send her to the city of non-existence. The first seemed to him expedient, and he made his plans accordingly, as we have seen. He left Ostad-ben-Hasan to keep watch, and instantly inform him if anything of importance should happen.

A still more impressive lesson of Hasan's evil temper and his arbitrary tyranny was given just before they started, and this vision of horror kept arising in Agapê's mind, making her shudder and filling her with hopeless despair. One of the two Chinese palankin-bearers tried to escape. He was caught and hauled roughly back before Hasan, who, without giving him time even to kiss the ground and exhibit his regret, stabbed him to the heart with his dagger. Then, flinging the dead body out of the room, he ordered his crouching servitors to put it into a sack and safely dispose of it. This quick and dreadful deed of violence made the impression that Hasan desired. Every one present was given to understand that no ordinary person controlled their destinies, and that human life was valueless in his eyes.

This scene impressed Agapê most painfully, for Hasan had more than once hinted that he would not spare her if she crossed his will. Yet not for one moment during all the time of that long and weary night journey across the plain, and the unrelentingly rapid ascent of the mountains in the early morning, did she cease to plan her escape. The sight of the sun, the beauty of the day, kindled the dying embers of hope in her heart. She had faith that Omar, with the aid of the Sultân and Nizâmu'l-Mulk, would leave no stone unturned to trace her, and bring her back in safety. It seemed incredible that Hasan could have kept so perfectly from rumor the mysterious transactions in the house where she had been imprisoned. Wonderful iris-winged Hope! how she finds her way into the darkest hearts, and lights up the gloomy recesses with her joyous radiance! Without her life would be a dreary waste. She is the mirage that beckons the lost and weary traveller onward, and sometimes, though not always, brings him through to the other side of the waste. So now, though Agapê knew not what was going to become of her, nor why she had been so hastily removed from Nishāpûr, she felt less heavily the incubus of Hasan's fierce personality, though he never for a moment relaxed his hold upon her.

As for him, he found a strange delight in looking at her in her boy's costume, which, in his eyes, rendered all the more fascinating the suggested contours of her pretty form; yet no casual observer would have suspected that the slender fellow dressed in the simple pilgrim garb, and mounted on the handsome horse, was a Grecian princess, abducted from the Sultân's anderûn! Hasan talked little with her; for her replies were not encouraging to sprightly converse, and he himself was too deeply concerned with evolving his weighty plans to indulge in sprightly converse. Thus they rode for hours without exchanging a word. Hasan had at first determined to go to Isfahân by the longest and speediest possible stages, to leave Agapê there in the guardianship of of his trusty friend Abul-fasl, and then return and perfect his plans at Nishāpûr and Marv; but to Isfahân it was a long and difficult journey, and, especially in midsummer, he could not well be so long absent, so he had arranged to leave her for a brief time with another of his trusty friends at Mashad. Here he could easily come to see her, and work on her mind, and the friend would willingly supplement his endeavors. This plan had accordingly been agreed on, and Ostad-ben-Hasan knew where he could find his father for a few days; for he calculated to be away at least a week.

So far all Hasan's plans were working admirably. He reached Mashad safely, and found his friend there prepared to do his bidding. Hasan gave him to understand that Agapê was his wife, whom he was disciplining instead of divorcing.

"Believe nothing she says," were his words, and the friend, a stupid, thick-headed fanatic, whom Hasan had impressed with a sense of his holiness, acted accordingly. Here at Mashad Hasan devoted himself absolutely to winning her favor, and the genius that he displayed in flattery and in promises, in doing for her what women best love, and in brilliant conversation, amazed even Agapê. That she was not somewhat dazzled by Hasan's pictures of his coming greatness, and of what he would do for her, would have been natural; but she could not forgive him his high-handed abduction of her, and her heart still turned to Omar as the needle turns to the pole. She was too crafty to display her resentment, or to let Hasan know of her love for Omar. She thought by apparently yielding somewhat to his advances she might cause him to relax his watchfulness and allow her a chance to escape. She was no longer dressed as a boy-pilgrim, but, at Hasan's desire, wore the ordinary costume of the Persian woman, and, being Greek, it mattered not to her whether she wore the veil or not, nor had she, as a Greek, the modern prudish fear of displaying natural charms; so that in the somewhat tenuous costume of the anderûn, she was neither self-conscious nor immodest. On the other hand, she was skilful enough to avoid all undue familiarities, and she kept Hasan at a distance. He would have compelled her to become his legal wife had he not desired to win through willingness what he was wise enough to despise when taken. He had only a few days to spend there at Mashad, for a long absence would cause suspicion, so he made the most of his opportunities. But like a boat that floats down stream the instant the rower ceases to row, so he found himself, each time that he began, floated down where he had begun the time before. And Agapê, with a childlike innocence which was the height of art, thus kept her wooer like the lover on the Greek vase. He made no progress, and yet seemed to himself to be progressing. Did not the famous, wise Penelope, in the same way, for years deceive her suitors? Thus went several days, till suddenly an event occurred which changed all their lives.

CHAPTER XXII.

HASAN'S FLIGHT.

It usually happens in life that there will be long stretches of uneventful days; then, in quick succession, following one on the heels of another, crises, excitements, disasters, triumphs come.

The unusual episode of an embassy from Europe which was attended with cruel disappointment to one member of it, was hardly a thing of the past when at the Arg occurred one of those tragedies so common in autocratic courts and especially in the East. The pride of Sultân Malíkshāh's heart was his young son, Berkiyarok, a graceful, black-eyed boy of about fifteen years of age. As the heir apparent to the sultanate he was being trained as carefully as was possible in all the accomplishment and studies of the day. He was excellent in riding horseback and in hunting, and in all the exercises with sword and lance. His favorite amusement was chugan or polo, and he was exceedingly skilful in it. The day after the departure of the embassy, Berkiyarok was matched in a game against his cousin Ibrāhîm Niyâl. It was an exciting game: the horses were full of life and agile as squirrels. The ball flew into the middle of the field, and Ibrāhîm Niyâl and Berkiyarok dashed off in order to intercept it. Then happened a dreadful thing: Ibrāhîm, perhaps accidentally, but apparently with malice prepense, dashed violently against the young shāhzādá or crown prince as if to crush him. The prince's pony being far lighter, was knocked over, and the boy himself was thrown headlong and fell heavily on the ground. He was picked up for dead and taken to the palace.

The Sultân, good-natured as he ordinarily was, now showed the undercurrent of cruelty that flowed deep down in his soul. He was convinced that Ibrāhîm Niyâl had endeavored to kill the young prince in order to clear the way for himself to the throne. Although Berkiyarok was fortunately not killed but only stunned, Malíkshāh would listen to no excuses. He immediately deposed Ibrāhîm Niyâl from his office as governor of the Province, and when this order had been promulgated he had two executioners throw him on the ground and tear out his eyes. The Sultân had for some time suspected his nephew of harboring undue ambition and had been warned to beware of him. Such domestic dramas had been before and Malíkshāh would take no chance. Yet, when he saw the bleeding, eyeless sockets of the young man, an hour before so bold and handsome, almost his own flesh and blood, he groaned in spirit and was sorrowful; he repented of his harsh judgment, but done was done and now he was safe. It was kept perfectly quiet; few and only confidential servants knew of what had happened. A day or two later Ibrāhîm was taken to Mashad and given over to the guardian of the sacred shrine of that city, who was to take care of him till he was well again.

Of course, Nizâmu'l-Mulk knew about this barbarous punishment; he would have fain stopped the Sultân from carrying it out, but when his protest was unavailing he was wise enough to hold his peace. But when Malíkshāh a few days later suddenly decided to return to Marv and proposed to make Hasan governor of the Province of Khurāsân in place of Ibrāhîm Niyâl, the Wazîr had no hesitation in advising him to wait a little: to wait at least until Hasan should have returned from Resht.

He did not want to make a direct charge or even to hint that Hasan had been the one to whom Agapê's disappearance was due, but he knew, as we have said, that Hasan had managed to enrich himself substantially from the clippings of the fleece, in other words, by his cleverly conducted dealings with the tax problem. Nizâmu'l-Mulk did not wish to appear jealous, especially when he himself had recommended Hasan to preferment, and he could not help confessing that the new treasurer had accomplished marvels in his work.

While the affair was thus hanging, a great excitement was aroused in the Court by the arrival of the eunuch Zālým. He still showed the signs of his illness; one could see at a glance that he had undergone a trying experience. He was so weak that he could hardly walk, and his poor little squeaky voice was like the fluting of a cicada. But when he was brought before Nizâmu'l-Mulk, and told his story in a straightforward way, and when the last part of it was confirmed by the watchman who had taken such good care of the poor fellow, no doubt remained that Zālým was telling the truth. He could not explain the reason of the assault; it had been so sudden that he had no idea what kind of men had attacked him. His appearance, therefore, brought with it no clue to the mystery; his sorrow over the loss of Agapê was so genuine that not a shadow of suspicion rested on him: he knew no more of the princess's whereabouts than Nizâmu'l-Mulk himself. At last the Wazîr asked in a casual way if Omar Khayyâm had ever seen Agapê. Under the pledge of the strictest secrecy he then confirmed what Omar himself had told the Wazîr. She was going that very afternoon to meet him. At first Nizâmu'l-Mulk was tempted to express himself pretty bitterly regarding the faithfulness of a hājí bu'd daulá who went off to river pavilions with the ladies of the anderûn and let them meet strange men! But when he saw how distressed the poor fellow was, how conscience-stricken, though he knew perfectly well the fault was not his, he did not press the matter: the Wazîr himself would have been the last to cast the first stone! Had he not himself taught Agapê the way, had he not made her acquainted with Omar, had he not wished that Omar should like the girl well enough to take her for his wife?

He took another course.

"Do you remember the Treasurer Hasan ben Sabah?" asked the Wazîr.

"I should never forget his eyes! They seem to burn your soul."

"Have you ever seen him talking with Agapê?"

"No," replied the Agâ Zálým. "He has never talked with her or spoken to her, so far as I know."

Then, suddenly remembering what had happened, he added:

"But one day he stopped me, and spoke most impertinently regarding her."

"Can you repeat what he said?"

"No; but the substance of it was that Agapê was doing wrong in meeting Omar, — but he did not say much. I refused to listen to him, and he was angry."

Nizâmu'l-Mulk's quick mind saw in this statement a confirmation of his suspicions. He resolved to know if Hasan was in Resht, and instantly sent a trusty courier to investigate. In an incredibly short time the courier returned, and reported that Hasan was not there, and had not been there. Happening a little later to be called into consultation with the Sultân, he gently hinted that perhaps Hasan ben Sabah might know more about Agapê than any one suspected. He told him how his secretary had said that he had gone to Resht, but that he was not there. Moreover, he now craftily mentioned the fact that he had discovered Hasan taking bribes on the right and on the left. The Sultân was furious. He for his part now began to recall the derogatory remarks that Hasan had made concerning the Wazîr; how he had insinuated more than once that if he were Wazîr things would be managed more economically, or with greater promptness. In fact, the Sultân, in his mind's eye, saw Hasan the centre of a plot in which Ibrāhîm Niyâl was the figure-head. He was for having Hasan instantly arrested and executed, but again Nizâmu'l-Mulk counselled a little deliberation.

"Besides," he said, "Hasan is not in the city. He went ostensibly to Resht on business connected with the revenue, and it is time now for his return. Let us send, and ask his secretary."

To this the Sultân offered no objection, and Hasan's son was summoned. He showed the greatest coolness and address in all his replies, betraying no uneasiness or hesitation, seeming to have implicit faith in Hasan. The Sultân, however, in trying to extort some damaging information regarding the treasurer, nearly lost his temper; and, as we have seen, when that happened, he was apt to be relentless and cruel. But he only threatened to have Ostad-ben-Hasan tortured, and when the young man showed no change in his preternaturally solemn face, and no apparent dread of anything that might happen to him, the threat was not carried into execution. It is certain that no torture would have extorted an incriminating word from his lips.

Malíkshāh, however, in his conduct of the examination said enough to awaken Ostad's apprehensions, and as soon as he was dismissed, he wrote a full account of all the circumstances, and sent it to his father by a trusty messenger, as had been agreed on between them.

The next morning he became perfectly convinced his father would be arrested the moment he returned to the city. With all secrecy and exactness, with a shrewdness worthy of his origin, he succeeded in penetrating the designs of the Sultân; he learned that the Court was going to return very shortly to Marv, that Nizâmu'l-Mulk had persuaded the Sultân to appoint Omar the governor of Nishāpûr, and that Hasan ben Sabah was to be put to death. Ostad even learned that the nominal charge against him would be of permitting irregularities in his accounts, but that he was suspected of being concerned in the disappearance of Agapê. He knew that Hasan might return at any moment, and that the utmost despatch was requisite in order to prevent the catastrophe. He therefore gathered together his few effects, secured a horse, and set forth by the caravan route to Mashad.

Hasan had already received his missive, and was naturally somewhat alarmed, but when he saw his son appear, bathed in perspiration from his swift ride, he realized that not a moment was to be lost. His only hope was to reach Isfahân as soon as possible, and find an asylum with Abul-fasl.

It chanced that a caravan was just about starting for Isfahân, and as the journey was long and dangerous, Hasan resolved to join it in his usual and familiar guise of a pilgrim who had been visiting Mashad-i-mukaddas, — Mashad the Holy, — the shrine of the great Imâm. When he thought of the chances that he might have had as treasurer of Irân to enrich himself, he regretted that he had abducted Agapê, but then he saw that his initial mistake had been in giving rise to any possible suspicion of his financial rectitude. He should have waited till he was actually treasurer; then his opportunities would have been vastly enlarged. But he comforted himself for his ignominious flight by the thought that he had in Isfahân the means for furthering his ambitions. There was no use of indulging in regrets. He had surely sacrificed another brilliant chance, this time by his own folly; he would take the lesson to heart, and next time be wiser. Even as he came to this conclusion, sprouted the germ of the idea which from this time grew in his mind like the deadly upas-tree.

Henceforth there was no hesitation in his course, no doubt as to its ultimate success. How he succeeded history tells. But now the one necessary thing was to escape before Malíkshāh's kazakî should arrive and apprehend him. He made the report current that he had gone the day before on business to Habushân, in exactly the opposite direction from Isfahân, and then, the time having come to start, he went to get Agapê. Ostad-ben-Hasan had started on to the caravanserai, where the company of pilgrims, merchants, and camel-drivers were to assemble. A disagreeable surprise awaited Ḥasan: Agapê was not to be found. Not a sign of her was visible.

No time was to be lost, but Hasan made a search for her in every room; she had vanished. With deep curses he hastened to the stable, and here another disagreeable surprise followed on the heels of the first. His favorite horse was gone. He thought it possible that Ostad might have taken it, but when he joined him at the rendezvous his hope was dashed. He was obliged to content himself with an inferior steed, and to go without his prize. His disappointment was bitter, and it seemed to him for a moment that the struggle before him was hardly worth while after all, that he might as well give in to his misfortune, let the Sultân's men capture him, and then throw himself on Malíkshāh's mercy, appealing to Nizâmu'l-Mulk's friendship. But the caravan was starting; the long line of heavily laden camels was already heading for the desert, and the guards were hurrying up the stragglers. Hasan, without saying a word, let himself be drawn along. The die was cast.

Six hours later the Sultân's kazakî came dashing into Mashad. They scoured the place, but when they were informed that Hasan had departed the day before, they came to the conclusion that it was useless to follow him. Perhaps Nizâmu'l-Mulk was not any too anxious to have Hasan brought back to undergo the punishment which he would have been powerless to prevent.

Agapê had not for an instant given up her design of escaping at the first possible moment. The arrival of Ostad's warning letter, followed by Ostad himself, had thrown the whole household into excitement. As a great wind on the ocean causes a restless rising and falling of the water in the harbor, so even in the quiet shelter of the anderûn was felt the reflex of this storm that threatened Hasan. Agapê knew not what the trouble was, but she surmised that it concerned herself; she thought it possible that Hasan, after his sudden departure from Nishāpûr, might have been tracked by the Sultân's spies. This surmise was strengthened by Hasan's coming to her in evident perturbation and ordering her to exchange her woman's costume once more for the pilgrim garb that she had worn. She obeyed, and tied into a bundle all her other clothes. Then for a moment, and for the first time since her arrival at Mashad, she was left alone. She thought she saw in this her opportunity; she slipped out, and, to her amazement and delight, met no one in the court. Hasan's horse was waiting at the door. Agapê, without saying a word, but with a charming air of authority, took the reins from the groom's hands and leaped into the saddle as if the whole had been prearranged. By the time Hasan appeared she was far away and beyond his reach.

CHAPTER XXIII.

PRINCE AND POET.

Prince Kreiton refused, at the last moment, to go back to Byzantium with the embassy. He still hoped against hope that his daughter might be found, and his form and sad face became familiar to the inhabitants of Nishāpûr, who, contrary to their reputation, treated him with respect as he went about the streets, looking for the lost. At Court he was an honored guest, and everything was done to appease his grief, to give him comfort, to aid him in the prosecution of his search.

A close friendship sprung up between him and Omar. It was a consolation to him to talk with the poet about Agapê. Omar told him how she had hungered for her beautiful distant fatherland, with its marble mountains and turquoise sea; how she was constantly planning to go and find out whether her father was still living. He praised the girl's sweet and sunny nature, and her intellectual superiority, her wit and knowledge.

It pleased the prince to talk with Omar about the

ancient Greek authors which Agapê had loved to study under his guidance. Every little thing about her which Omar could tell was as balm to the poor man's soul, and Omar never wearied of hearing the prince tell of Agapê's childhood and girlhood. Such a relationship between a father and a daughter was new to Omar's experience, but it appealed to the chivalry of his nature.

As the days went on, with still no news of Agapê, the prince's heart grew heavier, but at the same time he was supported by his Christian philosophy, and it pleased him to talk with Omar about that, and to compare it with the epicureanism which Omar himself professed. Omar made surprising progress in speaking Greek, and he found great delight in hearing the prince repeat Homer and the noble passages from the dramatic poets. The prince was interested in Omar's astronomical apparatus, and, like true philosophers, the two men, in their discussions on mathematics, poetry, and religion, often forgot for a time the ever present anxiety about Agapê.

When it became evident that Hasan had disappeared with Ostad as mysteriously as he had first appeared, when messengers despatched to various of the principal towns of Khurāsân brought no tidings, Nizâmu'l-Mulk determined to make one more effort to get a clue to their whereabouts. He succeeded in finding the house in Mashad, where Hasan had lodged, and he established beyond a doubt the fact that a woman corresponding to Agapê had accompanied him thither. It required drastic measures to extort even this information from the owner of the house in Mashad. The man was a willing tool to Hasan, who, whatever his other mistakes in action, never failed to select with consummate good judgment the agents of his powerful will. The Wazîr got also one important additional item of fact, and that was that Hasan had taken his departure from Mashad without Agapê. Whither the vanished treasurer had gone he either could not or would not tell, though Nizâmu'l-Mulk had the man confined and threatened with the loss of all he possessed.

Agapê, then, was alive, but where was she? What had become of her? She slid from one darkness of mystery into another: she appeared like a star on a night of storm, when it shines out for an instant not clearly, but dimly, from behind a dense cloud, only to be swallowed again and seen no more. But the fact that she was alive, or had been alive even after they had begun to mourn for her as forever lost to them, was a comfort to all of them.

Meantime reasons of state recalled Malíkshāh to his capital at Marv. News had come of the successful spread of his troops eastward, even to the Chinese wall. This conquest having been accomplished, he was now anxious to turn his attention to the west. Parts of Asia Minor were won during the reigns of Togrul Beg and Alp Arslân, as Prince Kreiton had known to his cost, but the complete reduction of the country was now to be finished by Malíkshāh. The arrangements for this great campaign were to be made at Marv, and the Sultân was anxious to begin the work as soon as possible. He regretted his summary treatment of Ibrāhîm Niyâl, and still more the necessity for it, for his nephew had administered the Province of Khurāsân with ability. He regretted Hasan ben Sabah's defection, for he recognized in him a man of marvellous capacity. He was ready to appoint Omar governor of the Province or of the city, and during a conversation with him, proposed that he should take Ibrāhîm Niyâl's place.

"I have every confidence in you," said the Sultân, "and I should feel greatly reassured to have the Province left in such able hands."

But Omar remarked, wisely and well:

"The sun of your Majesty's favor shines brightly on me. I kiss the ground at your feet, but beg to be excused from this honor; for though I would gladly serve you in any capacity, and give my life freely, still my ability does not lie in administration but in scientific work; and, moreover, as I am cordially detested by all the Mollâhs, — and I cordially reciprocate their feelings, — I should not succeed in the lofty position to which your Majesty would propose to call me."

The Sultân instantly recognized the propriety of Omar's objections, and said nothing further in regard to it. Nevertheless the rumor spread that Omar was to be appointed governor, and created great excitement, especially among the priestly and more bigoted classes, who felt that religion was insulted by such an appointment. Some of the Mollâhs, headed by Al-Ghazzâli, even went to Nizâmu'l-Mulk and protested against appointing an infidel and scoffer to rule over them; and a mob of the more unruly citizens collected in front of Omar's house, and uttered some threats against him. But the Wazîr assured the "Proof of Islam" that the appointment was not made, and Omar himself appeared with perfect unconcern, at his house door, and made the mob a clever address, as his manner was, and with such eloquence and wit that the crowd was restored to good humor, and dispersed without doing any harm.

This rumor got into history however, and in some of the biographies of Omar it may be read that Malíkshāh appointed him governor of Nishāpûr. But the Sultân assured Omar that he would not forget the scheme of revising the calendar, and that as soon as the arrangements could be made, he would send for him.

A week later the new Governor of Khurāsân was appointed. He was Malíkshāh's youngest brother, who had been serving with distinction in the great campaign that had served to spread the sway of the Seljûk Turks over wide and populous provinces hitherto boasting their independence. He was sharp, abrupt, incisive, with a stiff, military carriage; a man accustomed to be obeyed, and well adapted to control Nishāpûr, of whom it used to be said by its enemies: "Stranger, beware, lest thou go to Nishāpûr, for in that town neither merit nor lineage is a safeguard, and the respect due to human nature is ignored."

The Sultân especially commended Omar to his friendship, and the poet found him ever a firm and judicious patron and protector, especially in his later years, when he needed shelter from the storms of fanaticism that raged through Nishāpûr.

Prince Kreiton decided not to go with the Court to Marv, but to wait until he should know something definite about Agapê. He felt that if she were alive she would surely return to Nishāpûr, and he wished to be there to receive her. Moreover, he found more consolation in being with Omar, who was able to converse with him and to enter into his feelings, than at Court, in spite of all the Sultân's kindness. Malíkshāh readily consented to this, and granted the prince an ample allowance for his expenses.

When all these things were decided, the day was set for the departure of the Court. Early in the morning the great drums at the Arg were beaten, and, with the promptness characteristic of the Wazîr, the imposing procession started on its way. The streets were lined with picturesque throngs, gathered to see the departure of the Shāhinshâh, as the Persians called their ruler. It was a fiery, hot summer's day, and the people gathered in dense crowds around the chief masjid, where a preliminary service was to be held. When this was over, and all the ceremonies were fulfilled, the long succession of stately horses, proud of their distinction, and with their embroidered trappings, and splendidly decorated saddles, the ungainly camels, disdainfully bearing their heavy loads, the sumpter mules, with tinkling bells, the palankins, from whose windows curious eyes gazed stealthily forth, and all the multitude of retainers and servants passed through the Shamâli Dâr, or North Gate, and the visit of Malíkshāh to Nishāpûr was at an end.

CHAPTER XXIV.

THE PASSING OF A FLOWER.

NEARLY three years had passed away. Once more it was early summer in the beautiful valley of Nishāpûr. The roses were all in bloom, and the breeze was fragrant with the breath of a myriad flowers, — mignonette, violets, lilies, and forget-me-nots, poppies, acacias, and fruit-trees, the jujube and mango, the pipal-tree and peaches, plums and cherries.

On a faultless day two men were sitting together on a terrace, overlooking the garden of a pleasant house in the city.

One, a stately man grown old before his time, for he was not more than sixty, was speaking in a melancholy tone:

"Nay, I have at last given up hope. Years have passed, and not a sign of my daughter."

And he shook his lion-like head, with its mane of snowy hair, and sighed deeply.

The other, laying his hand affectionately on the old man's arm, said:

"Agapê heard not from you for four years, and still she did not despair. May it not be that she found some unexpected means of going to Athens in search of you?"

"Oh," said Prince Kreiton, "that is impossible. She would not have left you so inexplicably without a word."

And Omar's heart knew that the prince was right. But again, and for the hundredth time, he went over the old argument: Agapê had undoubtedly been abducted by Hasan ben Sabah; she had been with him at Mashad; when Hasan left Mashad she did not accompany him. That was all that was definitely known. She had probably tried to escape from Hasan, and had perhaps been —

But this probability Omar never liked to acknowledge. He could not bear to think of the fair and beautiful girl captured and enslaved by the rude barbarians of the mountains. This, of course, was the most natural hypothesis, and so emissaries had long before been sent up among the Bukharians and Turkmans, and other fierce tribes among the mountains, offering a large reward for the Greek girl's return. It had been all in vain. Nothing had been heard about her, and it was now going on the third year since her disappearance. The old prince had long before made up his mind that in making her escape from Hasan she had attempted to cross the mountains, and fallen over some precipice and perished. He tried, at least, to deceive his paternal pride into accepting such a fate for his daughter, rather than to imagine her subject to a living death.

Just at this moment a shrill scream in the street startled the two men. It was a woman's voice. Omar, followed by the prince, rushed to the door of the house, and saw two men, dressed in the Turkman costume, dragging away a young and slender youth. There was something so familiar about him that Omar's heart gave a bound; darting down the street, he overtook the men.

It was Agapê!

At the sight of Omar, she, with almost superhuman force, tore herself away from the two men, and threw herself into his arms. The Turkmans, with angry and threatening gestures, attempted to snatch her away again, but when they saw the prince appearing, with all the dignity of a Kadi, they desisted, and, with a torrent of words, seemed to appeal to him for justice. It would have been a comedy if it had not been so tragic. As usual, a crowd began to collect. Fortunately Omar saw, among the persons hurrying up, a young Persian who had once been among the Turkmans, and had a considerable knowledge of their language. Calling him as interpreter, he brought Agapê and the two Turkmans into the court of his house. Then, for the first time, Agapê caught sight of her father, and at the same instant he recognized the poor girl. It was too much for her; she swooned away, the words, "O phile pater!" dying on her lips.

Omar's mother now appeared, and took charge of Agapê. Through 'Abdul Faru-'dîn, Omar learned from the Turkmans that they had brought the youth to the slave market of Nishāpûr, with the intention of selling him; but that he had broken loose, and fled like a deer.

Omar asked why they had wanted to sell him. They replied that he was no good; not strong enough to work.

"What would they sell him for?"

They would undoubtedly have asked a high price if they had realized the relationship, and the extraordinary reunion, — how they would have leaped with joy had they known of the reward that they might have claimed! But they supposed that Omar, out of good nature, was buying the run-away slave, and they named a reasonable sum, which Omar did not even try to diminish. The transaction was speedily consummated, and the two Turkmans, depositing in their pouches the purchase-money, which was in silver, and bowing with a certain graceful condescension, took their departure.

When Omar went to his mother's room he found that Agapê had recovered her consciousness, and was lying on the divân with her head pillowed on her father's breast. He was inexpressibly shocked at the poor child's appearance; his eyes filled with tears; a sob choked him; he could not speak. There was no need of her telling her experiences. The story of her sufferings was written on her waxen cheek, her bloodless lips, in the wide, pathetic gaze of her ever beautiful dark brown eyes.

Ziba-khanùm quickly prepared for her some tempting food, and Omar, going to his storeroom, brought her a cup filled with choicest wine.

Her spirit was not all gone. In her weak, trembling voice she said, as she took it into her transparent hands, quoting the words of the old Greek epigram:

"'How was I born? Whence am I? Why did I come? To depart again. How can I who know nothing learn anything? Being naught, I was born. I shall be again, as I was before. The tribe of the voice-dividers is naught. But come, give me the joy-bestowing stream of wine! For this medicine is the antidote of ills!'"

Omar never forgot those melodious words, and afterwards, long afterwards he imitated them in more than one of his rubāiyât.

It was evident to Omar's mother that the girl could not live long. Familiarity with sickness and death had made her wise. But Omar saw only the pathos

"THE STORY OF HER SUFFERINGS WAS WRITTEN ON HER WAXEN CHEEK."

of the change in his beloved Agapê, and dreamed that now she was safe, and, reunited to those who loved her and would care for her, she would be restored to her ordinary health. Prince Kreiton also was blinded by his joy and surprise. It had been seven years since he had left Agapê at Bagdâd, and he had expected great changes in her. Her sufferings had not aged her, but had reduced her flesh and made her more like the child he remembered.

She was too weak to talk much. The extraordinary strength she had shown in escaping from the Turkmans had been like the exertions of one suffering from a fever and had brought the inevitable reaction. All she could do was to lie patiently with a look of unutterable peace and happiness on her pale, sweet face, a shadowy smile on her lips, and such love in her eyes! She never wearied of looking at her father, or at Omar, who would sit for hours by her side holding and caressing her delicate hand.

Not before a week had passed did she feel like telling them of her dreadful experiences, and then in such little chapters that it was long before they learned the whole. She told it, as it were, backwards, giving some of the last details first, but when she had finished, and they knew how false Hasan had been, and how he had held out to her such glittering but delusive inducements to be, like him, false to her friends and her love, they execrated him as a traitor and villain.

Agapê's account of her escape from him stirred them to admiration at her quickness of plan and action. We already know how she eluded her watchful guardian and rode off on his favorite horse. She had nothing with which to buy food; she had only one change of attire: the Persian dress which she had just exchanged for the pilgrim garb. She was an utter stranger in Mashad, and knew not whither to turn or what to do. But her one fear at the time was of being overtaken. So she rode on boldly as if she knew her way. The pilgrim garb frees from much idle curiosity, and though her horse was a beautiful creature, and covetous glances were cast at it, her right to it was not challenged. She knew by the sun the general direction of Nishāpûr, and she thought that if she once struck the caravan route she should recognize it.

She hoped that she might catch up with some caravan travelling over the mountains. She rode on and rode on, and the city of pilgrimage was far behind her. The great golden ball, weighing sixty mâns, that glittered over the tomb of the great saint, the Imâm Razwa, vanished from sight. The night approached; she was famished; she had nothing suitable with which to feed the noble animal that had borne her so faithfully. She tethered him to a bush, gathered some of the wild kerta grass that grew abundantly on the mountain-side, and she herself slept on the ground. The next morning she found a flowing spring of sweet water, and plenty of mulberries and other small fruits. She still pushed on, being now evidently in the regular caravan road.

Suddenly she was surrounded by armed men. She could not understand a word they said, but they made her prisoner and bore her off to a remote little hamlet far up on the mountain. It was evidently a robbers' den, held by a few outlaw Turkmans. Thinking that their prisoner was a young boy, they made her tend their sheep, and, though they treated her harshly and often struck her, she found her lot preferable to the refined insolence and poisoned flatteries of Hasan. She knew that it was absolutely essential for her happiness to keep the secret of her sex from her captors, and she succeeded for two years, during which time she was out, exposed to all kinds of weather, the bitter cold of winter and the intolerable heat of summer. For a time the exposure had seemed to strengthen and toughen her, but at last the labors that the Turkmans had added to her share little by little, the care of the horses and the daily wandering with the herds, often with insufficient food, had broken her health, and at last the Turkmans had sent two of their number down to Nishāpûr to sell her as a slave.

How she had rejoiced when she saw the familiar bāzâr once more! She knew that Omar's house was not far away, and she had staked all on a quick and sudden flight, hoping that she might find the door open and dart in, thus eluding her pursuers. They, like every one else, had taken a fancy to the gentle youth, and the escape had been easier than she had expected it would be. But when they overtook her at the very door and began to drag her back again to the slave mart, she felt that it was of no use to make any further struggle.

Now what peace she enjoyed, lying under the shade of the palm-trees on Omar's terrace, looking down into the lovely little garden, listening to the tinkle of the fountain, and having Omar and her father by her side! It is the nature of some persons to go through the fire of sorrow and trouble and to come forth unchanged, or, if changed, sweetened and purified. So it was with Agapê's remarkable spirit. Trial and disappointment, long years of waiting, and now lassitude and illness, could not dim the brightness of her mind, the gentleness of her disposition, the warmth of her love. She was like gold from the refiner's fire. But it was more and more evident as the days went on that she was slowly fading away. There was no suffering, except from weariness; she did not like to move; but she made no complaint and did her best to seem bright and cheerful. She always had a winning smile for the aged Ziba-khanùm, who worshipped her and could not do enough for her. Above all, she enjoyed having her father and Omar sit by her side and talk about Greek and Persian poetry. Omar had become skilled enough in Greek to give Prince Kreiton some notion of the great epic, the Shâh-nāmáh, or Book of Kings, and Agapê above all liked to hear him repeat the charming lines about Zerdusht and how he reared before the palace of King Gushtasp a magic tree with beautiful foliage and branches, whereof if any one ate he became learned in all the mysteries of the future, and the fruit thereof made men perfect in wisdom and holiness; and she liked to hear, also, of the prowess of Isfendiyâr in the battle between Gushtasp and Arjasp, the sovereign of Chin, who led an army of demons into Irân. Then the two men would discuss the comparative merits of Homer and Firdausî.

As the summer days passed, even to listen to pleasant talk became too great an effort for her. She was content to recline on the soft pillows and let her father or Omar merely fan her. But one day she was roused to greater animation. Omar had immediately sent to Marv the news of Agapê's return and a brief account of all the circumstances.

Both the Sultân and Wazîr happened to be away, but on Nizâmu'l-Mulk's return, when he found a second missive from Omar telling of her long and patiently borne illness, he immediately set out for Nishāpûr. Agapê was overjoyed to see her old friend and protector once again. The flickering candle of her life for a little while burned up quite steadily, and they all felt encouraged, except Omar's wise mother, who saw in her renewed animation only the hectic fever of excitement. She was right. That same evening the reaction came, and the light fell so low that it seemed as if it would go into darkness. But she lingered on for several days more, conscious to the last, affectionate and thoughtful. She asked that the little scroll containing the poems that Omar had written for her might be laid on her breast and buried with her.

And so she, like so many others, —

> "*The loveliest and best*
> *That Time and Fate of all their Vintage prest,*" —

faded finally away. The same Death that took Zenophile and Zoe, Heliodora and Melissa, from their lovers, took also Agapê from those who loved her.

> "*Alas, that Spring should vanish with the Rose!*
> *That Youth's sweet-scented Manuscript should close!*
> *The Nightingale that in the Branches sang,*
> *Ah, whence and whither flown again, who knows?*"[1]

[1] E. FitzGerald's paraphrase.

Thus sang Omar a little later. To him death had no terrors. He saw its sad, pathetic side, not as men do who mourn as if there were no hope of immortality; neither with the fatalism of the ancients, who regarded life as the dearest gift of the gods, and its loss as the greatest of all losses. "Rather would I live above the ground as another's slave, with a landless man that had no means of livelihood, than bear sway among all the dead that are gone," said Homer, through the mouth of Achilles. But Omar's attitude toward death and life was indifference. The material heaven promised by Muhammád, the river Kausar running with its store of celestial wine and milk, the Tubâ-tree of happiness, the promiscuous crowd of Hūâr, waiting on the couches of the Faithful, — all this was to him like the "thunder of a distant drum." Nor was the material heaven pictured to the Christian any more attractive, with its golden streets and many mansions, its golden candlesticks and magical trees. He could say with calm indifference: "To one who understands the mysteries of the world, the joy and sorrow of the world are of equal account; since the good and the bad of the world will come to an end, what matter, since it must end?"

The death, then, of the Greek girl whom he loved was a part of the order of the universe. The pen had written at the creation of the world that it must be so; it was one more arrow shot by the bow of Fate. But deeply as he felt it, — for Agapê had been dear to his heart, — he was not one to be crushed by it. If it were better not to have been born, and better still, for one who had been unfortunate enough to be born, to go away, even though the absolute silence of the grave was never broken by any one of the myriads who had passed behind the veil; so then he could only envy Agapê, who now perhaps knew in a single instant of eternity more than he with all his learning, which was naught, could know in a lifetime of terrestrial existence.

He sang:

"*I am not the man to dread my non-existence,*
For that half seems pleasanter to me than this half;
This is a life which God has lent me,
I will surrender it when the time of surrender comes."[1]

Perhaps Omar, as a scientific man, was more curious and envious of Agapê's marvellous transformation than he was afflicted by it. There she lay, perfectly pure and beautiful, and yet cold and statue-like. On her lips the same patient smile; but the eyes had no recognition for father or lover. No sound would ever again come from her sweet mouth. Yet only a few brief moments before the animating soul was there! Where had it gone?

[1] E. Heron Allen's translation.

"*Earth could not answer; nor the Seas that Mourn*
In flowing Purple, of their Lord forlorn;
Nor rolling Heaven, with all his Signs revealed
And hidden by the sleeve of Night and Morn."

And as he looked at Agapê, this thought came to him:

"*Why, if the Soul can fling the Dust aside,*
And naked on the Air of Heaven ride,
Were't not a shame — were't not a shame for him
In this clay carcase crippled to abide?

"'*Tis but a Tent where takes his one day's rest*
A Sultân to the realm of Death addrest;
The Sultân rises, and the dark Farrâsh
Strikes and prepares it for another guest." [1]

Feeling as he did about his own death, he could not without hypocrisy fail to recognize that all was for the best. His philosophy, in other words, supported him.

Nevertheless, at the funeral, when the dear form was deposited in the guristân, or graveyard, his philosophy served him as an unsteady staff. The immense pathos of the young life that had vanished forever suddenly came over him, and he had to turn away and choke down the sobs that arose from his heart. A great warm heart beat in his bosom, and from that heart had been taken away what could never again be replaced.

[1] E. FitzGerald's paraphrase.

Prince Kreiton would have taken her, if he could, to Athens, where he knew she would have loved to lie, but it was impossible, and equally impossible to mark her last resting-place with a suitably carved marble tomb from the Grecian quarries. But the mountains near Nishāpûr furnished marble, and Nizâmu'l-Mulk procured a skilful carver, and a beautiful little mausoleum was erected to the memory of Agapê.

The prince, her father, remained a few weeks longer; then he bade Omar an affectionate farewell. They had become warm friends, and Omar found it hard to think that, in all probability, they would never meet again. An opportunity came for him to join a caravan going to the Caspian Sea. From there he could with comparatively little difficulty make his way to Byzantium.

So from Omar's life vanished the romance that still gleams in his poems with a pale, rosy reflection like a fading sunset.

CHAPTER XXV.

A NEW ERA.

GREAT victories had accompanied the Sultân Malíkshāh's arms in the west as well as in the east. The standard of the Seljûk Turks was carried far beyond the Jaxartes; and the savage tribes of Turkestân yielded their allegiance. Even the Tartars on the borders of China placed his effigy on their coins, and acknowledged him as their ruler when on their holy days they gathered in their temples. Multitudes of rich and prosperous cities paid him tribute: "From the Chinese frontier," says Gibbon, "he stretched his immediate jurisdiction or feudatory sway to the west and south, as far the mountains of Georgia, the neighborhood of Constantinople, the holy city of Jerusalem, and the spicy groves of Arabia Felix." Such a wide and beneficent reign had not been known in Asia since the time of Alexander the Great. All the internal dissensions, which always characterize reigns where the right of primogeniture is not firmly established, had been quieted, and peace reigned from the Chinese wall to the shores of the Mediterranean. The Sultân was now ready, under the stimulating influence of Nizâm-u'l-Mulk, to confer the blessings of culture and refinement wherever his victorious arms prevailed.

The Wazîr recalled to Malíkshāh his promise to bring about the reform of the calendar under Omar's superintendence. The time seemed favorable for such a momentous change, and a messenger was despatched to Nishāpûr, to bear to Omar the farmân that established his new commission, and bring him to Marv.

It came most opportunely. Omar's aged mother had just died, and he was sitting gloomy and alone in his deserted house, trying to cheer himself in composing a quatrain which should express this unusual mood. But it did not go, and he tried another with a more optimistic turn :

"*Like river-waters and like wind of the waste*
Passes another day with eager haste ;
I will not mourn for two days at least :
The day not come and the day that is past."

It was not like him to be gloomy long. He had too many occupations, and when one is busy the sorrows of life do not press so darkly. But associated with the death of Ziba-khanùm came back the remembrance of Agapê. The summer was over; the roses had done blooming; the chill winds were beginning to blow down from the mountains.

The darkness of the shrouded sky seemed to let through no light. At such times, if ever, a man is justified in melancholy retrospections. The phantoms of the Past rise before him: the faces of those whom he has loved and who have vanished behind the veil seem to hover in the shadows, almost palpable and yet evanescent like forms in fleeting clouds. Lost opportunities renew their glamour mockingly. It requires all one's philosophy to throw off depression when one sits alone in one's ancestral home, out of which has just passed the dear mother full of years and honor. It must be; 'tis the lot of all, and, being the lot of all, is for the best. And yet the heart hungers for what it has lost. Morbidness easily takes possession of one at such times.

Omar needed at this moment the stimulus of change. He had not as yet adjusted himself to the new conditions, and his mind was restless and introspective. He was sitting thus before a lighted brasier one day toward the end of the joy-killing month of Ramazân. A knock at the door aroused him. It was the messenger from Nizâmu'l-Mulk. He brought Omar the letters, and in addition a beautiful warm cloak lined with the fur of the jerboa, so that in crossing the mountains he might not suffer from the cold.

The invitation, which of course from the Sultân amounted to a command, was the electric shock that

Omar needed. He was instantly awake and alert. It needed no long preparation. He had few things to put away, few things to take with him. The complicated paraphernalia of a modern traveller were then unknown. Dismissing the one Chinese servant with an extra coin, and leaving his house in the general care of a neighbor, he fastened the door, and within an hour after the arrival of his summoner he was mounted on a strong horse and well on his way to Marv.

Marv, situated in the great oasis beyond the mountains northeast of Nishāpûr, was the jewel of the desert, and, like Tadmor, a crown of beauty for the Sultân's brow. It was intersected by four wide and splendid canals, supplied with water from the Murg-âb, or Bird River. Lined with palaces, these waterways gave the city a peculiarly rich and magnificent aspect. There were three great mosques, whose tapering minarets and bulbous domes, embowered in trees, made a noble and picturesque vista for the eager traveller, approaching through the level sea of the wide-stretching desert. Here, as in Nishāpûr, under the stimulus of the Wazîr, who, says the Arabian writer, Ibn Khallikân, was "the ornament of his age," schools and colleges flourished; no less than ten libraries collected the works of the poets and historians; and the new Nizāmyîeh, or university, founded by Nizâmu'l-Mulk, was beginning to give the very best object-lesson of what it was then believed true education should be.

Omar was conducted directly to the palace. He found it more magnificent than anything that he had ever before seen. Here were collected the spoils of a hundred cities, — great gates, encrusted with pearls and precious stones, swung on noiseless hinges; thrones and chairs of ebony and ivory, carved by the cunning hands of Eastern artists, were scattered about in profusion; magnificent rugs of the softest colors were spread on floors of curiously designed mosaics; hundreds of costly pieces of armor, taken from conquered pashas and princes, were disposed about the walls, where also the horns of innumerable deer, mounted on brazen plates, betrayed the Sultân's love for the noble art of venery. Here, also, were trophies of the victory won by the Turks over the Greek Emperor Romanus. A thousand servants — pages, grooms, and men in waiting — executed the vast hospitality of the Sultân, and anticipated the slightest desire of even the humblest guest.

As soon as Omar was suitably lodged, Nizâmu'l-Mulk took counsel with him regarding his assistants in the great work of revising the calendar.

"In reality," said the Wazîr, "it seems to me that you are perfectly capable of doing this work by yourself, without any assistance. But there will be less danger of jealous criticism and open opposition, if it is known that the new calendar is recommended by a Commission consisting of seven or eight of the wisest men in the Sultanate."

"That is true wisdom," said Omar. "The mere mathematical calculation of the days and hours might be done by a schoolboy, but Islâm might see some danger in accepting a new method of reckoning time, devised by a man whom the Faithful love to call Núkuam-ne-bud, — not of good name.

"'*Not always over my nature can I prevail, — but what can I do?*
From my actions I suffer, and often I fail, — but what can I do?'"

he added, quoting the first couplet of one of his quatrains.

Nizâmu'l-Mulk laughed.

"'Tis fortunate that you have a friend in power that understands you," said he; "'tis fortunate, also, that Malíkshâh is a man of liberal views. Had the Sultân's brother Kadir Beg prevailed, when he beat the kettle-drums of revolt, and swept like dust over the land, you would have found a different master. We owe Allâh thanks! But whom would you suggest as your assistants on the Commission?"

"Might it not be well to raise the number to two and seventy, — one from each of the warring sects?"

"I fear they would tear one another to pieces."

"Yes," said Omar, "one of the Seniviye and one

of the Maniviye engaging in a quarrel over dualism would perhaps involve all of us in a pitched battle."

"Eight, or perhaps at most twelve, — one from each of the universities, — will suffice to give dignity to whatever recommendations may be agreed on. But would it not be well to have the general scheme already laid down before the members of the Commission assemble?"

"I have it all elaborated," said Omar. "Prince Kreiton, before he departed for Rûm, took the keenest interest in the scheme, and he aided me in several important particulars."

"Think you he might have been prevailed on to join the Commission?" asked the Wazîr.

"Possibly. But, since the question is complicated by the damnable prejudices of our race, who would have distrusted him, I doubt if it would have been wise. Personally, I should prefer him to any one whom Allâh might send."

"True!" said Nizâmu'l-Mulk. Then, after pondering a moment, he asked, "Have you any preferences?"

"Mâ shâ' Allâh!" exclaimed Omar, with a comic shrug of his shoulders. "If I select the like of myself, there will be woes! And if I select my opponents, I shall be in a hopeless minority. But I should like Nizâmi Urūzî of Samarkand. He promises to do great things in poetry, and his abilities will shine in this work."

"I will leave it to you to select your assistants," said Nizâmu'l-Mulk.

"The responsibility is great. There are few men equal to Nizâmi, — Kassāra'llâhu am sâla-hum! may God increase their like!"

"Take your own time, and when you have decided, let me have the list and I will procure the Sultân's assent."

Omar immediately set about the important matter of selecting the members of the Commission. It would have been easy for him to gather about him a little coterie of agreeable and talented men who should blindly follow his lead, and accept whatever he might dictate. It would have been easy for him to manage so as to arrogate all the credit of the great innovation. But he was guided by a higher motive than self-seeking. Scientific men have in all time been willing to sacrifice their own comfort and to prefer the triumph of the Truth, as they saw it, to any personal advantage. The old false story of Archimedes, at the siege of Syracuse, bidding the Roman soldier not to disturb the circles which he had drawn in the sand, is typical of the scientist's mental attitude. The bloody sword in the hands of Ignorance or Fanaticism absolutely fails to disturb the wise man's serenity or faith in his theories.

So Omar, utterly ignoring possible unfriendlinesses, chose his men with an eye single to their abilities. He took his time, as the Wazîr advised, and as there were all sorts of distractions, and the easy-going ways of the Orient were conducive to procrastination, several months elapsed before all the arrangements for the assembling of the Commission were completed.

At last, however, Omar was enabled to report to Nizâmu'l-Mulk that everything was ready.

According to the old manner of reckoning, "the irregular course of the lunar months" was taken as the basis of time, but the intercalary days had been neglected, and the result was that the date of spring was coming absurdly near to the domain of winter.

According to Omar's scheme, which, when it was brought before the Commission, instantly appealed to their common sense, the year was divided into proper months, with an apt apportionment of days, so that the errors of the past and the future were reduced to a minimum.

The absurd custom of the Urgurish-Turkish cycle of twelve years, named in succession after the Mouse, the Ox, the Leopard, the Hare, the Crocodile, the Serpent, the Horse, the Sheep, the Monkey, the Hen, the Dog, and the Pig, was done away with. In place, then, of the awkward and inaccurate system which had lasted so many generations, there was substituted a method of reckoning time which was simple and free from complications. This new calendar, called Tarikh-i Jelâli, after the dynasty to which Malíkshāh belonged, was officially promulgated, and became the law of the Sultanate. It always excited the admiration of the historians, and Gibbon, writing about it long years afterwards, declared that its accuracy surpassed the Julian, and approached that of the Gregorian style.

The manifold details of this work occupied the long, hard winter, and when spring again showed the white hand of Mūsâ on the bough, the Sultân resolved to celebrate the completion of it by a grand pilgrimage to Makka. Such a brilliant and splendid expedition of piety had never before been known. It consisted of the whole Court and hundreds of tributary rulers, and all of their vassels. Not less than a thousand princes sat daily at his table, and the cost of maintenance was defrayed by the generous Sultân. Over twenty-five thousand splendid horses and an innumerable multitude of camels stretched out the interminable line of the caravan as it proceeded across the desert. Ample provision for the comfort and convenience of the pious multitude was made in advance, and for years to come pilgrims blessed the memory of Nizâmu'l-Mulk, whose thoughtfulness provided so many places of refreshment for man and beast. At Makka, where the most imposing ceremonies were performed, and at Bagdâd, where the Sultân stopped on his return, munificent donations of alms were distributed.

The title of Hajji is given to those who have accomplished the visit to the Ka'aba; never before did the title become so common. Even Omar Khayyâm, little though he cared to claim the credit for a pious act performed in such a wholesale manner, was not sorry to visit the sacred city under auspices so favorable. Except in dress, which of course conformed to the conventional pattern, there was nothing about this pilgrimage that spoke of renunciation. The open table kept by the Sultân, who welcomed to it the humblest of the pilgrims, the easy stages by which they travelled, the chances for delightful talk, the gaiety of entertainment, — everything combined to make the journey a vast junket. It certainly availed to divert Omar, who found in the changing scenes and in the varied throng an endless source of study and amusement.

At Bagdâd the students of the universities, and especially those who were engaged in the study of Greek philosophy, which at his suggestion Nizâmu'l-Mulk had added to the curriculum, flocked to see the celebrated Hakîm, or doctor, the fame of whose exploits had spread throughout the realm. Omar did not care to be lionized, and he modestly kept himself as far as he could in the background. He did not refuse to meet the literati of Bagdâd, nor did he shut the door in the face of his admirers, as some of his enemies asserted. Nor was it true, either, that he took advantage of his easily acquired reputation of a Hajji to impose on his acquaintances a belief that he had become more orthodox. He returned as he went, the same keen-minded, wise, liberal, noble-hearted poet and philosopher that all who knew him loved.

CHAPTER XXVI.

THE MAKING OF A PROPHET.

HASAN BEN SABAH was not molested during his journey. Nevertheless he deemed it expedient not to go immediately to Isfahân, lest he might be tracked thither. Accordingly, he and his son managed to elude observation, and quietly dropped behind. Then the two struck off to the town of Kerej, situated about sixty farsâkh from Isfahân in the hill country of Irâk. This was the seat of the Arab family of Al Ijli, whose possessions in camels and date-palm plantations and other estates were beyond estimation. Hasan ben Sabah knew the head of this family, and he had no hesitation in going boldly to him and demanding hospitality. This was freely accorded, and Hasan and Ostad found themselves comfortably established in the patriarchal mansion of the old sheikh. Here they abode for several months. There happened to be also staying at Al Ijli's house an Arab called the Refik Emir Dharab, who had been sent up into Asia from Cairo charged to spread the esoteric doctrines of the Ismailites. He was a graduate of the so-called Darul-Hikmat, or House of Wisdom, at Kahira, a university founded at the very beginning of the eleventh century, and sustained by the Kaliph, at an expense of what would be in our money over a million of dollars. It was furnished with books and mathematical instruments, and the students, who were not required to pay any fee, but were admitted free, heard the learned professor discuss abstruse questions, and were registered in nine grades. They wore kaftans, or robes, which in form and color were like those now worn in the English universities, were in fact the legitimate ancestors of the modern graduation robes. The doctrines of the Ismailites were here promulgated under the guidance of the Dai-'l Dût, or Grand Master. The missionaries of this sect spread into many parts of Asia, and caused much trouble to the Abbas family, who claimed sole right to the succession of Muhammád as Imâm al Muslimîn, or Head of the Faithful. Those who found dynasties need to take heed that the stream of power does not and cannot flow in more than one channel. It has been said that all schisms arise from ambition, and all heresies are the fruit of overweening aspiration. The great question whether seven or twelve is the most sacred number has led to rivers of blood flowing, and the successive apparitions of ambitious men claiming to be the twelfth and last descendant of Muhammád, Ben Hasan Askeri, who, having slept for a certain or uncertain number of ages in an African cave, should awake and come forth as El Mahdî, the Leader, and announce the end of the world, prove how deep-rooted the superstition has been and still is.

If the Mahdî was claimed by many as the Twelfth and last Prophet, Ismaïl, son of Jafir Sadik, or the Upright, was the Seventh and last Imâm, and the adherents of his family for several hundred years were a thorn in the flesh to the Abbas family, who, in 1011, in the reign of the Kaliph Kadirbellan, brought it about that a great assembly of legal lights met secretly, at Bagdâd, and investigated the claims of the Fatemites, or descendants of Muhammád's daughter, and pronounced them unfounded. On the side of the Seven was the fact that there were seven heavens, seven seas, seven planets, seven colors, seven tones, seven days of the week; hence, beginning with Ali, there were seven Imâms, ending with Ismaïl.

The Twelve had no such array, — only the twelve signs of the zodiac, the twelve months, the twelve tribes of Israel, and, by some jugglery, twelve joints in the hand. So when the claims of the Seven were set aside, dissatisfaction still prevailed.

Now Hasan ben Sabah had been brought up to believe in the lore of the Twelve Imâms; and, naturally, when the clever Refik tried to bring him round to the other view, many wordy battles ensued. But while it pleased his combative nature to take the off side, it pleased Allâh to render the soil of his mind receptive, and the seed took root. In other words, he found in the doctrine of the Ismaïlites the intoxicating fruit of which he was in search, in his as yet somewhat undetermined plans for achieving power.

While pretending to defend his hereditary views, he was learning from Amîr Dharab many interesting and curious secrets. It was evident to him that, if he could combine something of the mysterious ceremonial that obtained in the Lodge into which he had once been initiated with a modification of Ismaïlite sophistries, he might pose as a new prophet of a new sect, and win a tremendous following.

This practical development of his dreams and aspirations was worked out by him with the utmost care and deliberation. He took no one into his counsels. After the Refik went on his way, never suspecting what a revolution his words had worked, Hasan still stayed on in Mikhaïl Al Ijli's house. He would run no risk of having his plans interrupted by a premature arrival at Isfahân, where he knew it was more than possible that Malíkshāh's emissaries were on the lookout for him. And when at last he determined to set forth, he left his son Ostad in the friendly care of the old sheikh's son, whom he had won to a most unquestioning admiration, so that he was certain that if he should say "Come with me" he would have left all and followed him.

Hasan managed to reach the beautiful city of Isfahân just before sunset, and, disguised as usual, rode through the well-guarded gate without detection.

With the greatest caution he made his way to the mansion of his old friend, Abulfasl, who was amazed and delighted to see him once more.

"How did you manage to avoid arrest?" asked Abulfasl. "And yet I need not ask. I myself should not at first have known you in your disguise. There were great rewards offered for your apprehension, and a price was set on your head. But you are perfectly safe with me. I will conceal you as long as you like."

Abulfasl was as good as his word. He had received Hasan's ill-gotten wealth and placed it in safety, and now, at Hasan's desire, he disposed of it at the bāzârs, and converted it into ready money. Abulfasl, however, on hearing Hasan boast of what great things he was going to do, came to the conclusion that his friend's mind was affected.

"Give me two good friends like yourself," said Hasan, "and I will soon get the better of that boor of a Turk who happens by good fortune, and by no wits of his own, to be on the throne."

Abulfasl looked at him in amazement, and, alarmed by the wild, strange look in his eyes, prepared for him some aromatic drinks which he thought might soothe his perturbed spirits.

Hasan was not content to remain long inactive. His teeming brain constantly impelled him to go forth and begin the great work which he now felt certain was to occupy the rest of his life. And yet even now he compelled himself to restraint. He would not precipitate matters by inconsiderate haste. He confirmed himself in his theories by discussing them with the wise Abulfasl. One day he fell ill, and a physician was called to see him. His name was Abu Nadshm Saradsh, and Hasan quickly discovered that he was also an Ismaïlite, and even more deeply grounded in the doctrines. Abu Nadshm became greatly interested in Hasan, and, finding that he was ready to acknowledge fellowship with him, took him, as soon as he had fully recovered, to a Daï, or missionary, named Mumin. Mumin at first hesitated to accept his allegiance, because he distrusted him, knowing that he had served as treasurer to Malíkshāh, and enjoyed greater dignities than he. But just at this time Abdul Melek ben Attash, the head of the Fatemite mission of Irâk, happened to come to Isfahân. Hasan's pretended zeal greatly pleased him, and he immediately made him also a Daï, but told him he must go to Egypt, and serve for a time in the Court of the Imâm Mostansar, Kaliph of the Fatemites.

Mostansar having been informed of the coming of his distinguished convert, and possibly expecting all the more from him because he had fallen into disgrace with Malíkshāh, sent a deputation headed by the Grand Master of the Dai'l Dowwat, the Sharif Tahre Kaswimi, and other distinguished persons to meet him at the border. He was escorted to Cairo with great pomp, and was lodged in one of the most commodious residences in the city. The Kaliph, a bigot and fanatic, found in him a kindred spirit, and loaded him with honors. It was generally supposed that, in recognition of his genius and zeal, he would be appointed First Minister.

There is a saying to the effect that history repeats itself, and Hasan found that this saying was true in his case. He was just on the point, as had happened before when he was in Egypt, of attaining this important office, when again an untoward event seemed to block his ambition. The Kaliph Mostansar had two sons by different wives. The question arose which of them should be regarded as his successor. His own favorite was his eldest son Nezar, and he finally formally proclaimed him the heir apparent. But Bedr Jemâli, the chief Amîr of the army, a man of great intelligence, had a decided preference for a younger son, Most 'Ali, a youth of stronger and less pliable nature than Nezar's.

Bedr Jemâli, who had enlisted a powerful party in support of his candidate, went to Hasan, and urged him to join him. But Hasan, who thought he saw in Nezar a possible tool for his own purposes, had already cast in his lot with the Kaliph's party.

The Amîr was deeply offended, and, taking advantage of his almost unlimited powers, managed to implicate him in a technical offence, and had him arrested and confined in the Castle of Daimiat.

The Kaliph was extremely indignant, and was preparing to rescue his unfortunate convert, when Heaven, or rather the earth itself, interfered to liberate him. A slight earthquake shock took place, and the tower in which he was confined fell in ruins.

Calmly as if he had expected it, he walked out without having suffered a scratch. He had been in prison before and had escaped, but never in such a miraculous manner. But his tribulations were not ended. The rumor of his escape reached the ears of Bedr Jemâli, who a second time seized him, and would have put him to death had it not been that a ship was about sailing for some port on the African coast. Hasan was conveyed aboard of this ship, and the captain was ordered not to let him disembark until the very farthest end of his voyage was reached.

The ship had hardly reached the Mediterranean before a mighty tempest arose, and all on board were momentarily expecting to go to the bottom. Now the greatness of Hasan's character asserted itself. With his long hair and beard wildly waving he stood on the deck, and in his clear and inspiring voice, which could be heard above the whistling of the wind and the roar of the waves, he declared to the frightened sailors with all the assurance of a prophet that no harm should befall them.

"Listen to me," he cried, "I have had a revelation from heaven. We shall weather the storm. Our Lord hath promised it."

The sailors and the captain himself, involuntarily calmed and reassured by such a commanding figure and such an expression of authority, recovered their courage, and, working with renewed zeal, managed the ship with great skill, and escaped destruction. The tempest itself seemed to submit to Hasan; the superstitious sailors declared that he had commanded the winds to subside, and that they obeyed him. And when he, with glowing eyes, announced to them his mission, and with perfect assurance told them that instead of going toward the setting sun he was bound to return to Asia, and as if in corroboration of his prophecy the wind suddenly shifted, and blew strong and free from the west, every man on board came to him and swore that they would follow him to death.

How then, as the vessel, instead of bearing him, a weak and powerless exile, into unknown African lands, flew, as if conscious of her mission, toward the Syrian coast, his ambitious heart swelled within him! He knew now that by his apparent victory over the elements, by his real victory over the men that manned the ship, he was on the right road. The little band that would land with him, converting their possessions into weapons, would be the nucleus of an army that might, that surely would, within a few short months, bear him to the glittering eminence of power that he had seen himself in his visions occupy.

"Let Malíkshāh tremble on his throne," he said.

CHAPTER XXVII.

A CLOUD ON THE HORIZON.

After a day of dazzling sunshine, where not a cloud flecks the tender blue, the sun sinks into a downy bed lying low on the horizon. The weather-wise prophesies: "To-morrow we shall have a storm."

So on the cloudless sweep of Sultân Malíkshāh's reign, after a long period of uninterrupted calm, arose the threatening cloud that portended change.

One day a messenger arrived at Marv, and demanded an immediate interview with the Sultân and his Wazîr.

He was admitted, and, bowing low, said:

"O Master of Irân and Defender of the fortunate in Religion, may the evil eye of disaster be forever averted from your august Majesty. I am sent to you by his Excellence, the orthodox and pious 'Ali Mehdi, Governor of Rûdbar, whose face has turned saffron from his anxiety in behalf of the province over which he extends his wise and beneficent hand."

"What is the message?" asked Malíkshāh, impatient at the circuitous discourse which, like a river through a plain, makes a slow and ambiguous descent to the sea of satisfaction.

"His Excellence, the pillar of orthodoxy, 'Ali Mehdi, sends from the bow of his Faithfulness your unworthy servant as a broken arrow, around the neck whereof is wound the parchment of his message."

"The message!" reiterated the Sultân.

"A wolf has broken into the pasture and is ravaging the sheep," said the messenger. "And the wolf has brought other wolves with him, and the pack of wolves is too large for the shepherd to drive out."

"You speak in parables," said Malíkshāh. "Who is the wolf, and where are the shepherd dogs?"

"The wolf, O glory-cheek of the Faithful, is that dog of a heretic, Hasan ben Sabah, who, with a pack of devouring devils, with the name of Ismaïl written on their foreheads and denying the validity of the Kaliph of Bagdâd and the authority of the Master of Irân, — whom may Allâh keep perpetually on the throne of his father, — is spreading over the regions north of Kaswîn and threatening Dirhem and Irâk. To that faithful shepherd, 'Ali Mehdi, he sent an impertinent message and demand for the surrender of the fifty castles. And when the light of the Faith — that brave and noble warrior and shepherd, 'Ali Mehdi — flung back his message into his jaws, Hasan, by treachery and overpowering numbers, seized the largest and strongest of all the castles of Rûdbar, that invincible burg Alamût, the Hawk's Nest, built to last forever by Hasan ben Seyd Bakerî, and already two centuries have dressed its mighty walls in gray and — "

"Hyāsan Allâh!" interrupted the Sultân, turning pale with anger. "We will soon drive out this wolf and all his brood. We have already a score to settle with him."

Nevertheless, as Malíkshāh had nothing but scorn for Hasan ben Sabah, he resolved, before wasting force on him, to send a special messenger to him, demanding the surrender of the castle and evacuation of the province.

"Diplomacy costs less than bloodshed," he said, "and who is Hasan that he should defy me when I demand?"

Nizâmu'l-Mulk was inclined to take the threatened storm more seriously than the Sultân did, and would have resorted to drastic measures at the very first, but he did not press the matter. He suggested, however, that an army under command of the Amîr Arslāntâsh should be in readiness to make an immediate attack on the Castle of Alamût, in case Hasan ben Sabah should still remain recalcitrant. The Sultân, with excellent judgment, determined on Omar Khayyâm as his ambassador.

"Hasan ben Sabah," he said, "will behave respectfully to Omar, and will listen to him with greater consideration than to a stranger."

Accordingly, Omar was summoned a second time from Nishāpûr, whither he had retired after the completion of his labors on the new calendar. He was not averse to undertaking this important mission, but when, in a friendly and confidential conversation with the Wazîr, he talked the matter over, he had no hesitation in expressing his opinion that any such velvet treatment of Hasan would prove perfectly idle and abortive.

"We know the man," he said; "he is not sugar to melt in water; but I will do my best to persuade him."

No time was wasted. In two days Omar, provided with a suitable escort of Kazakî fully armed and equipped, set forth for the Province of Rûdbar, or the Land of Rivers. The Amîr followed more leisurely with a regular army of about ten thousand men, which it was supposed would be sufficient to drive out the intruder. Arslāntâsh was ordered to keep concealed so that Hasan might not suspect his presence or, at least, might have no idea of his strength.

'Ali Mehdi's messenger had not exaggerated the

impregnability of the castle seized by Hasan. Built of great blocks of gray granite carefully hewn and fitted, as if it were the work of the Jinnát, or demons, it frowned down from the summit of a towering crag, which was accessible only by a narrow, winding way, easily defensible by a handful of determined men. Elsewhere there was no approach. No scaling-ladders could ever reach from the foot of the gorge half way to the first small grated windows. Even should an invading host successively cut down the defenders at each turn of the stairs and penetrate through the tunnelled passages, it would have at the very top found a drawbridge spanning an almost fathomless gulf between the two spurs of the mountain, — a bridge as dizzy and aerial as that of Al A'râf, which is fabled to divide heaven from hell.

When Omar with his mounted escort stood at the foot of the castle, and his herald blew a challenging blast, a sentinel dressed in white, except his hat, his girdle, and his boots, which were red as if dyed in blood, threw open a small wicket gate and shouted down:

"Kîm galán — who is there?"

"An envoy to Hasan ben Sabah. Is he within?"

"He is within. From whom comes the envoy and concerning what?"

At Omar's bidding the herald told the sentinel that he, Omar Khayyâm, had come to bring a personal message to Hasan ben Sabah. Would he be received?

There was evidently some method of internal communication. Had the sentinel been obliged himself to go up to the castle, it would have taken a good half hour. But within a few moments the sentinel again thrust his head out of the wicket and bade Omar and his escort enter at a gate a little farther to the left. It was so cleverly constructed that it seemed to be a part of the very foundation, and yet from the inside it was seen to be as solid as heavy oak and wrought iron combined could be.

Once within, Omar was amazed at the sight. The wall of the castle enclosed a vast space, a hidden valley, where a large population were busily engaged in providing for the sustenance of Hasan's followers. On the sunny slopes of the mountain-side there were vineyards and gardens, and an abundance of the purest water came flowing through a multitude of conduits, so that there was never any possibility of a garrison, even though it were driven to the last resort in the isolated tower, perishing from thirst.

Omar's men were commanded to remain below, while he himself and one other, under a guard of Hasan's Fedāvîye, or Dedicated Youths, all, like the sentinel, dressed in white with the significant relief of red, were conducted through great iron-barred doors and gloomy arched passageways through turns and over many stairs, until at last they were introduced into an enormous room, the massive ceiling of which, consisting of great carven blocks of marble, rested on seven solid monolithic columns, the capitals of which were carved each in a different pattern, though not elaborately. In this anteroom there were scattered about a multitude of men singly or in groups. It was evident at a glance that they belonged to different orders of some great society, and Omar's chief guide, proud of the impression which this strange scene produced, explained that a certain stately, patriarchal-looking officer with a flowing robe of white was a Daï-al Kirbâl, or Grand Prior, and the group of younger men who bowed ceremoniously as he passed them were Refikât, or Associates.

Omar was kept waiting a few moments; then a gorgeously embroidered curtain or portière at one side of the assembly hall was drawn aside and disclosed a still more imposing apartment. At one end of it was a raised daïs, on which stood a magnificent throne. In it was seated in truly regal splendor of apparel the Sidna, or Supreme Regent, of the new order, — Hasan ben Sabah. Beside him stood the Grand Priors, and ranged around him in a semicircle, the symbolic colors of their raiment blending in a sort of barbaric magnificence that was calculated to impress the eye of even the coolest beholder. The prominence of white as typical of innocence and of red as typical of blood was due to the immense numbers of Fedāvîye, who, having been initiated, were ready for any kind of service, and now flocked about their leader eager to hear the Sultân's message.

If Omar had deemed it possible that he might have private speech with his old schoolmate, he now saw that it was most unlikely. A vast gulf of ceremony separated them, and whatever stream of bitter reminiscence regarding Hasan's treatment of poor Agapê may have poured through the hidden caves of Omar's mind, he would not have deemed it prudent or politic to bring it to the light before such an assemblage of Hasan's devoted followers.

Profound silence reigned as Omar stood with simple dignity before the waiting assemblage. He remembered Hasan's boast, and confessed to himself that the regal state with which he was surrounded, and of which Hasan was the central figure, seemed like a swift fulfilment of his prophecy.

Then suddenly broke on his ear the deep bell-tones of Hasan's wonderful voice.

There is no instrument which has a greater majesty of power than a human voice when properly used in speech or song. The stringed instruments may give out a melody to enchant the heart, and yet your ultimate praise is modified by the "almost human" which you add. The organ fills the mind with solemn and religious thoughts, and in its place in a cathedral, where the light falls through pictured windows and the very atmosphere seems sacred, its vast and noble harmonies seem almost heavenly. But a man of genius, gifted with a sympathetic and flexible voice, can sway a throng of his fellows by its means, as the wind sways the ocean, stirring them to every possibility of passion, from the lowest depths of fanatic anger to the loftiest heights of generous enthusiasm. Such a voice had Hasan. It rang through the throne-room of his castle, — clear, vibrating, deep, and sonorous, clear and distinct to every person present. Hasan ben Sabah indulged now in none of the filigree decorations dear to Oriental orators. His address was absolutely simple and direct:

"What is your message, Omar?"

"Hasan ben Sabah, my master and yours, the Dîn-parwár, the Defender of the Faith, Malíkshāh, Sultân of the Turkish and Persian Empire and ruler of this province, demands your instant evacuation of this Castle of Alamût, the dispersal of your lawless followers, and your absolute submission to his authority."

Hasan's lip curled with scorn. Yet he spoke calmly and assuredly:

"Your master, but not mine. I refuse to acknowledge allegiance to that Turkish usurper. As for me, I call these my faithful ministers and followers to witness that I act not on my own behoof, but under the direct influence of the Spirit of Allâh, whose name I am allowed to bear."

A mighty roar of assent burst from the mouths of all present.

Omar waited till silence was restored. Then, stepping one step nearer to the throne, he said:

"Hasan ben Sabah, if you refuse to yield to the Sultân's reasonable demand, I am commanded to warn you that he will immediately take measures to expel you from the fortress and from the province. I have delivered my message."

Hasan made no direct reply. But taking a jewelled dagger from his belt, he called out a number, evidently at haphazard, and beckoned to one of the Fedāvîye, who were ranged in a semicircle around the throne. The youth, a swarthy, ferocious-looking Arab, instantly stepped forward, and, accepting the dagger from Hasan's hand, made him a deep obeisance, and, repeating the solemn formula of his order, in accordance with which he swore to obey the Sidna for life and for death, plunged the weapon into his heart, and fell back dead without a groan. Four of the novices, throwing a scarlet cloak over his dead body, bore it out without saying a word.

Then Hasan, again calling out a number which was instantly answered by the Initiated Youth to whom it corresponded, pointed to the open window overlooking the sheer precipice hundreds of feet below, and cried:

"Paradise and all its glories for those who unquestioningly obey. The mystic leap!"

Omar would have seized the fellow by his red girdle and forcibly detained him, but the youth was resolute in facing his fate.

"I obey!" were the words spoken by lips that blenched not, and, the victim of this barbarous tyranny, walking resolutely to the window, without even looking around, sprang out into the air. A moment of breathless silence ensued. Then the sound of a dull, sickening thud was heard far, far below. The double tragedy was over.

Hasan with an awful dignity and majesty rose, and, casting a look of triumph over the throng of his faithful followers and at his old schoolmate, said in the deepest tones of his marvellous voice:

"Omar, return and report to your Turkish master, the Sultân Malíkshāh, what you have seen. Every one of these whom you behold, and thousands more, are sworn by the solemnest of oaths to obey me to the death. Tell him — since I have left the mill, what have I to do with the millstone? — I defy his threats. I will not yield allegiance to him. Nor has he power enough to drive me from this province or from this castle. Tell him this!"

Omar was wise; he knew that further parley was useless. Accordingly he prepared to withdraw. He said:

"I have delivered my message. I will faithfully report to the Sultân what you have said. I regret that you impose on me such a duty. But I have warned you. On your head be the consequences. I will now return."

Hasan made no attempt to detain him. Escorted by the same body of soldiers, he passed through the anteroom, down through the winding passages and subterranean stairs, the gloomy arches reverberating to the tramp of their feet and the clank of their weapons; and after an interminable time he rejoined the rest of his men, who were patiently awaiting his return. They had waited the more patiently because during his absence a most hearty and appetizing refection had been prepared for them, and they had employed the time to advantage. But to Omar, by some neglect, either accidental or intentional, nothing in the way of refreshments had been offered. This was so contrary to all Eastern usages, that no one could fail to remark on it. Was it meant as an insult to him, or to the Sultân whose ambassador he was? This question he debated with himself as he rode out of the great gate of the castle.

CHAPTER XXVIII.

THE ASSASSINS.

Hasan allowed Omar and his suite to ride some distance away. Then he despatched a messenger on a swift horse to overtake them.

"Our Sidna," he cried, "begs Omar ben Ibrāhîm to turn back for a little space. He desires private talk with him."

Omar was at first inclined to refuse the invitation; his better judgment advised it, but thinking that possibly Hasan might have changed his mind regarding his message to the Sultân, he came to the conclusion that it was his duty to comply.

This time, as he reëntered the castle, he was met by two of the Chief Priors, who received him with a particular assiduity which contrasted strangely with the cold formality of his previous visit. He was offered the privilege of a bath, and then he was conducted to a dining-room, where he was met by Hasan, and seated at his right hand. The repast was ample, and elegantly served, a dozen of the

"Aspirants" acting as waiters, and bringing in the various courses as they came along. It seemed as if Hasan were trying by the magnificence of this dinner to atone for his former inhospitality. The presence of the two Grand Priors, and of Ostad ben Hasan, whom Omar would hardly have recognized, clad as he was in the white garb of the mystic order, served as an effectual barrier to any intimate conversation, even if Omar had felt like unbending from his dignity to enter into unrestrained dialogue with the man whom he regarded as primarily responsible for the death of Agapê.

But when the dinner was finished, and the attendants had brought perfumed water in brazen ewers to pour over their hands for the customary ablutions, Hasan dismissed the other guests, and begging Omar to come with him, led him to a room which might perhaps be called a library. It was of noble proportions, with arched ceiling, the panels of which were filled with symbolical designs carved in marble. It was one of the apartments adopted by Hasan for his own private use, and furnished with an elegance and luxury which would have been remarkable even in our day.

When the two men were seated on the wide divân that ran on the side of the room next the outer wall, so that they could look out of wide windows into a garden furnished with every manner of fruit-tree, and with graceful fountains tossing their scintillating jewels high into the air, Hasan began:

"Omar, you are a poet, and no one delights in your verses more than I do. Poets are prophets, and are able to read the book of Fate with clearer insight than ordinary mortals. When, therefore, I told you at Nishāpûr that I should rise high, that my sun would eclipse the moon of Malíkshāh, you knew in your inmost heart that I was not idly boasting, and you were not surprised when you heard how I had returned, with ever growing power, till the Sultân began to tremble on the toppling throne of his usurpation, and sent his idle threat by the very man who best knew how idle it was."

Hasan's eyes were kindling; his powerful features were lighted up by a strange glow. No one could doubt that he believed in his own preëminence. Omar listened with keen interest. He saw that he was dealing with a man who was destined to do terrible things; but he said nothing. Hasan went on:

"Omar, friend of my youth, I told you at Nishāpûr that if you would cast in your lot with mine we would drive the Turk from our ancient kingdom of Irân. It is not too late now. I shall accomplish my destiny. When I went to Isfahân I told my faithful old friend, Abulfasl, that if I had two friends like himself I would soon drive that Turkish boor from

Irân. Abulfasl is not a poet; he thought I was crazy, and prepared aromatic drinks and saffron meats to drive out the evil spirits. When I saw him last I had already won this castle, and I proved to him, as I shall prove to you, that I have power enough to make good my promise. I asked him then, 'Which of us was crazy, you or I? And for whom should the aromatic drinks and saffron meats have been prepared? You see I am keeping my word.' Perhaps you think as others have thought, that I would simply destroy and not build up. Atheism, or what the rabble call atheism, may be fitted for the unsettling, for the destruction of states, but not for the foundation of dynasties. Lawlessness may be well enough for you and me, for us the rulers, but morals and religion are the safeguards of the people. We must, at least, make the people believe that we are pious. I, even I, have performed the tapassa. I have gone for a week without food, steadfastly pronouncing the name of God, —for Muhammád declares that fasting brings us to the door of the heavenly palace; and I have ever found it so."

Omar knew that this was the veriest hypocrisy. Indignation swelled his heart. He could no longer contain himself.

"What did you do with that poor Greek maiden, the Princess Agapê?" he declared, suddenly.

"Oh, I remember; you were wont to meet her clandestinely, and break the law of the Prophet in her company. I had regard to her eternal welfare and rescued her from such contamination. Had she been willing to listen to me, I would have made her more famous than the Queen of Saba, who won the love of the Sultân Suleymân. But she refused to listen to my words of wisdom, and I know not what became of her."

"She returned to her father and to me," said Omar. "She died in my arms. More unfortunate was she than Basûs, the most beautiful woman of Israel. But, though she owed all her misfortunes to you, she refused to curse you."

"It was certainly very generous of her," said Hasan, with a sneer. "Why should she have cursed me when I would have done so much for her? But she is dead, and henceforth I say 'Sow not in unfruitful soil.' We will speak no more of her. I have now other more important things to talk about."

Omar had a sharp and indignant reply on his tongue, but Hasan rose and said:

"Now I am going to show you how I win converts. Come with me."

He led the way through several apparently empty apartments, all furnished and decorated with sumptuous magnificence, as if Asia and India, and even

Europe, had been robbed of their treasures to enrich this barbarous abode of fanatic indulgence. Carved ebony chairs, adorned with elephants' tusks, cunningly wrought into weird and grotesque designs; divâns, inlaid with mother-of-pearl, and disposed with swans-down cushions in gorgeously embroidered covers; great crystals of the purest water, like drops of liquid air fixed and glowing with light, patiently fashioned by the artist-artisans of China; bronze figures, brought overland from Japan; a marvellous array of precious rugs spread on the mosaic floors, and the cold solidity of the walls protected from dampness by hangings of exquisite designs.

Arriving at a room comparatively dark, Hasan touched a gong-bell, and instantly unseen hands pulled apart heavy silken curtains. A strange scene was presented to Omar's wondering eyes. A handsome youth whom he had noticed among his escort stood blindfolded between two maidens of exquisite loveliness clad in gauzy raiment, which only the more enticingly revealed the symmetrical contours of their Huri-like forms. Ranged at a little distance were concentric semicircles of beautiful maidens, standing motionless and, as it were, breathless, as if painted, or rather sculptured from living marble. The two guides conducted the youth to a cushioned seat beneath an oleander-tree in fullest bloom, every branch laden with a multitude of white blossoms, breathing intoxicating perfumes, and when they had seated him there, they deftly unbound the bandage from his eyes. As they did so, the semicircles of maidens, drawing closer, began to sway to and fro in a most enchanting dance, while an invisible chorus broke forth in a song so soft and seductive that it would have charmed an anchorite.

CHORUS OF HASAN'S HURIS.

After the toils of terrestrial life,
After the burden and heat of the strife,
After thy trials and sorrows are done—
Welcome to Paradise, Fortunate One!

Here blooms the Tuba-tree, full of delight,
Here rise the fountains eternally bright,
Here fragrant rivers of wine ever run—
Welcome to Paradise, Fortunate One!

Maidens celestial shall fan thy desires,
We are all thine, as we sing to our lyres,
Bliss never-ceasing for thee hath begun—
Welcome to Paradise, Fortunate One!

The youth with eyes widely staring looked first at one, then at another. One of the tenuous-clad maidens, flitting off to a little table of teak-wood studded with jewels, seized a golden ewer, and pouring out a cup of flashing wine, bore it back to the youth, and, seating herself by his side, threw her soft, round arm about his neck, put the seductive liquor to his lips.

Omar could hear him ask in a trembling voice: "Where am I?" and the ringing answer, sweet as the music of angels, "Thou hast won the victory; this is the crown; thou art in paradise, as the Prophet foretold."

"He believes it!" whispered Hasan in Omar's ear. "It accords with his dreams; he has tasted the Indian hemp; he is intoxicated with hashish. When he is recovered from the delirium he is ours!"

Even as Omar looked, the youth, feeling the lips of the simulated Huri on his, swooned and was instantly borne away by two stout slaves who were in waiting. The silken curtains were drawn, and the radiant, marvellous scene was shut out, but Omar heard the chorus of the Hūrân again as still another of Hasan's postulants entered into the charmed circle of his maleficent paradise.

"I brought you back and have shown you this," said Hasan, with triumphant security, "that you might see how certain I am of accomplishing my designs. Each day sees hundreds flocking to my standard. Yesterday a caravan of five hundred camels, bringing countless treasures, came to me from the Reis Mozaffir, who has agreed to turn over to me his castle of Kirdkuh, and to renounce his allegiance to the Turkish Sultân, Malíkshāh."

Omar knew perfectly well that Mozaffir had been one of Nizâmu'l-Mulk's fast friends, and as a faithful servant to the Sultân had been entrusted with an important province in the north.

"There are fifty other castles," Hasan went on, "which I shall soon occupy with my faithful. There are Dirkul and Tambur and Firushkuh and Kain and Tun, — rich and well fortified. Within six moons, perhaps in less time by your new and improved method of reckoning, — which, I assure you, I will adopt, at least, if you will join us, — I shall have the whole of Kufisân under my sway. Omar, join me and I will make your name to ring through the ages!"

Omar shook his head. He had no temptation to be unfaithful to his benefactor; but before he could speak Hasan went on:

"You shall be free to think as you please. Do you imagine that I believe as the brainless rabble do? Is my mind less acute than yours? Do I not know that Muhammád was a crazy poet, that the quarrels between the Shiites and the Fatemites are based on the most senseless of genealogies? Do you suppose I really make any distinction between seven and twelve? Is one number more sacred than another? But the great mass of people, — the Jaherî, the exoteric, — they must, for their own good, be given fables for truth, husks for corn! You and

I despise them equally. For us, who are adepts, who have reached the highest grade of worldly wisdom, there may be freedom from close observance of Islâm; but the blinders of custom must be tied over the eyes of ignorance.

"Yes, come with me, Omar, Prince of Poets, join me and I will make you head of the Seven Grades of Learning. What keener delight than to teach my Daïs, my faithful missionaries, how most successfully to flatter the prejudices of mankind and win power over them, as one trains a fiery steed! Think of the Tarîl, that allegoric instruction which shows men, who have passed through the ordeal, that there is something deeper and higher and wider than the Qurân! All this shall be put into your hands, you shall be master of it!"

"Nay," said Omar, quoting from one of his own quatrains as his manner was, "'The hereafter will fill all hours, and the world is but for a moment; sell not the Kingdom of Eternity for the sake of a moment.' It may be that you will drive Malíkshāh from the throne as you threaten to do; but he is my generous friend and benefactor, and no temptations that you could hold out would cause me to swerve from my duty to him. I must now return."

Hasan's face grew threatening; a black look of wrath came into his eyes, contracting his shaggy brows. "Know you not," he said, in the deepest bell-tones of his portentous voice, "that I have you in my power?" He touched his gong, and instantly from every door advanced a score of his fanatic followers with sparkling daggers in their hands.

"If I speak the word," exclaimed Hasan, "your last moment is come. A hundred blades will be in your body; you will be cut into a thousand pieces."

Omar, who had risen to go, stood there a moment; not a muscle of his face quivered; he looked straight into Hasan's eye.

"I fear not death," he said; "you who are the murderer of innocent maidens may well threaten to kill the ambassador of your Sultân! A worthy deed to be remembered by. Do your worst. I defy you!"

Hasan could not help respecting Omar's courage. Perhaps, if he had shown the slightest weakness or shadow of quailing, he might have given the fatal word; it is certain that no fear of consequences, no respect of conscience or law, would have restrained him and his men, who stood there enclosing Omar with a circle of daggers, sworn to kill or to die; indeed many of them not many months later, penetrating to the inmost shrines of royalty, buried those same daggers in hearts as innocent as Omar's.

But it pleased Hasan this time to experiment rather than to act; he was glad to have a truthful man carry the report and message to Malíkshāh.

Accordingly he bade his band of assassins retire, and in a moment the gorgeous room was as empty as before.

"Return to your Turkish master. Are you not ashamed — you, a Persian of purest blood — to be a slave to a Turk? Tell him what you have seen! Tell him my dagger will be buried in his heart before your orange-tree bears its first golden fruit! He has not deceived me. His army tried to hide from the Hawk of Alamût. Can ten thousand hide from the eye and scent of the eagle? I am ready for a siege or for a battle in the open field. Go!"

Two taps on the gong brought a special guard of four men who should conduct Omar outside the castle. As he was leaving the room where Hasan stood a terrible and relentless figure, Hasan's voice thundered forth:

"Omar Khayyâm, one more chance is yours. But I warn you,—the fate of Nizâmu'l-Mulk and of Malíkshāh will teach you what you, too, may expect."

And Omar, as he passed along the echoing corridor, heard his ill-omened voice saying in Arabic, "Hail to the Prophet and his family: Allâh the Best of Rulers satisfies us!"

CHAPTER XXIX.

THE SULTÂN'S PAVILION.

WHEN Omar rejoined his escort, he found that Hasan's Daïs had taken advantage of his absence to tamper with their fidelity, and they had succeeded in seducing a number of the younger men as well as the handsome youth, the beginning of whose initiation he had witnessed. He now saw that he ought not to have turned back. Hasan had used the opportunity the delay afforded to win adherents by his usual underhanded and wily ways. He did not know how severely the Sultân might blame him for allowing such a defection. He mounted his horse and, ordering his men to follow, rode with the greatest possible despatch toward the mountain pass where Arslāntâsh, the Lion Stone, was lying in wait, ready to march against Alamût. As soon as Omar came within sight, the Amîr himself, who had been in hourly expectation of his return, met him and brought him to his tent that he might hear his report. Like a true soldier, Arslāntâsh rejoiced at the prospect of immediate action. He saw himself forcing his way through the great halls of the castle, slaying the fugitive followers of the false prophet, and tracking Hasan himself to his ultimate refuge while his men ransacked the treasures which fanatic enthusiasm had poured into his grasping hands.

"What does this Hawk call himself?" asked the Amîr.

"He scorns the title of Sultân, which he says is Turkish," replied Omar, "and as his rôle is religious as well as political, since he makes no claim to be a descendant of the Prophet, he contents himself with the simple title of Sheikh. His followers call him the Sheikh ul Jebal, the Old Man of the Mountain, and they in turn take their name from him and are known as the Hasanites, though because their initiation begins with hashish they are also known as the Hashish Eaters, or Assassins. And they have renamed the castle the House of Fortune."

"Well, we will clean out this nest of Assassins!" exclaimed Arslāntâsh, confidently. "And we will turn the House of Fortune into an abode of Misfortune."

Within half an hour the ten thousand men under his command were on their way to the castle, which he was burning with zeal to capture and destroy.

Omar with his escort set out for his long ride across the mountains to render his report to Malík-shāh. It was a journey of several days, taken with decent leisureliness as became an ambassador of the Sultân. Nizâmu'l-Mulk received him with his usual friendly courtesy, and listened with eager attention to Omar's picturesque description of his experiences at Alamût.

"No," said the Wazîr, "I cannot blame you for heeding Hasan's invitation to turn back. It was clearly your duty to do so, nor were you to blame that some of your men were foolish enough to be seduced by his specious promises. But let us go to Malíkshāh."

Omar had almost completed his account for the second time when a sudden interruption broke it off. A messenger had arrived, haggard and pale from a long and breathless journey, and demanded instant admission to the Sultân, as his tidings were of the utmost importance.

He came in, and precipitated himself at Malík-shāh's feet, and kissed the hem of his robe. When the Sultân commanded him to rise and speak, it seemed as if his tongue clave to the roof of his mouth. But at last, by dint of questioning, the man was able to tell his story.

"Arslāntâsh," he said, "had advanced to the foot of the Castle of Alamût with all his forces, and, after demanding its surrender, proceeded to lay regular siege to it. Once Hasan made a sortie with a troop of soldiers dressed like darvishes, in black leather leggings and yellow turbans, and, shouting 'Ya Allâh! Ya hu!' made a desperate onslaught which Arslāntâsh repulsed with great difficulty. Many had fallen on both sides. From a prisoner we learned that Hasan had seventy companions, all well-armed and sworn never to surrender. On the second night a great misfortune had occurred. Abu 'Ali, one of Hasan's most devoted adherents, hearing that he was besieged in his castle, came with a force of only about three hundred men, and, taking advantage of the darkness, fell with a desperate onslaught on Arslāntâsh and completely defeated him; Hasan's troops hearing the tumult, or perhaps getting word, also emerged from the gates and joined in the pursuit of the Amîr and his fleeing men. Arslāntâsh himself was killed by an arrow which pierced his eye, and of all his troops scarcely ten escaped. A few threw down their arms and surrendered. I was fortunate enough to find a riderless horse, and, as soon as daylight dawned and I could see where to go, succeeded in eluding the enemy, and here I am. O Light of the Faith, may your shadow never diminish!"

This tidings caused the greatest excitement, and even consternation. That Malíkshāh, whose victorious arm had ground to powder the most formidable Khans of Bukhâra and won cities from the Emperor of Byzantium; who had taken as his standard the darafshî Kāwānî, the sacred leather apron of the famous blacksmith Kāwâh, of Isfahân, the jewelled standard of Persia; who was recognized by the Kaliphs as the Imâm al Muslimîn, — that he, Malíkshāh, should be flouted by an adventurer of evil reputation, a man to whom he had been a benefactor, was too monstrous!

Nevertheless, he now saw the mistake he had made in underestimating his powers. He would put him down with ruthless hand. He immediately ordered his chief Amîr, Kizil Zarîk, to take all the troops of Khurāsân and proceed against Hussein of Ain, while Nizâmu'l-Mulk should reduce the Castle of Alamût and bring Hasan to him alive or dead.

This order came as a surprise to the Wazîr. The look of the Sultân was almost threatening; his order was peremptory. For several weeks there had been a slightly chilling atmosphere about the Court, and Nizâmu'l-Mulk had not failed to notice it, though he thought himself too secure in his powerful position to allow it to trouble him. He understood perfectly well the cause of it. Malíkshāh's youngest wife, Khātûn Alyalaluiya, was engaged in an intrigue to secure the succession to the throne for her son, Māhmûd, at the expense of Barkiyarok, whom the Sultân had already designated as his heir. She had tried to induce Nizâmu'l-Mulk to side with her. But the Wazîr, who had been the young Barkiyarok

Mirza's tutor, remained true to him, and refused to countenance this Palace revolution. His influence would have been preponderating, and Khātûn became his bitter enemy, whereas she would have been more than friendly to him if he had been willing to meet her half way. It was the old story of Yusûf and the wife of the Egyptian Lord Treasurer. So well did Khātûn use her influence against the Wazîr, that the Sultân insensibly cooled toward him.

And now this order removed Nizâmu'l-Mulk from the Court, and made him responsible for the peace of the realm, as if he were commander-in-chief of the army. What for any other man would have been a promotion was for him a degradation, and he understood it so. But the Sultân was not unmindful of Omar's services or ungrateful. He summoned him a second time, and, after he had asked him many questions regarding his interview with Hasan and the appearance of the castle and its inmates, he said:

"Omar Khayyâm, you are not only most excellent among poets, but you have acquitted yourself with credit as my ambassador entrusted with a peculiarly trying and responsible mission. I have arranged with my Governor of Nishāpûr that your pension is to be paid to you regularly, as long as you live, and may many happy days be yours!

Moreover, whenever it may please you to return to your home and resume your work in your observatory, then you are at liberty to do so. This will express to you my appreciation of your services —"

Malíkshāh extended to Omar a costly ring set with magnificent pearls, and commanded a slave to bear to his room a bag full of gold coins, — enough to keep him in comfort for many days.

"I shall in all probability come to reside again in Nishāpûr," continued the Sultân. "If I do, I promise you we shall have some more talks by the river. I am, you know, a restless man; already twelve times I have crossed the whole of my dominions. But life is short, and there are still many things left undone. In spite of all my successes, I could envy the poet of Nishāpûr, who is content to watch the stars, to dream by the river."

Then suddenly changing his tone, he said:

"Nizâmu'l-Mulk told me you had composed a quatrain on the new calendar. I beg of you repeat it for me."

"Was it this?" asked Omar.

"'*Ah, but my Computations, People say,*
Reduced the Year to better reckoning? — Nay,
'Twas only striking from the Calendar
Unborn To-morrow and dead Yesterday.'"[1]

[1] FitzGerald's paraphrase.

"Alas!" exclaimed the Sultân, "there is no dead yesterday. It lives in to-day, and will live to-morrow. Omar, I could wish that once more, even this day, I might with you drown remembrance in your rosy wine. A presentiment of misfortune glooms my mind. I was wrong to send the faithful Nizâmu'l-Mulk against the Sheikh of the Hashish-eaters. Something tells me I shall never see him again. Has he gone? Let us have one more day of careless ease!"

Malíkshāh summoned a slave:

"Have the atabeg Nizâmu'l-Mulk instantly brought to me!"

The slave silently withdrew, and within a few moments the Wazîr appeared at the entrance of the Sultân's room. Although his face was perfectly calm, it could be seen that he came with the expectation that he was about to meet the death-stroke of royal disfavor.

Imagine his surprise and pleasure when he was met by the Sultân with a sweet but melancholy smile, when he found his master gracious and affectionate as of yore, and with him his friend Omar, beaming on him with his serene and handsome face.

Thus sometimes when, as one goes to bed, one looks out on a world wrapped in gray and impenetrable fog, and says, "Ah, to-morrow we shall not see the sky," but in the night the wind suddenly changes, and when the day dawns not a shred of mist clings to tree or shrub, but the sun rises from behind the cloudless mountains, so it was with Malíkshāh's Wazîr. He had, as it were, shivered in the chill atmosphere of disfavor, and, still expecting to find the sun of Royalty shrouded, and perhaps the lightning of wrath flashing from the cloud, he suddenly emerged into sunny, smiling skies.

"We must have one more day together before we separate," cried the Sultân. "Allâh only knows when we three may meet again. See to it that no one disturb us. We will dine in the summer pavilion. Nor will we even think of the future. Wait, how is it, Omar, Star of Improvisers?"

"Ah! fill the Cup," said Omar.

> "*Ah! fill the Cup. What boots it to repeat*
> *How Time is slipping underneath our Feet;*
> *Unborn To-morrow, and dead Yesterday,*
> *Why fret about them if To-day be sweet!*"[1]

"'Unborn To-morrow, and Dead Yesterday' again?" exclaimed the Sultân, frowning slightly. "Let us have no death's head at our feast!"

The arrangements were perfected, and the three men proceeded together to the beautiful pavilion, made of costly wood and filled with rare flowers.

Here the Sultân had his favorite musicians play,

[1] FitzGerald's paraphrase.

and the sound of the lutes mingled pleasantly with the tinkle of the fountains dropping into porcelain bowls, and the sighing of soft breezes among the swaying fronds of the palms.

After they had feasted on game brought from the mountains, and on frozen sherbets and other delicious dainties, and the Sultân's trustiest servants had provided them with the richest wine that Omar had ever tasted, Malíkshāh turned to Nizâmu'l-Mulk, and, reaching to him his hand, said:

"Forget, old friend, the events of the past few months. Woman should not be allowed to come between men. I know, and have known all the time, that my interests were dearer to you than your own. But for the sake of peace one sometimes shuts one's eyes. I assure you, here and now, — and I will swear by the Qu'rân, — that I will take your advice and make no change in the succession. Now for good cheer!"

This gracious tribute to his Wazîr's faithfulness and wisdom was naturally most grateful both to him and to Omar, and whatever atmosphere of apprehension or presentiment may have at first hung oppressive on their spirits was suddenly lightened. The influence of the cheer-inspiring wine also began to be felt, and Omar was called on to repeat some of his quatrains in praise of the generous Ruby Kindled in the Vine!

"Come, fill the Cup," he sang, "and in the fire of
spring
Your winter-garment of Repentance fling:
The Bird of Time has but a little way
To flutter, — and the bird is on the Wing!

"Whether at Nishāpûr or Babylon,
Whether the Cup with sweet or bitter run,
The Wine of Life keeps oozing drop by drop,
The Leaves of Life keep falling one by one.

"Waste not your Hour, nor in the vain pursuit
Of This and That endeavor and dispute;
Better be jocund with the fruitful Grape
Than sadden after none, or bitter Fruit."

These and many more Omar repeated, but the Sultân and Nizâmu'l-Mulk could not help noticing that, in spite of his joyous voice, there was an undertone of sadness in many of his quatrains. When, for instance, toward the end he repeated the following rubā'iyât:

"Yon rising Moon that looks for us again —
How oft hereafter will she wax and wane;
How oft hereafter rising look for us
Through this same garden, — and for one in vain!"

"And when like her, O Sākî, you shall pass
Among the guests Star-scattered on the Grass,
And in your joyous errand reach the Spot
Where I made One — turn down an empty Glass!"[1]

[1] FitzGerald's Paraphrase.

There was no doubt in their mind whom he meant by *one!*

"Have you never heard from your old Greek Prince Kreiton?" asked the Sultân.

"Only once since he returned to Byzantium," replied Omar. "He sent me a manuscript containing a copy of some of the poems of Anakreon, and with it a few brief lines in appreciation of his visit at Nishāpûr and of the Sultân's generosity, and referring with deep feeling to his lonely old age without his daughter, without Agapê. He also said —"

But Omar paused without finishing his sentence.

"What also did he say?" demanded Malíkshāh.

"He said that his younger daughter, Leukonoe, was the image of Agapê, and —"

"Ah! I see," said the Sultân, "he invited you to come to —"

"Yes, to Athens he invited me."

"Do you not feel drawn to go?" asked Nizâmu'l-Mulk.

"Yes, I should like to see the Western lands," replied Omar, "and if I were young once more I might be tempted, but I am growing old and, if Leukonoe is like Agapê, it would be too painful —"

The afternoon was waning, and the soft light came through the interwoven foliage of the terrace.

"We must now return to the actualities of life," said the Sultân. "It is too late to recall my order for you to go in person against the chief of the assassins, but I have no doubt of your success, and if we once have Hasan in our power, we will devise together a plan for his punishment. I can not avoid a certain admiration for his audacious genius."

"I will do my best to take him alive," said the Wazîr.

"Why should I not go with you?" asked Omar, addressing the Wazîr. "I have been in the castle. I might be able materially to help in case it were captured," he added, turning to the Sultân.

"I have no objections, if you would like to accompany him," said Malíkshāh, after a moment's thought.

Nizâmu'l-Mulk showed in his noble face how deeply gratified he was at Omar's suggestion. The matter was accordingly decided, and the three friends separated.

CHAPTER XXX.

TO WHAT LENGTHS HATRED WILL CARRY.

THE Wazîr, armed with his mace as well as with his bow and arrows, and clad in a full suit of armor which had been made by a Nishāpûr armorer, after the pattern of one captured from a Greek general, arrived with a powerful army, and encamped on the banks of the Shâh-rûd, or King's River, not far from the Castle of Alamût.

Accompanied by Omar and his subordinate generals, he reconnoitered the castle, and came to the conclusion that it was not to be captured by ordinary means. It would rèquire a long siege, but might it not be possible first of all to cut off the stream or streams of water that supplied the castle? And yet the extent of the structure was enormous, and these streams came from various sources, and, moreover, its own drainage-surface was so arranged that a single rain-storm would furnish drinking-water enough to last for days. This seemed impracticable. It was a serious undertaking in many ways. Other large and important castles not far distant had come into possession of Hasan's followers, either by treachery or by the treasonable action of their governors, and constant watch had to be maintained against surprise.

Hasan himself was kept informed by spies of all that took place. His power and influence had been strangely augmented by a tragic occurrence in his own household. One of his most resolute and faithful Priors had been found with a jewelled dagger thrust through his heart. This dagger was known to be Ostad ben Hasan's, and accordingly the young man was charged with the crime. What was a meritorious action when directed against any one whom Hasan considered an enemy was worthy of punishment when its victim was one of Hasan's allies and friends.

The Grand Council of the Order was convened, and Ostad was formally tried in accordance with their rites and customs. Hasan himself, unmoved by the fact that it was his own son, presided over the solemn tribunal, and when the vote was taken, and, having been counted, was found almost unanimously in condemnation of him, without hesitation pronounced against him the penalty provided by their rules, and himself handed him the poniard by which he was to put an end to his own life in presence of the whole assembly.

One of the Grand Priors, urging the extenuation that Ostad had confessed, and that the murder had been committed under unusual provocation, tried to induce Hasan to mitigate the sentence. But the father refused to change. He had the keenness to perceive that such relaxation of the stern laws of his Order would be deleterious to that terrifically strict discipline that he had succeeded in maintaining, and consequently he had looked on with stern and cruel eyes while the sacrifice of the life of that strange and enigmatical son was performed.

It was felt by all that Hasan's impartiality was absolute, and that in the interests of the Order he would not spare himself any more than the humblest Lasik or Aspirant, in the whole hierarchy.

Accordingly, when it was known that a dangerous and difficult service was required of one or two of the Fedâviye, there was not one that had taken the oath who did not burn with zeal to be chosen.

The lot fell to the son of the Arab sheikh at whose house Hasan had spent so many months. When the lot was announced Hasan took the young man by the girdle and led him into an adjoining room. He was there informed what his duty was. It was the custom at Alamût for the Fedâviye selected for a specially dangerous service to be given an intoxicating draught of hashish, so that, after the delicious delirium had passed, the desperation born of the reaction might nerve him to any deed of valor. Every delight that imagination and the excitation of the senses could inspire in a human being was thought the proper stimulus for one who might and probably would perish in the desperate deed. The stern and strenuous régime prescribed for the rank and file, the frequent fasts, the plain and almost forbidding food, the abstinence from all relationship with women, the daily exercise in arms, with sword and bow, contrasted powerfully with this foretaste of paradise, — with its wine and music, its enticing damsels lily-armed and scented with musk, its sudden ending in the madness of an almost divine delirium, its awakening to do and to die! No wonder there was immense ambition and rivalry among the fearless and zealous adherents of Hasan ben Sabah to be chosen for any desperate deed of daring.

Abdīshû knew perfectly well that he was expected to take advantage of this privilege of intoxication and license; but when he was invited to enter the inner apartments of the castle, to prepare for the mystic rite by perfumed baths and other ceremonies, he informed Hasan ben Sabah that he preferred to forego the ordination.

"It will require the very coolest and clearest head to accomplish this task," he said. "I do not wish to cloud my mind by any licensed follies, nor do I need hashish to nerve my arm. I have good enough reason to hate Malíkshāh and his Wazîr, and my hate is all the stimulus I need. It will save time to let me start immediately."

Hasan applauded this decision. He remembered that Togrulbeg had once made a great requisition on Al Ijli's family for camels, and that the old sheikh had felt that the payment was far too small. A large edifice of hatred can be erected on one small coin, and Abdīshû found in this transaction of a preceding Sultân a sufficient cause for deadly rancor, and justification for any treachery. To such lengths will hereditary resentment go.

It was early evening. Darkness had fallen early. A fog filled the valley, and no one in the castle would have suspected the presence of a vast army encamped on all sides of it. Nor was the castle, with its mighty battlements and frowning towers, manifest to a single eye in all the host. A curtain as dense as the veil of Nonentity shut enemy from enemy, indeed shut friend from friend. The sentinels, walking their rounds, occasionally met and exchanged peremptory greetings, though their voices were muffled in the mist. By Nizâmu'l-Mulk's orders a powerful guard invested each one of the entrances of the castle, so that in case any sortie were attempted it might meet with swift rebuttal. Around the whole castle the lines were closely drawn, and it seemed as if it were impossible for human being to make way out through the hedge of armed men.

But the builder of the castle had begun, and

Hasan had completed, an underground passage which was tunnelled through the living rock, was led by zigzags and slopes, up and down, was provided with gates and bolts, and finally emerged far beyond the valley in a glen or gorge. The outlet was curiously and cleverly concealed among vast masses of precipitated rock and a dense growth of underbrush.

Through this labyrinth a man was silently and cautiously making his way, occasionally pausing to listen; for though the chances were slight of his discovery, he would not allow even the beating of his heart to prejudice his escape. He had no light; his only guide was the narrowness of the walls, which sometimes approached so close together that he could barely squeeze through. Then again it dipped, and he could hear the drip, drip of water falling into crevices; occasionally the air grew dense and unwholesome, but at last he finished his laborious expedition, and emerged from the inner darkness which was palpable into the outer darkness which was scarcely less impenetrable.

He had no star by which to direct his course, no lodestone to point his way. The cold mist blew into his face, and condensed into rain in the meshes of his curly young beard. He was fearless and alert. His senses were keen. Noiselessly as a panther he made his way down the ravine, which he knew would bring him within a short distance of the environing army. His plan was all made, and he proceeded skilfully to carry it out. Fortune favored him.

Coming from outside he crept up near one of the outer pickets, and, seizing his opportunity, stabbed him through the heart from behind, and at the same instant threw his jubbá, or seamless jacket, over his head, so that his yell was stifled before it escaped into the air. Then seizing his victim, he picked him up, and carried him back into the underbrush from which he had come.

The Persian whom he had killed was about his own size, and he quickly stripped him, and, exchanging his clothes for the dead man's and concealing the body in the bushes, he hastened back and took his place as sentinel. How it was that no one detected the substitution, or missed the murdered man, is one of those mysterious details that make us say, Truth is stranger than Fiction. He fell as naturally into the discipline of the camp as if he had been trained to it all his life, and if he made any blunders of awkwardness they were not noticeable.

When day dawned the mist precipitated itself into a pouring rain; the wind blew fiercely, and the mountain-sides became roaring torrents. Abdīshû managed, in spite of the rain, to secure sufficient information to assist him in his design. He easily learned every division and part of the camp, the strength of the army and its weakest sides, and, after the guard had been changed for the evening, he profited by the pitchy darkness to crawl out of his own quarters without being discovered, and to approach the more sheltered esplanade, where the Wazîr and the chief officers were encamped. The heavy rain still falling made the torches gutter and burn low. No one believed that in such a storm, and in such a night, there would be any sortie from the castle, or that any danger was abroad.

CHAPTER XXXI.

LIFE GOES LIKE THE WIND.

In his water-proof tent Nizâmu'l-Mulk, who had just finished his evening refection in company with Omar, was remarking:

"O Khayyâm, we were unadvised not to have taken shelter in Dirkul; but it is too late now to complain, and we are fairly comfortable in spite of the damp air. What say you to a game of Strategy?"

This game, which corresponded pretty closely with our modern chess and got its name from the Hindu *chaturanga*, had its origin more clearly defined than we now see it. It was played with the four members or divisions of the army — the elephants, the horse, the chariots, and the foot-soldiers. What is now called the castle was then termed *rukh*, the hero; there was a queen, *farzên*; for the knight stood *asp*, the steed, and *fil*, the elephant, took the place of the later bishop. The very name check-mate appeared in the word shâh-mât. It was then, as now, a game which required deep thought and serious attention. The skilful player could see into the future, and pre-determine the motions of his subordinates. What delight to make the apparently unimportant move that should condition the very success of your play; to be so far-seeing that not one of your opponent's apparently unimportant moves shall escape your attention or leave its significance unperceived!

It was Omar's favorite game, and he and Nizâmu'l-Mulk would often spend hours in its intricacies. They were well matched, and their duels were often closely drawn and most exciting.

When Nizâmu'l-Mulk invited Omar to join him in a game, and the attendants were making ready the table and arranging the lanterns, Omar quoted two quatrains recently composed by him, and referring to the lantern and game:

"'*We are no other than a moving row*
Of Magic-Shadow-shapes that come and go
Round with the Sun-illumined Lantern held
In Midnight by the Master of the Show;

"'*But helpless Pieces of the Game He plays*
Upon this Chequer-board of Nights and Days;
Hither and thither moves, and checks, and slays,
And one by one back in the Closet lays.'"[1]

"Yes, and did you not compose one with the same thought, comparing life to our great game of chugân?" asked Nizâmu'l-Mulk.

"Was it this:

[1] FitzGerald's paraphrase.

"'*The Ball no question makes of Ayes and Noes,*
But Here or There as strikes the Player goes,
And He that tossed you down into the field
He knows about it all — He knows — He knows!'"

"Yes, that was it! 'Tis a beautiful fatalism," continued Nizâmu'l-Mulk. "It often seems to me that we are, as you say, 'the helpless Pieces of the Game He plays,' and that we are moved about just as we move our elephants and horses. Your figure is fine, I shall never forget it, 'We are the pieces; Heaven plays the game; we are moved about on the chess-board of existence.'"

"I prefer another that I have recently composed," said Omar.

"'*The Morning Finger writes; and having writ,*
Moves on: not all your Piety nor Wit
Shall lure it back to cancel half a Line,
Nor all your Tears wash out a Word of it.'"

"I better like your quatrains about Fate than those in praise of wine," said Nizâmu'l-Mulk.

"How would it be, if by wine I meant also the divine intoxication of the spirit of God?" asked Omar, with a smile. "It is possible to read that esoteric signification into them, and once when Hasan ben Sabah did my humble house at Nishāpûr the honor of a visit, he predicted that in time to come that would be the interpretation of them. It struck me as not a bad idea, and since then I have composed several that certainly might bear that double meaning. I rather like it myself. Besides, it serves to annoy the overvirtuous, and you know I love to stir up those that have no imagination. Those that deserve to understand will understand."

"Methinks you have become more spiritualized, if I may use that expression, since our poor little friend Agapê died," said Nizâmu'l-Mulk. "I understand you; it is hard for you to show your serious side to people, and they do not read between your lines. But I do, and I know that you are deeply religious."

Omar did not try to deny the assertion; he had studied the mysteries of the skies too thoroughly to be really irreverent, though some of his poems are audacious in expressing what has come to be the feeling, or at least the hope, of thousands; and even in his day there were many men of philosophical minds who were, like him, dissatisfied with the husks of Islâm, and yet who had not, like him, worked out a philosophy of their own.

But as he also made no reply, Nizâmu'l-Mulk said: "Come, now, let us have our game and see which will first cry kisht ba shâh!"

They sat down and were soon deeply engrossed in their mimic duel. The servants holding the lanterns watched with keen interest the meditated moves, sometimes ventured as by intuition, at others only after careful deliberation. The rain was still pattering on the tent, and the roar of the torrents mingled with the gusty swooping of the storm-wind bending the distant forests.

Suddenly a tall, slender young man, dressed in the garb of a Khurāsân foot-soldier, darted through the closed flaps of the tent, crossed the intervening space, and, before any one could lay hands on him, exclaiming, "Mâ shâ allâh! Thus perish all tyrants and robbers!" drove his poniard into Nizâmu'l-Mulk's back, and left it sticking there. He also aimed a blow at Omar, but the table was between them, and the poet, by his very act of springing to grasp the assassin, escaped any serious injury. The men with the lanterns were so dazed by the suddenness of the attack that they stood like dummies, and not till Omar, who never lost his presence of mind, shouted to them to stop the man did they realize that, if they had acted with instant promptness, they might have tripped him up and captured him.

But Omar missed his grasp; his foot became entangled in a rug, and he fell prostrate, thus escaping the assassin's blow; but Abdīshû took advantage of the confusion to dart by the guards and hide himself in the darkness and rain. The moment he was out of the range of torches he ceased running, and, being dressed like one of the regular soldiers, there was nothing about his appearance to excite suspicion.

So even while he heard behind him the beating of the great drums and excited shouts, he slowly and cautiously made his way toward the outskirts of the camp.

Meantime Omar Khayyâm, who had quickly got to his feet, issued peremptory orders, which were heeded as if he were actually in command. He summoned the chief amîrs, who were directly responsible to the Wazîr, and the ablest surgeons connected with the whole army.

But nothing was to be done. It was evident that the moment the dagger was withdrawn, life would follow the fatal point. Nizâmu'l-Mulk himself realized this, and, although every breath that he drew was attended by the keenest anguish, he used the precious moments of consciousness to give his last directions. Omar had detached from the dagger a little roll of parchment, in which was written in Persian characters a brief and terrible message from Hasan ben Sabah:

"Hasan forgets not insults: he repays."

But Omar kept it from the knowledge of his friend, and Nizâmu'l-Mulk never knew that he was the victim of the basest ingratitude that ever stained the character of living soul.

"Take my hand — Omar — old friend — a Allâh, I am — passing away — in the hand of the wind — tell the Sultân — I should have tried — to do my best — but — the moving Finger! — Omar — to you I confide my son — Abul Mosaffer 'Ali — be a father to him — bear a message to — Shirîn Khānúm — the pain — is too great — remove the dagger — let me die!"

The surgeon saw that his strength was failing rapidly under the stress of his agony, and took it on himself to concede to the Wazîr's demand. He pulled the dagger from the wound; it was followed by the red blood mingled with foam from the lungs; blood also gushed from his mouth, and in a moment more Nizâmu'l-Mulk lay lifeless on the rug.

Thus passed away the greatest man of his day, — a man of whom the poet El Bekri said:

> "He was a precious pearl, fashioned of pure nobility by the Merciful One; nay, so goodly was it that the age knew not its worth, and the Creator, jealous for its honor, returned it to the shell."

The news of the assassination spread like wild-fire through the camp; almost a panic succeeded; it was felt that if Hasan's emissaries could penetrate undetected even into the headquarters of the commander-in-chief, anything else unexpected and dreadful might occur. The storm was increasing in severity;

the wind blew like a tempest, and many tents were levelled to the ground. A general alarum was beat, and the whole army was called to arms. The pickets were doubled, and a thorough search was made for the miscreant who had done the vile deed. But Abdīshû's propitious star never deserted him. He succeeded not only in eluding the sentinels, but also in making his way back into the Hawk's Nest, where the report of his success was received by Hasan with a fiendish delight.

In the morning the fury of the storm had passed. The sun had sufficient power to penetrate the mists which the conquering north wind drove before it, far away across the wide continent. But there was no sun of Joy to dissipate the pall of sorrow that hung heavy over the camp. It was decided that the Wazîr's body should lie in state throughout the day, and the army was permitted to view the noble face for the last time. It bore no trace of suffering, but wore an expression of absolute serenity, as it were of joy.

Had there been any way of reaching Hasan in his castle, had there been any way of tearing the castle from the beetling precipice, there would have been not one stone left on another by night; but it was impregnable; it frowned down on the angry host as an island crag stands unmoved amid the onslaught of the ocean in a tempest. Its tremendous battlements towered above their loftiest scaling-ladders; its small windows were above the reach of their arrows, and no fire which could be kindled around their solid gates would suffice to burn a way into the long and winding passages, protected by more than one portcullis and with recklessly brave defenders at every oilet, so that one man might keep back a host.

Thus Hasan was able to laugh his foes to scorn. He was amply provisioned; there was no possibility of his water supply running dry; his most dangerous enemy was dead at his feet. He inwardly gloated over his triumph, but before any spectator he was as calm and unmoved as if he were only a farmer preparing to do a spring ploughing. Like a volcano which outwardly smiles back to the smiling sun, bearing aloft rank upon rank of prosperous villages embowered in vineyards and olive plantations, but far down within its secret channels glows the tortured lava burning with desire to rush forth and destroy, so Hasan, calmly regulating the affairs of his Order, calmly listening to the report of his secret emissaries, who returned to tell of their success in making way with this, that, or the other ruler whose influence stood in the way of his ambitions, seeming to all who saw him the very embodiment of impassive, cold, and heartless power, was inwardly quick with consuming passions. Even when his heart gave a bound at hearing of Abdīshû's unexpected success he gave no sign. He listened to the young Arab's glowing account of his adventurous visit to the Wazîr's camp; he nodded with grim appreciation when Abdīshû told how he had cleared the way by plunging his dagger into the sentinel's back; he almost smiled when he told how he had succeeded in entering the tent where Nizâmu'l-Mulk was playing chess.

"With whom was he playing?" demanded Hasan.

"I think it was Omar, the chief astronomer," replied the Arab.

"Would that you had killed him also!" exclaimed Hasan. "But since you have accomplished so much I will let my eyes come together concerning the omission."

"Indeed I struck at him," explained the Arab, "but I had left my second dagger in the heart of the Wazîr, and I had no weapon left."

"Alhamd lillâh!" exclaimed Hasan with assumed piety. "Praise God for so much! You have earned your promotion. In the coming moon you shall be made a Refik."

The Arab bowed. Such praise from Hasan meant more than many more words would have meant in the mouth of another man.

CHAPTER XXXII.

IN OLD EMBERS NEW FLAMES.

Omar Khayyâm himself undertook to carry the news of the assassination of Nizâmu'l-Mulk to Marv. It was arranged that the body of the murdered minister should be brought as speedily as possible to the capital, where it might be buried, or, if it were thought best, it might be taken to the city of Tûs, the revenues of which had for many years been diverted to his private use. The inhabitants of that region were proud of him, for he was born at Radagan, near Tûs.

Omar travelled post, and in less than a week was at the palace. Malíkshāh was amazed to see him, but welcomed him with his usual gracious affability. It was hard for Omar to speak, and the Sultân saw that some trouble weighed on him.

"Khayyâm," he said, "something unusual disturbs the serenity of your mind. Does Hasan ibn 'Ali ibn Ishak Tūsî send you to me with evil tidings? Speak and have no fear!"

Omar's voice trembled, as he made his reply:

"Your Majesty, I bring bad tidings, but not from the Wazîr. He, whom I was privileged to call my friend, the great Regulator of the Realm, has been foully dealt with. As we sat together in his tent, under the very shadow of Alamût Castle, an emissary of the Sheikh ul Jebal succeeded in eluding the vigilance of the guards, and, before any one could interpose, plunged a dagger into his lungs from behind. He lived only long enough to express his fealty to his Sultân, commended to me the care of his young son, and died. The miscreant escaped; it was stormy, and exceedingly dark. Even now the train bearing his body is on its way to Marv. I hastened on in advance to apprise your Majesty of the terrible occurrence."

Malíkshāh was stricken dumb with horror. His only consolation was that before Nizâmu'l-Mulk had started he had given him one last mark of his confidence and esteem, and had not sent him thus to his death, supposing that his sovereign's heart was alienated from him.

"Nizâmu'l-Mulk's wife has gone to Tûs," said the Sultân. "She must be notified. The cruel tidings must be gently broken to her. I have confidence in your tact. Will you undertake also this trying mission?" asked Malíkshāh, after he had somewhat recovered from the first shock.

Omar, of course, willingly complied with a command so graciously expressed, and started immediately for Tûs.

Shirîn Khānúm, the Wazîr's only wife, was a woman as remarkable in her way as Nizâmu'l-Mulk was in his. She was one who thought for herself. Like some of the Moorish women in Spain, she had thrown off the trammels of her religion, and actively participated in the questions that interested her husband. She was able to read and write, and she composed very creditable verses. Moreover, she was refined and beautiful in person and manners. Omar had often seen her, and talked intimately with her, and he felt for her the worship that a poet feels for a woman who can appreciate and understand him. He knew perfectly well that Nizâmu'l-Mulk would never have retained his responsible position under two emperors, had it not been for the wise counsels of his beloved wife.

It was with strange feelings, therefore, that Omar undertook the errand to Tûs. As guardian to Abul Mosaffer 'Ali, the Wazîr's son, a youth rapidly approaching maturity, he would be obliged to see much of Shirîn Khānúm. How would she like such a relationship? Omar knew that she was friendly to him, that she liked to talk with him, and was able to keep up her end of an argument, even when it treated of pretty abstruse questions. And now he was going to her to announce the death of her renowned husband!

He was expeditious in setting forth, and expeditious in his journey; for the Sultân advised him to bring Shirîn Khānúm immediately back to Marv, where his intention was to erect a magnificent tomb to the martyred Wazîr. He reached Tûs without adventure, and found Nizâmu'l-Mulk's residence without difficulty. Shirîn Khānúm received him graciously. She was sitting on a divân in a beautiful room decorated in what is called ardish-work, where bits of mirror are inlaid in quaint mosaics in the plaster. Her son, a handsome youth, with regular features and his father's kindly eyes, was sitting with her. She immediately ordered her farrâsh to bring refreshments, but her quick eye and keen psychic intelligence told her that something was wrong. It did not become her to ask Omar outright what trouble bent his dark brows; but the question trembled on her lips. Sometimes words are unnecessary. Omar, his generous heart bursting with anguish at the loss of his friend, and the difficulty of telling his widow the circumstances, was at a loss how to begin. Is there not a sort of language that souls united in internal harmony understand without words? It seemed as if Shirîn Khānúm read Omar's very soul:

"You come to bring me bad tidings!" she cried.

"My husband — has anything happened to him! Oh, Allâh, have mercy! He is dead!"

"Baji!" said Omar, with an infinite tenderness in this word which means so much and so little. "My sister, my dearest friend and benefactor said to himself these words:

"'*If thou desirest Him, be separated from wife and children,*
Bravely move thine abode from relatives and friends;
Whatever is, is an hindrance on the road for thee;
How canst thou journey with these hindrances? Remove them.'"[1]

It was a strange impulse which induced him to quote one of his own poems at such a moment; but it was a happy impulse. Although Shirîn Khānúm had said, correctly, "My husband is dead," Omar's reply seemed to make the effect of the announcement a little less dreadful.

"He was wounded doing his duty," continued Omar. "He breathed out his life in the service of his Sultân. His last word was a message of love to his wife. The Sultân sent me to you to bear his deepest condolences and to be your escort back to Marv. I await your command. Pray, regard me as your faithful servant."

No man, however kindly he may be, can feel satisfied with his manner of breaking tidings of disaster to those who are to suffer from it. But, after all, it

[1] E. Heron Allen's translation.

is not so much the words that one says as it is the spirit in which they are said. Omar's presence was comforting, the sight of his beautiful face softened by sympathy was a benediction. Consequently Shirîn Khānúm was calmer than she would have believed it possible. She allowed Omar to give the necessary orders for immediate departure. There were many things which required wise direction. The Wazîr's son would inherit his father's estate, and as a large part of it was situated in his native province and in the city of Tûs, it seemed well to take some preliminary steps for its maintenance; this Omar was enabled to do. Fortunately Nizâmu'l-Mulk had kept his wife informed of his finances, and, moreover, he had left in her hand a sort of will, called Wasiyat, for the guidance of Mosaffer 'Ali, in case, as seemed probable, he should come into his father's place. These details consumed several days before they were satisfactorily adjusted.

Omar had constantly fresh reason for admiration for Shirîn Khānúm's dignified character, her keenness of perception, the delicacy of her sentiments, the ripeness of her judgment, and the serenity of her grief; she allowed herself no transports of despair, but in every way showed herself the worthy consort of Nizâmu'l-Mulk.

When at last Omar arrived with Shirîn Khānúm and her numerous following of servants at Marv, he found the Sultân very ill; he was suffering, it was said, from a mysterious malady, the nature of which baffled the physicians. Omar, who had expected that all the arrangements for Nizâmu'l-Mulk's funeral would have been made on a scale commensurate with his fame, was admitted at once to the Sultân's sick-room. Malíkshāh had asked if Omar were yet returned, and when told that he had just arrived with the family of Nizâmu'l-Mulk, he desired to see him. Omar was shocked at the Sultân's appearance, but he was quick enough to suspect the cause. The moment his eyes met the Sultân's he read in them his own thought: Malíkshāh was slowly dying from the effects of poison, and he needed not his sovereign's whispered word:

"The Sheikh ul Jebal has stricken me also! He is the evil genius of my reign."

He extended his hand; the bloodless fingers showed how the flesh was wasted.

"Some slow and deadly poison has been administered to me. I am doomed."

Omar tried to encourage the Sultân. But the fixed idea that his case was hopeless had taken possession of his mind.

"No!" said Malíkshāh, "Hasan ben Sabah has taken from me the very staff of my sovereignty. I was quickly punished for having distrusted for even a moment that noblest and most generous of servants. If I had hearkened to his advice, I should not have permitted the persecution of the Christian pilgrims. I had nothing against them; now I know all Europe will come in defence of the holy places and will inflict on Islâm frightful losses. It was a woful mistake."

Malíkshāh referred to a persecution of the pilgrims to Jerusalem which had been instigated a few years before by the Mollâhs, and which Nizâmu'l-Mulk opposed. The Sultân allowed himself to be overpersuaded. This led directly to the Crusades.

Malíkshāh, with the prophetic eye of approaching dissolution, seemed to see the cataclysm that followed his death. He knew well enough that without the organizing and controlling hand of Nizâmu'l-Mulk, the vast empire which he had so laboriously constructed would fall apart as the empire of Alexander had collapsed. Could he have foreseen even with the clairvoyant vision of genius that within less than a decade Antioch would be besieged, Askalon fall, and Baldwin reign as king of Jerusalem?

No, the details were lacking, but in the mists that blurred his fading eyes his imagination saw overwhelming armies and stricken banners, and sacked cities and desolated plains.

Malíkshāh was dying, and not even the glory that had crowned his reign could console him in the foreboding prognostications which his experience and his wisdom and the melancholy engendered by the subtle poison coursing through his thickening, sluggish blood only too truly implanted in his mind.

But he found no little pleasure in Omar's presence, in his cheerful philosophy, which bore with equal equanimity the sorrows and the joys of life, in his wise reflections, in his wit and perspicacity. Ill as he was, and conscious of his approaching end, melancholy in his inclinations, he insisted on Omar's staying with him for several hours every day. He bade him repeat his more inspiring quatrains, especially those referring to the greatness of departed kings and to the inevitableness of death. Often and often he made Omar repeat the morning rubâ'ı; he never wearied of it:

"*Awake! for Morning in the Bowl of Night*
Has flung the Stone that puts the Stars to Flight:
And lo! the Hunter of the East has caught
The Sultân's Turret in a Noose of Light!"

And this:

"*Irâm indeed is gone with all his Rose*
And Jamshŷd's Seven-ringed Cup where no one knows;
But still a Ruby kindles in the Vine,
And many a garden by the Water blows."

This, too, pleased him :

> "*The Worldly Hope men set their Hearts upon*
> *Turns Ashes — or it prospers ; and anon,*
> *Like Snow upon the Desert's dusty Face,*
> *Lighting a little hour or two — is gone !*
>
> "*Think, in this battered Caravanserai*
> *Whose Portals are alternate Night and Day,*
> *How Sultân after Sultân with his Pomp*
> *Abode his destined Hour, and went his way.*"

Is it not a pleasant picture to see the Sultân and the Poet in this familiar intercourse ? Omar, with his fine face aglow, his eyes resting affectionately and tenderly on the weak and weary monarch, who lay so patiently on his royal couch demanding and ever demanding the music of those exquisite lines :

> "*Up from Earth's Centre through the Seventh Gate*
> *I rose, and on the Throne of Saturn Sate,*
> *And many a knot unravell'd by the Road ;*
> *But not the master-knot of Human Fate.*
>
> "*There was the Door to which I found no Key ;*
> *There was the Veil through I might not see :*
> *Some little talk awhile of Me and Thee*
> *There was — and then no more of Thee and Me.*
>
> "*So when that Angel of the darker Drink*
> *At last shall find you by the river-brink,*
> *And offering his Cup, invite your Soul*
> *Forth to your Lips to quaff — you shall not shrink.*

"*Why, if the Soul can fling the Dust aside*
And naked on the Air of Heaven ride,
Were't not a Shame — were't not a Shame
In this clay carcase crippled to abide?

"*'Tis but a Tent where takes his one day's rest*
A Sultân to the realm of Death addrest;
The Sultân rises and the dark Ferrâsh
Strikes, and prepares it for another Guest.

"*And fear not lest existence closing your*
Account, and mine, should know the like no more;
The eternal Sākī from that Bowl has poured
Millions of Bubbles like us, and will pour."[1]

A man who thinks overmuch of himself may be unhappy because he thinks the world does not think highly enough of him. Any fancied insult or neglect strikes the iron into his soul. But the truly great man recognizes of how little importance he is, how small a space his orbit fills, and therefore accepts whatever homage the world gives him as far above his deserts. He demands nothing and gets much; while he who expects and demands great rewards must necessarily be disappointed because his realization can never equal the hunger and thirst of his expectation. Malíkshāh was a really great man, and these quatrains of Omar, though they pointed directly to the insignificance

[1] E. FitzGerald's paraphrase.

of the most opulent and powerful of mortals, expressed the mood of the dying monarch.

What had he of consolation? The Qu'rân could really give him little. To one who has enjoyed the highest heights of earthly enjoyment, the prospect of a material heaven is a cheerless continuation of a diet of the apples of Sodom. But Omar, with his serenity of epicureanism, though he had nothing positive to offer, and only a magnificent and poetic expression of the negative, or rather the unaffirmative, met the eternal question with such sweetness of confidence that, even if a man were swallowed up into the Ocean of Nonexistence as a pebble-cast disappears in the Haft Qúlzum, or Seven Seas, it was all well, it was a part of the scheme of the universe. To a conceited man, whether monarch or peasant, such marked depreciation of the individual would have been painful. Malíkshāh, feeling like another Oriental monarch that all was vanity, — his conquests, his wealth, his titles, his popularity, his fame, his life, — enjoyed the poetic statement, especially when it came in such exquisite strains from Omar's rich and well-trained voice.

The last lines that Omar was privileged to recite were those two finely imaginative quatrains:

"*I sent my Soul through the Invisible,*
Some letter of that After-life to spell:

And by and by my Soul returned to me,
And answer'd 'I myself am Heaven and Hell:'

"*Heaven but the Vision of fulfilled Desire,*
And Hell the Shadow from a Soul on fire,
Cast on the Darkness into which Ourselves,
So late emerged from, shall so soon expire."[1]

That day his visit was shortened, as the Sultân's strength was failing; indeed, he saw him only once again. The slow but deadly poison was working its destined end. Just five and thirty days after the assassination of Nizâmu'l-Mulk the Sultân Malíkshāh expired.

During his illness every arrangement for the succession was perfected, and Barkiyarok became Sultân without any shock.

On the very day that he first mounted the throne a singular discovery was made: when he woke in the morning a dagger was found firmly imbedded in the felt farsh at the head of his couch. On a parchment were written these words:

"*Were not the Sultân's favor dear this dagger had been thrust into his heart.*"

It was signed with Hasan ben Sabah's signature.

This warning was sufficiently startling. It was felt that no one was safe. A great sense of uneasiness pervaded the palace, making deeper the gloom

[1] E. FitzGerald's paraphrase.

caused by the death of Malíkshāh and his Wazîr. Who could have approached so close to the royal couch? Some slave, doubtless. Barkiyarok had no doubt of it, and every person who had access to the neighborhood of his apartment during that night — every slave and guard — was executed the following day.

But owing to various political complications the Sultân withdrew his armies from the Rûdbâr district, and left Hasan ben Sabah in complete control of that mountainous region. Hasan took this retreat as tacit confession of his independence, and made no further attempt to take the life of the Turk whom he despised.

CHAPTER XXXIII.

IRÂM IS GONE WITH ALL HIS ROSE.

After participating in the imposing ceremonies incident to the burial of the Sultân and his great minister, Barkiyarok entered upon a comparatively uneventful reign. He appointed his brother, Sanjar, governor of Nishāpûr, and sent his younger brother, Māhmûd, who had been the cause of some agitation in favor of his appointment as heir to Malíkshāh, on a military expedition to Asia Minor. Barkiyarok had little of his father's energy, but he had considerable tact, and thus was enabled to hold together the larger part of the empire.

Omar, who had remained in Marv, was all the time acting in consultation with Shirîn Khānúm in regard to the best interests of his ward. At his suggestion, Barkiyarok gladly took him as his own special page, and promised to initiate him into the duties that would lead him ultimately into much the same position that Nizâmu'l-Mulk had so marvellously graced.

Omar found ever increasing delight in his acquaintance with the stately, dignified, and beautiful woman whom he had revered ever since he first saw her.

In place of the hot fire of passionate desire burning in his heart, — such as he had known for Agapê, — there came the chaste white flame of worship. He knew that even as Shirîn Khānúm had been the true and faithful wife to his friend, so it was right that he might hope that in time she might graft her affection on him. Did not the Sacred Book say that if a widow went out from her husband's home there was no crime in what they did for themselves in reason? And God is mighty and wise!

The report came that Nishāpûr was in a state of great ferment, owing to Sanjar's attempt to drive out the Keramiyah heretics, who believed in a strange form of anthropomorphism. He was led into this act of persecution by the Hujjâ-tu'l Islâm, who represented that they were a dangerous and pestilential sect.

Sanjar, who inherited Malíkshāh's partiality for Omar, sent him a letter stating that the riots in the city had caused great bloodshed, and that perhaps it would be advisable for him to stay away till the trouble was quelled.

On the very evening of the day that he received this friendly warning, a startling incident occurred.

He was seated in front of a little fire of sweet-scented wood which was burning on a basis of argol, for the night was cool. He was pondering over the possibilities of inducing Shirîn Khānúm to live in Nishāpûr; he was picturing to himself how delightful it would be to have for a fireside companion a woman of such beauty and accomplishments, so gentle, so true, so capable of entering into his inner studies. "Like the mistress of the Impostor of Seruj," he said to himself, "she has understanding and discretion, sharpness and wit, a hand with fingers, and a mouth without teeth!" By which he meant that her tongue was not froward or apt to scold.

Suddenly a tall youth flung himself on the felt at Omar's feet:

"I approach you as deserving of death!" he cried. "Kill me!" and he extended to Omar a glittering dagger with a jewelled hilt.

"Who are you?" demanded Omar; but no sooner had he asked the question than it flashed on him he had seen the youth before. The scene rose before his mind: the chess-board with its beautiful ivory figures, carved in China, the silent lantern-holders looking on at the game, the concentrated face of the great Wazîr planning the move that was never made, the swift rush of the assassin, the deadly blow struck from behind, the attempted arrest, the confusion, the escape of the miscreant!

"Who are you, and what do you want?"

"I am a wretch who swore to take your life," stammered the youth. "It was I who stabbed Nizâmu'l-Mulk. Here is a dagger! Take it and kill me!"

"Why did you not fulfil your oath?" asked Omar.

"Because you are a poet and a wise man. I love your poems, and I prefer to break my oath and be put to death by you."

"You are a strange man!" exclaimed Omar. "Are you one of Hasan ben Sabah's fanatic followers?"

"I have been till now. But having broken my oath, I cannot return except to die."

"Why did you kill Nizâmu'l-Mulk? Was it not a cowardly thing to do, — to creep up behind a man and stab him in the back?"

"That is Hasan's way of waging war on his enemies. He has made us believe that this is God's will. We swore to obey him in all things, — even till death."

"Hasan was my friend," said Omar. "Can he have fallen so low? He urged me to join with him. Bi Khodâ, 'twas well I scorned his specious arguments."

"But again I say," continued the youth, who was none other than Abdīshû, "I am deserving of death! Kill me!"

"Nay," said Omar, "your secret is safe with me. Once I wrote 'I verily believe Thou wilt generously pardon me on account of my shame, because Thou hast seen what I have done.' If I could write thus of God pardoning me, can I do less? I will not cause your punishment. If you thought you were doing your duty, you braved all possibilities to accomplish it. I have naught against you, so far as I am concerned."

"But what can I do? Where can I go? I am not afraid of death, but I cannot return to the Hashish-eaters. I have learned to despise them and hate them. They are repugnant to me."

"Where is your home?"

"My father is the sheikh of the village of Karej, not far from Isfahân."

"I have heard of him. His name is Yusûf al 'Ijli?"

"That is his name, and he befriended Hasan; but if I were to return to my home, the sheikh of the mountains, the head of the Order of the Batiniyeh, would swoop down on my father's home and leave it a wilderness. I cannot go home."

Omar pondered for a moment. During that moment a sudden project flowered in his mind.

"Your secret is safe with me," he said. "But I am going to put a terrible burden on you. Hasan ibn Ishak Tūsî, whom we knew as Nizâmu'l-Mulk, left a widow. You shall enter her service and guard her interests. As for me," he continued, "I start within a week for India. Perhaps you may go also."

It would be hard to describe the gratitude of the young Arab, who thus found himself enabled to do penance for what he now regarded as a despicable crime. He had learned to compare the insignificance of the affront which he had burned to revenge with the blood-guiltiness that now weighed on his soul. The Qu'rân emphasized the doctrine of *As-sinna bis-sinn,* the tooth for the tooth, but here was an innocent man murdered foully because a few camels had not been paid for at a fanciful price! So he welcomed the hard service: of being frequently in the presence of the woman whom he had so terribly injured, and of bearing in his heart the knowledge which she might not share. He kissed the edge of Omar's robe, and said:

"I gratefully accept your command."

In view of the perturbed condition of Nishāpûr,—and something of the same ferment was taking place in Tûs,—it occurred to Omar that perhaps Shirîn Khānúm might not be averse to visiting some of the cities of Upper India. A large part of India was then under the sway of the Ghaznavide princes, who were nominally though not really superior to the Seljûks. It was not a difficult journey to visit India, and there was a constant succession of great caravans starting from Marv and penetrating Kashmir and the land of the Sikhs, and even to the Pan-jaub, or, as the Persians called it, the Páng Rûd, the Five Rivers.

Barkiyarok approved of Omar's journey, and gave him orders to collect information regarding those distant regions. The Sultân himself suggested that Abul Mosaffer 'Ali should go with him. He had often travelled with his father when the Wazîr was required to accompany Malíkshāh on some great journey, and he was delighted at the idea of accompanying Omar to the mysterious lands beyond the Himalyas.

It required no long argument after that to induce Shirîn Khānúm to join the party to the south. She could not endure the idea of separation from her son, and she confessed to herself that to be under the protection of her husband's lifelong friend, a man whom she respected and admired, was in itself a consolation in her bereavement.

It is not in the province of this history to relate the details of Omar's journey. The fruits of it may be found rather in the impressions of Indian philosophy, that are seen in his later poems, than in any actual record of his experiences. He met some of the eminent Vedantic philosophers, and discussed with them his theories of life, his philosophy, and theirs. He had imbibed something of Plato's idealism, and he and they were in accord as regards all things being only symbols or ideas; but they taught him not a little about what might be called the theosophy of that day. His own liberality of view, his catholicity, made it easy for him to see all that was fine and inspiring in their ancient literature and in their religion.

He was absent more than a year, and when he returned he found that the rioting and disturbances at Nishāpûr had almost ceased. He therefore went back to his own home. Shirîn Khānúm returned to her former home in Tûs; but as long as she lived, she and Omar were the best of friends. She remained faithful to the memory of Nizâmu'l-Mulk, and he never realized his dream of bringing her to Nishāpûr and he was content to have it so. He occupied himself with his astronomical and mathematical pursuits. He still took pleasure in sitting on his terrace and listening to the nightingales singing in the neighbouring gardens. Occasionally, but not so frequently as when life was in its prime, he composed and polished one of his quatrains. Abdīshû would gladly have followed him and remained his servant all his life, but Omar knew that his life would not be worth an hour's purchase if he came into reach of Hasan ben Sabah's long arm, and advised him to settle in India.

The Governor of the city, Sanjar, found no less pleasure in his society than his father had done, and often invited him to the palace and seated him by his side on his ivory throne. Protected by this powerful friend, he was enabled to live at ease, even when his heretical notions would have exposed him to fanatic outrage. But by the advice of Shírîn Khānúm he went often to the services at the Mesjid, and outwardly conformed to the observances of Islâm. He could do so without hypocrisy, for his liberal mind enabled him to find the Truth under almost any form of worship.

His great fame attracted many students to him, and with the young he had an extraordinary influence. Though he had the reputation of being such a lover of wine and pleasure, he recommended his young friends to seek the One, the Ruler of the Universe, by trying to purify the soul, by controlling with firmness all the carnal desires. He showed them in what happiness consisted. He himself was well acquainted with the philosophy of Greece, and especially Plato's, and he used often to talk to an eager group of his admirers about politics and civic economy as represented in Plato's republic. His ideal was a state founded on love, — a perfect state in which the centripetal and centrifugal forces are so accurately balanced that there is never any discord.

Among his pupils was more than one poet who afterwards became famous. Anwari studied with him, and Nizâmi of Samarkand, who told the poetic tale of Alexander's conquest, was his favorite disciple.

Nizâmi says:

"Once I chanced to find the learned Omar in Balkh and had a joyous meeting with him, and as he talked he said: 'My grave shall be in a place where every spring the north wind shall scatter roses over it.'"

With a deeper meaning he himself wrote:

"*Ah, with the Grape my fading life provide*
And wash the Body whence the Life has died,
And lay me, shrouded in the living Leaf
By some not unfrequented Garden-side.

"*That e'en my buried Ashes such a snare*
Of Vintage shall fling up into the Air
As not a True-believer passing by
But shall be overtaken unaware."[1]

Sultân Barkiyarok passed away, and Sanjar came to the throne in his place; the younger brother, Mahmûd, was sent against Hasan ben Sabah. But Hasan ben Sabah, unmoved by any display of force, sat still in his impregnable castle and laughed to scorn the efforts to dislodge him.

Many were the princes whom his dreaded emissaries sent untimely into the darkness. But he himself seemed to bear a charmed life. He lived

[1] E. FitzGerald's paraphrase.

till well into the twelfth century, never during his latter years leaving his sumptuously furnished quarters, but reaching out into distant regions, and making his ruthless influence felt. The Crusaders came to know him quite too well, and they bore back to Europe frightful reports of his unscrupulous fanaticism, which sacrificed the Lord of Emessa, and attacked Count St. Gillies. When, full of years, he felt death approaching, he summoned the Daï Kurbusurgomid to Alamût, and appointed him his successor as head of the Order. He had expected great things of Abdīshû, and would have probably made him the second Sidna, but the young man's defection and disappearance — for he remained in India — had greatly disappointed him. The sect of the Assassins lingered on for a few years, but it missed the master-mind that had so skilfully guided it so long, and before half a century had passed it had vanished, leaving only an evil memory behind. It was finally destroyed by Hulugu, the Tartar Conqueror of Bagdâd. The same year that Hasan died, Omar also died. And this was the manner of his death:

The Imâm Muhammád of Bagdâd happened to be visiting him, and Omar, seated in his favorite position under the palm-tree in his little garden, was reading a chapter in the "Book of Healing," — that chapter of the Qu'rân entitled the "One and the Many," when he suddenly ceased, and, placing between the leaves a golden dinar to mark the place, he addressed the Imâm Muhammád, and said:

"I feel that my last hour has come; call my friends, that I may speak once more to them."

And when his friends—his pupils and some of his neighbors—had assembled around him, he got to his feet in the manner prescribed by the ritual, and, turning in the direction of Makka, in a clear voice repeated the evening prayer. Then, kneeling, he bent his brow to the ground, and said:

"O God! Verily I have known Thee so far as the power within me extended; forgive me, therefore. Verily my knowledge of Thee is my recommendation to Thee."

Then he arose once more, and repeated to his friends his last quatrain:

"'*I am weary, O God, of my utter badness;*
Of my idle days, of my anguish and sadness.
Ever as life out of death thou bringest, so bring me
From my non-existence for Thine Honor and Gladness!'"

After this he bade his friends and disciples one by one farewell, and when he had thus dismissed them, he went and lay on his divân.

The Imâm accompanied them to the door, and when he returned, he found that Omar had peacefully and silently breathed his last. Such was the end of Omar, the poet and astronomer of Nishāpûr.

The report of his death was received with sorrow by a wide circle. Even those who criticised his heresies realized how great he was, how much he had done for his native town and province. He was buried in a costly tomb. When, some years later, Nizâmi happened to be passing through Nishāpûr, he remembered what Omar had said about his grave, and he went in search of it, and found it in the midst of a garden, where pomegranate and other fruit-trees shaded it, stretching forth their branches over the garden wall. And the blossoms of the rose-bushes and of the fruit-trees had fallen in such abundance that they hid it from sight. And Nizâmi marvelled at the wise Omar's saying and prophecy, and when he went to Omar's house he was told that it had been his wish to be thus laid away, so that the blossoms might be strewn over his last resting-place.

The rose-bushes still bloom over Omar's tomb; but Nishāpûr lies in ruins. Of all the myriads who in his day were living in that beautiful city of the plain, he alone speaks in deathless voice to men of other tongues and other religion. His message is heeded because it expresses the modern mood of epicureanism and agnosticism, and perhaps of pessimism. Our restless, discontented hearts find comfort in the beautiful utterances of a man who, almost a thousand years ago, faced bravely and unflinchingly the same problems that we must face, and, in spite of the ruthless wheel of the sky, found joy and peace in the Day as it passed, and had faith that the Maker of the Pots was a good fellow, and that all would be well.

He lived in a day of strenuous life; he mingled with the great men of his time, and his poems show that he preserved his independence, his sublime individuality, his serenity, his keenness of vision, unimpaired till the end.

Farewell, then, Omar the Tentmaker! We of a later day, we of a happier civilization, though perhaps not more advanced, claim you as one of us. We love and revere your memory. Hail and Farewell!

TAMÂM.

SELECTIONS FROM

L. C. PAGE AND COMPANY'S

LIST OF NEW FICTION.

The Road to Paris.

By ROBERT NEILSON STEPHENS, author of "An Enemy to the King," "The Continental Dragoon," etc. Illustrated by H. C. Edwards.

1 vol., library 12mo, cloth **$1.50**

An historical romance, being an account of the life of an American gentleman adventurer of Jacobite ancestry, whose family early settled in the colony of Pennsylvania. The scene shifts from the unsettled forests of the then West to Philadelphia, New York, London, Paris, and, in fact, wherever a love of adventure and a roving fancy can lead a soldier of fortune. The story is written in Mr. Stephens's best style, and is of absorbing interest.

Rose à Charlitte.

An Acadien Romance. By MARSHALL SAUNDERS, author of "Beautiful Joe," etc. Illustrated by H. De M. Young.

1 vol., library 12mo, cloth **$1.50**

In this novel, the scene of which is laid principally in the land of Evangeline, Marshall Saunders has made a departure from the style of her earlier successes. The historical and descriptive setting of the novel is accurate, the plot is well conceived and executed, the characters are drawn with a firm and delightful touch, and the fortunes of the heroine, Rose à Charlitte, a descendant of an old Acadien family, will be followed with eagerness by the author's host of admirers.

Bobbie McDuff.

By CLINTON ROSS, author of "The Scarlet Coat," "Zuleika," etc. Illustrated by B. West Clinedinst.

1 vol., large 16mo, cloth **$1.00**

Clinton Ross is well known as one of the most promising of recent American writers of fiction, and in the description of the adventures of his latest hero, Bobbie McDuff, he has repeated his earlier successes. Mr. Ross has made good use of the wealth of material at his command. New York furnishes him the hero, sunny Italy a heroine, grim Russia the villain of the story, while the requirements of the exciting plot shift the scene from Paris to New York, and back again to a remote, almost feudal villa on the southern coast of Italy.

In Kings' Houses.

A Romance of the Reign of Queen Anne. By JULIA C. R. DORR, author of "A Cathedral Pilgrimage," etc. Illustrated by Frank T. Merrill.

1 vol., library 12mo, cloth $1.50

Mrs. Dorr's poems and travel sketches have earned for her a distinct place in American literature, and her romance, "In Kings' Houses," is written with all the charm of her earlier works. The story deals with one of the most romantic episodes in English history. Queen Anne, the last of the reigning Stuarts, is described with a strong, yet sympathetic touch, and the young Duke of Gloster, the "little lady," and the hero of the tale, Robin Sandys, are delightful characterizations.

Sons of Adversity.

A Romance of Queen Elizabeth's Time. By L. COPE CONFORD, author of "Captain Jacobus," etc. Illustrated by J. W. Kennedy.

1 vol., library 12mo, cloth $1.25

A tale of adventure on land and sea at the time when Protestant England and Catholic Spain were struggling for naval supremacy. Spanish conspiracies against the peace of good Queen Bess, a vivid description of the raise of the Spanish siege of Leyden by the combined Dutch and English forces, sea fights, the recovery of stolen treasure, are all skilfully woven elements in a plot of unusual strength.

The Count of Nideck.

From the French of Erckman-Chatrian, translated and adapted by RALPH BROWNING FISKE. Illustrated by Victor A. Searles.

1 vol., library 12mo, cloth $1.25

A romance of the Black Forest, woven around the mysterious legend of the Wehr Wolf. The plot has to do with the later German feudal times, is brisk in action, and moves spiritedly from start to finish. Mr. Fiske deserves a great deal of credit for the excellence of his work. No more interesting romance has appeared recently.

The Making of a Saint.

By W. SOMERSET MAUGHAM. Illustrated by Gilbert James.

1 vol., library 12mo, cloth $1.50

"The Making of a Saint" is a romance of Mediæval Italy, the scene being laid in the 15th century. It relates the life of a young leader of Free Companions who, at the close of one of the many petty Italian wars, returns to his native city. There he becomes involved in its politics, intrigues, and feuds, and finally joins an uprising of the townspeople against their lord. None can resent the frankness and apparent brutality of the scenes through which the hero and his companions of both sexes are made to pass, and many will yield ungrudging praise to the author's vital handling of the truth. In the characters are mirrored the life of the Italy of their day. The book will confirm Mr. Maugham's reputation as a strong and original writer.

Omar the Tentmaker.

A Romance of Old Persia. By NATHAN HASKELL DOLE. Illustrated by F. T. Merrill.

1 vol., library 12mo, cloth $1.50

Mr. Dole's study of Persian literature and history admirably equips him to enter into the life and spirit of the time of the romance, and the hosts of admirers of the inimitable quatrains of Omar Khayyam, made famous by Fitzgerald, will be deeply interested in a tale based on authentic facts in the career of the famous Persian poet. The three chief characters are Omar Khayyam, Nizam-ul-Mulk, the generous and high-minded Vizier of the Tartar Sultan Malik Shah of Mero, and Hassan ibu Sabbah, the ambitious and revengeful founder of the sect of the Assassins. The scene is laid partly at Naishapur, in the Province of Khorasan, which about the period of the First Crusade was at its acme of civilization and refinement, and partly in the mountain fortress of Alamut, south of the Caspian Sea, where the Ismailians under Hassan established themselves towards the close of the 11th century. Human nature is always the same, and the passions of love and ambition, of religion and fanaticism, of friendship and jealousy, are admirably contrasted in the fortunes of these three able and remarkable characters as well as in those of the minor personages of the story.

Captain Fracasse.

A new translation from the French by Gautier. Illustrated by Victor A. Searles.

1 vol., library 12mo, cloth $1.25

This famous romance has been out of print for some time, and a new translation is sure to appeal to its many admirers, who have never yet had any edition worthy of the story.

The Rejuvenation of Miss Semaphore.

A farcical novel. By HAL GODFREY. Illustrated by Etheldred B. Barry.

1 vol., library 12mo, cloth $1.25

A fanciful, laughable tale of two maiden sisters of uncertain age who are induced, by their natural longing for a return to youth and its blessings, to pay a large sum for a mystical water which possesses the value of setting backwards the hands of time. No more delightfully fresh and original book has appeared since "Vice Versa" charmed an amused world. It is well written, drawn to the life, and full of the most enjoyable humor.

Midst the Wild Carpathians.

By MAURUS JOKAI, author of "Black Diamonds," "The Lion of Janina," etc. Authorized translation by R. Nisbet Bain. Illustrated by J. W. Kennedy.

1 vol., library 12mo, cloth $1.25

A thrilling, historical, Hungarian novel, in which the extraordinary dramatic and descriptive powers of the great Magyar writer have full play. As a picture of feudal life in Hungary it has never been surpassed for fidelity and vividness. The translation is exceedingly well done.

The Golden Dog.

A Romance of Quebec. By WILLIAM KIRBY. New authorized edition. Illustrated by J. W. Kennedy.

1 vol., library 12mo, cloth $1.25

A powerful romance of love, intrigue, and adventure in the time of Louis XV. and Mme. de Pompadour, when the French colonies were making their great struggle to retain for an ungrateful court the fairest jewels in the colonial diadem of France.

Bijli the Dancer.

By JAMES BLYTHE PATTON. Illustrated by Horace Van Rinth.

1 vol., library 12mo, cloth **$1.50**

A novel of Modern India. The fortunes of the heroine, an Indian Naucht girl, are told with a vigor, pathos, and a wealth of poetic sympathy that makes the book admirable from first to last.

"To Arms!"

Being Some Passages from the Early Life of Allan Oliphant, Chirurgeon, Written by Himself, and now Set Forth for the First Time. By ANDREW BALFOUR. Illustrated by F. W. Glover.

1 vol., library 12mo, cloth **$1.50**

A romance dealing with an interesting phase of Scottish and English history, the Jacobite Insurrection of 1715, which will appeal strongly to the great number of admirers of historical fiction. The story is splendidly told, the magic circle which the author draws about the reader compelling a complete forgetfulness of prosaic nineteenth century life.

Friendship and Folly.

A novel. By MARIA LOUISE POOLE, author of "In a Dike Shanty," etc. Illustrated by J. W. Kennedy.

1 vol., library 12mo, cloth **$1.25**

An extremely well-written story of modern life. The interest centres in the development of the character of the heroine, a New England girl, whose high-strung temperament is in constant revolt against the confining limitations of nineteenth century surroundings. The reader's interest is held to the end, and the book will take high rank among American psychological novels.

A Hypocritical Romance and other stories.

By CAROLINE TICKNOR. Illustrated by J. W. Kennedy. 1 vol., large 16mo, cloth . . . **$1.00**

Miss Ticknor, well known as one of the most promising of the younger school of American writers, has never done better work than in the majority of these clever stories, written in a delightful comedy vein.

Cross Trails.

By VICTOR WAITE. Illustrated by J. W. Kennedy.
1 vol., library 12mo, cloth **$1.50**

A Spanish-American novel of unusual interest, a brilliant, dashing, and stirring story, teeming with humanity and life. Mr. Waite is to be congratulated upon the strength with which he has drawn his characters.

A Mad Madonna and other stories.

By L. CLARKSON WHITELOCK, with eight half-tone illustrations. 1 vol., large 16mo, cloth . **$1.00**

A half dozen remarkable psychological stories, delicate in color and conception. Each of the six has a touch of the supernatural, a quick suggestion, a vivid intensity, and a dreamy realism that is matchless in its forceful execution.

On the Point.

A Summer Idyl. By NATHAN HASKELL DOLE, author of "Not Angels Quite," with dainty half-tone illustrations as chapter headings.
1 vol., large 16mo, cloth **$1.00**

A bright and clever story of a summer on the coast of Maine, fresh, breezy, and readable from the first to the last page. The narrative describes the summer outing of a Mr. Merrithew and his family. The characters are all honest, pleasant people, whom we are glad to know. We part from them with the same regret with which we leave a congenial party of friends.

Cavalleria Rusticana; or, Under the Shadow of Etna.

Translated from the Italian of Giovanni Verga, by NATHAN HASKELL DOLE. Illustrated by Etheldred B. Barry. 1 vol., 16mo, cloth . . . **$0.50**

Giovanni Verga stands at present as unquestionably the most prominent of the Italian novelists. His supremacy in the domain of the short story and in the wider range of the romance is recognized both at home and abroad. The present volume contains a selection from the most dramatic and characteristic of his Sicilian tales. Verga is himself a native of Sicily, and his knowledge of that wonderful country, with its poetic and yet superstitious peasantry, is absolute. Such pathos, humor, variety, and dramatic quality are rarely met in a single volume.

Published by

Facsimile Publisher
Ashok Vihar, Delhi-110052 (India)
Website: www.facsimilepublisher.com

Distributed by

Gyan Books Pvt. Ltd.
5, Ansari Road, Daryaganj, New Delhi-110002 (India)
E-mail: books@gyanbooks.com, Website: www.gyanbooks.com

2 222000 014025